MARBLE
SUN

Copyright © 2025 by E. G. Sparks

Cover Design: *Infixgraph Designs*

Copy Editing: *Lisa Fox*

Interior Formatting: *Fox Formatting*

ISBN (paperback): 979-8-9880450-4-5

For my loving parents.

PROLOGUE

T he Soaz climbed the last steps to the overlook. He flicked the heavy metal hatch open with ease and strolled to the metal barrier. Thick angry clouds smeared the sky gray. Sizable but sparse raindrops drummed against the metal roof. But the drizzle didn't bother him. He wrapped his long masculine fingers around the railing with force and stared down at the tiny flickers of lights in the distance. Life in New Seattle was bustling as usual. But all that would change soon.

Everything had gone according to the plan. The Soaz smirked, an action that pulled at the scar splitting his lip and trickling down his tattooed neck. The sharp ping of pain in his back replaced his cheerful expression with a deep scowl. None of the Fringe's medics could find an antidote for the shot his little brother had stuck him with. The substance had immobilized him during their fight, making him vulnerable and under Xavier's mercy. His cretin of a brother should have ended him then and not turned his back and left.

His little brother had grown too soft over the last few weeks. And because of what? A female? Even if she was a scrumptious morsel to toy with... And the toying had given the Soaz something to look forward to lately.

A deranged smile split his face. He planned to leave the Fringe for the Northern Institute soon to visit the newest prisoner. A fragile small warrior with an angelic face and silky blond hair he dreamed of wrapping his fist around again. His *nightshade*. Above all, he craved her scent and blood. As soon as the institute was finished with her, he would take his incorrigible warrior with him and mold her into the proper, enhanced Earthbounder. The rule of the old guard had ended with the attack on Invicta and he would deal with the council in time.

The Soaz never regretted volunteering for the experiments. Even as a child, he'd recognized that indifference to the suffering of others was a key trait of powerful leaders. He'd tested it on his own mother first. Hafthor, his father and Invicta's Magister, didn't need to encourage him to lie. Once again his father had misjudged his son's potential. Hafthor might have ruled with a tight fist, but the Earthbounder mindset limited him.

Ever since his own Earthbounder genes had successfully melded with the demonic genome, Damian's eyes had opened to a new world—no, a universe—of new, uncharted possibilities. He would build an empire. But first he needed to mop up some trash, including his little brother and his band of rejects.

It played into his hands that most Earthbounders and Magisters remained blind to the truth. He needed these pawns for a little longer. Until his army of enhanced warriors rose in numbers.

The clouds darkened in the distance and winds howled in the ravine.

The Soaz withdrew a wooden box out of his pocket. The only item of interest his men had recovered from Xavier's room. A letter "D" was engraved on the bottom, and since he knew Xavier had opened their mother's gift to him when Arien disappeared, he felt confident this one was their mother's gift to her other son. The box wouldn't open to anyone but the rightful recipient, so he'd get his confirmation soon.

He stared at it for a prolonged minute, asking himself whether he wanted to know. He never doubted his mother's seer abilities. She'd been the best seer who ever lived in the last millennium.

The nail on his thumb extended. He slid it beneath the clasp and pried the gift open.

The light spilled from the box like liquid gold, illuminating the feather that lay nestled within.

The Soaz staggered back, a vision overtaking his mind.

He stood on the lip of a mountain, peering down at the red horizon. Tall tongues of fire licked at the buildings, swallowing them whole and slithering across to others. He beamed on the inside. He'd done it. The first step in reconstructing the world was its destruction. His mother's voice whispered in his mind, "You will set the world ablaze..."

A figure shifted by his side and he turned his head, curious to see his accomplice. A curtain of light blond hair obscured her face, ruffled by the winds.

His heart jolted as he threaded his fingers into her locks and pulled back. Softness imbued the angles in her profile. She swiveled her face toward him slowly. Lagoon-blue eyes glared at him, stubborn and defiant. The fire in the distance illuminated her skin with a golden sheen.

He despised her vulnerability but admired the quiet resistance. Her cheeks glistened with moisture. The same softness that could invoke pity in a weaker soul ignited something darker in him—an urge to wipe it away and replace with blank disregard. With one minor exception. She would disregard everyone but him.

Her place would remain beneath him and he'd remind her of it every single day...and night.

Damian lowered his head, eager to taste her. While the world burned around them, he'd partake in what was his.

Peering into her eyes, he paused. The clear blue surrounding her pupils clouded over. Her expression slacked. She blinked. Then the most beautiful vermilion spilled over the blue of her irises. She tilted her head, a small smirk pulling at the corner of her lips. The Soaz's eyes flared to pitch black, recognizing his similar within her.

His scarred lips parted. She was perfection. A perfect queen to sit by his side.

She gripped the back of his neck and yanked him toward her.

But instead of meeting her lips, Damian began falling into an endless dark space. And the pair of her fiery eyes morphed into dozens of red orbs.

Then they rushed him.

The Soaz gasped, patting his chest as if to reassure himself he was whole and standing.

The feather hovered above its enclosure for a moment suspended by some unseen force. It trembled and began to dissolve at the quill, where delicate fragments flaked away, drifting upwards like glowing embers.

Before the last pieces floated away, his mother's voice entered his mind again. "After fire, there is ash...and reckoning. She's yours..."

ONE

Shock waves rocked my body, leaving me convulsing as waves of pain and cold spread from my core. A blindingly sterile light pierced through my eyelids, burning inside the thin veil of skin. I flung my arm across my face, rough gauze-like fabric snagging my nose.

My breath came in short, ragged gasps. The air reeked of antiseptics and metal. I pried my eyes open despite the stabbing brightness and instantly regretted it. My vision blurred, shimmering with tears, and white walls and unfamiliar objects swam in and out of focus.

What in the actual hell? Where am I?

The square of white tape on my arm came into view, pinning down a small tube that snaked its way to the other side of a transparent wall. The sight of it flipped a switch inside me. My pulse roared in my ears.

No. Get it off. GET IT OFF!

With a strangled cry, I clawed at the port, ripping it from my arm in one desperate yank. A sting shot up from the puncture, and blood welled up. Red drops splattered the pristine floor. A high-pitched beep erupted from the IV drip outside the transparent wall, the sound cutting through the silence like a blade.

A figure in a white lab coat—one of the many in the vast space surrounding my holding cell—appeared, her face obscured by a mask. She moved methodically, her gloved hands disconnecting the tubes and carting away the blinking machine as if my outburst was nothing more than a routine inconvenience.

I struggled to sit, but the world tilted. My head swam, nausea threatening to pull me under. Propped on my elbows, I blinked at my surroundings—a cold, steel cot trapped in the center of a stark white void. A hangar-sized expanse stretched endlessly, sterile and soulless. Figures in white coats flitted between stations.

My chest heaved with shallow breaths. Too shallow. Too fast.

I forced myself to stand, my legs trembling so violently they barely obeyed. My palms slammed against the smooth transparent barrier that enclosed me. A ten-by-ten prison of glass-like walls.

No.

My eyes grew hot.

A sob clawed its way up my throat, but I swallowed it, letting the fear burst into fury instead. My fists pounded against the wall, each strike echoing uselessly in my cell.

"Let me out!"

A few heads turned, casting brief glances from behind microscopes and glowing computer screens. Expressionless and dismissive. They returned to typing, analyzing, and arranging samples in mini-fridges. Like I wasn't even there.

Panic surged, turning my blood to ice.

At the far end of the room, a stainless steel door slid open with a low hiss. My pulse quickened, and I shuffled to the other side of my cell, trying to get a better look. The woman who entered stood out sharply against the clinical background, dressed in black—tailored pants and a fitted jacket that emphasized her severe, angular frame. Her honey-blond hair was twisted into a tight bun, not a single strand out of place, and her lips curled in a faint sneer.

I would have recognized her anywhere—this was Mariola, the Magister of the Northern Institute. Her cold eyes found me—disparaging, slicing through me with a single glance. They judged, dismissed, and condemned.

She walked with a crisp rhythm, her heels clicking against the concrete floor, each step like the ticking of a clock counting down my fate. Two guards flanked her, both tall, burly, and broad-shouldered, their eyes trained on me with predatory focus.

I backed away instinctively, retreating deeper into my cell until my back pressed against the far wall.

The Magister placed her hand on a square etched into the barrier. A symbol flared to life under her touch into a cold, sterile white. A rectangle the size of an entrance appeared, shimmering like frost before icing over entirely. With a groaning hiss, the barrier rose, leaving a chill in its wake that crept along my skin.

My heartbeat thundered in my ears, each pulse vibrating through my skull.

She crossed the threshold into my cell, her black-heeled boots striking the concrete floor with finality. She halted a few feet in front of me, lifted her left arm, and folded her sleeve once, revealing a rose-gold bracelet. My gaze darted to my own wrist where my bracelet, thankfully, still hung. A perfect match.

Mariola's last words to me clawed their way back into my mind. She had called my mother...her sister. I tried to swallow. My throat felt dry as if I hadn't used it in days. Or had it been weeks since the Soaz—uh, Damian—sank a needle into my neck?

"You are… You're…my aunt?" I asked in a raspy voice.

Her smirk deepened, a glimmer of dark amusement curling her lips.

"You didn't lose your memories. That's good," she said.

A shiver coursed through me, but I forced myself to speak again. "What do you want?"

She stepped closer, scrutinizing me, and I resisted the urge to recoil.

"It's cunning, really," she said, her tone soft yet cutting. "How much you resemble her, and yet…how utterly different you are."

Her words sent a ripple of unease through me. My brows knit.

The Magister wheeled around, heels scraping against the floor as she began to pace toward the entrance.

"You see," she began, her voice measured but laced with venom, "your mother stole from me. Priceless research we worked on side by side until she blindsided everyone. But, it appears that instead of destroying the serum, she put it into her body. Into…*you*."

The floor seemed to tilt beneath me. My mother. What had she done? And why?

Fragments of answers started to align—the mystery of my ancestry, the demonic stain on my ancient Earthbounder blood, the strange power that had always set me apart, the Sky Ice crystal, and the realm it had come from—could all this be related?

Mariola paused at the threshold, readjusting her sleeve.

"What now?" I asked, the words tumbling out, barely above a whisper.

Our eyes met, hers glittering with a hatred so sharp it felt like a physical wound.

"Now," she said, her voice low, brimming with dark promise, "I take back what's mine."

She tilted her head toward the guards beside her. "You know what to do."

Their gazes snapped to me, their expressions hardening into something ruthless. They rushed toward me, boots thudding against the floor. My body tensed and I pressed harder against the wall as if trying to meld into it.

There was nowhere to run.

TWO

The men loomed over me, their leering gazes dripping with menace. Dressed in black tactical shirts, pants, and boots, they exuded a brutal, unyielding presence. These weren't just any warriors—they had to be Purebloods. The Magister's personal army.

My nails scraped against the glass wall behind me, clawing for something—anything—to anchor me. My fingers curled upward as if they could find a way out. I had no chance against them. None.

But instinct, honed by what little training I'd had, forced me to study them. Every detail. Every potential weakness. My pulse pounded as I hunted for vulnerabilities, even knowing the odds were stacked impossibly high.

"Like what you see?" I sneered. My unguarded mouth—a weapon as much as it was a curse—had always been my sharpest edge.

The closest warrior's grin twisted into something dark and predatory. A spark of cruel amusement flickered in their eyes as his companion reached over his shoulder, unsheathing an onyx blade with a deliberate, menacing swish. I had only seen the Earthbounders use this particular sword to dispatch Archons and a few other pesky demons. The weapon sent them back to the realm they'd come from. Why were they choosing to use it on me?

The cold glass burned against my semi-nude back. Heat flared against my shoulder blades, a warning ripple radiating outward. My wings stirred, readying themselves for a fight. Maybe it was time to skip the calculations and let them take over.

"A little pain," the closer man growled. His hand shot out, tangling itself in my hair. Then he yanked my head sideways, exposing my throat with a cruel jerk.

"A little blood," the second warrior drawled. My throat bobbed as my gaze locked onto the blade glinting in his hand and now poised at my neck.

The thudding in my ears roared louder, drowning out reason. I reached out to my wings, coaxing them with silent urgency. *Come out now; it's time.* But the familiar heat that coiled at my shoulder blades flickered, fading as if retreating several steps. Panic licked at me, but I pushed it down. *I trust you*, I whispered in my mind. In the past, I would have accused my wings of desertion. But I had begun differentiating between their moodiness and their protection of me.

The blade nicked my skin and I sucked in a breath. A searing burn spread across my neck like wildfire. So this was it? Magister Mariola would behead me and take her revenge on my mother. I squeezed my eyes shut.

The sword's edge slipped away, and the first warrior yanked me forward with brutal force. His snarl blasted hot against my face, and my eyes flew open. His gold-flecked brown irises churned in erratic swirls, a strange and hypnotic display of barely contained fury.

"Call on your wings," he said, his voice sharp enough to cut.

I blinked, my mind racing, my chest heaving. Beyond the threshold, the Magister watched, arms folded tightly, her expression carved from ice.

"I don't have all day, *niece*. Summon your wings," she said.

"Why?"

A slap cracked across my face, the sound reverberating in the enclosed space. My head snapped to the side, stars exploding behind my eyes. I swayed, unsteady, but the warrior's iron grip kept me upright.

I dabbed my lip with the back of my hand, smearing blood across my chin. The taste of copper filled my mouth. The wings hummed faintly, restless, but stayed buried.

A strained laugh bubbled from my throat. "They're not coming out," I rasped, meeting the Magister's gaze. My voice hardened. "No matter what you do to me. *Auntie*."

Her expression darkened. Heels clicked against the concrete. She gripped my chin, her cold fingers digging into my skin. Her pencil-thin brow arched. "You don't know who you're dealing with," she said, her voice dripping with malice. "But you'll learn."

Chills raced down my spine. This woman was devoid of mercy, a creature who could rival the king of cruelty himself —Magister Hafthor. Whirling on her heel, she strode outside the cell, tapping her smartwatch.

The metal door hissed open. A girl emerged, her wrists bound in front of her with handcuffs that gleamed under the sterile light. Two warriors prodded her to move faster with harsh shoving.

My chest tightened as my gaze locked on her. She blew a stray curl from her face, and everything inside me seized.

"No!" I roared, surging forward. My captors yanked me back, their grips like iron clamps.

Nelia's wide eyes found mine, shock and despair written across her bruised face. Her golden curls hung in limp, matted tangles on one side, a shadow of their usual luster. The pencil skirt and once-elegant blouse she wore suffered stains and tears. As Xavier and I had suspected, she hadn't left Invicta voluntarily. Hafthor had sent her without a warning, not even giving her time to change clothes.

After the week since her disappearance, she looked smaller, her frame hollowed and frail. What had they done to her?

"Let her go. You don't need her," I said through gritted teeth.

"On the contrary," Mariola said. "Your wings refuse to manifest, but there are ways to force them out." She gave a faint nod and a warrior stepped forward, his baton flashing as it slammed into the back of Nelia's legs. She let out a strangled cry and crumpled to her knees, her shoulders heaving.

My body trembled against the arms restraining me. "Stop it!"

Nelia peered at me, her bright blue eyes locking onto mine, shimmering with defiance despite the bruises shadowing her cheekbones and the pain. My heart ached with a visceral intensity. She didn't deserve this. None of it.

The Magister's unyielding gaze drilled into me, waiting for me to yield and call forth my wings for her twisted purposes.

Another strike landed on Nelia's shoulder, her body shuddering with the blow. She bit her lip to keep from crying out, but the sound slipped out anyway—a small, pained whimper that scraped across my nerves like claws.

"Stop!" The word burst from me again, ragged and pleading.

Mariola tilted her head, a mockery of innocence in her

gaze. "You know what I want. Bring them out, and she's free to go."

"Don't," Nelia mouthed, her voice barely audible. "Not for me."

I shook my head. How could I not do it for her?

I clenched my fists, feeling a warmth gather between my shoulder blades, the familiar heat of my wings stirring, uncertain, wary. They had sensed the threat to us before I even realized it and refused to unfurl. But now they wavered, sensing my desperation.

The warrior tightened his hold on Nelia's arm, twisting it painfully. She cried out, and something within me snapped. I took a breath, reaching deep into myself, calling forth that hidden power with every shred of focus and strength I possessed. "Please," I whispered to my wings, "just this once, for her."

The heat flared, a slow burn that ignited into a torrent of energy. Pressure built in my back, pulling and straining against my skin. My body arched involuntarily, a sharp, hot pain tearing through my shoulders as the wings emerged. The weight of them settled over me like a protective shield, each white feather dipped in silver and gold like a mosaic. But I had no time to marvel at them; the warriors had already drawn closer.

The onyx blade absorbed the light as it lowered, the tip skimming the ground. The warrior brandishing it positioned himself at my side, his expression an unsettling blend of duty and anticipation. Dread filled my heart.

Nelia screamed. "No! Please, don't do this to her!" She fought against the man holding her down, her slender frame straining uselessly. The sight twisted a knife deeper into my heart. I couldn't let her suffer because of me. I managed a small, bittersweet smile.

"It's fine," I murmured, forcing a calm I didn't feel. I held her gaze as long as possible, as though I could somehow transfer my strength to her, lend her the last of my resolve. The warrior at my side shifted, and I braced myself.

The onyx blade sliced through the air with a terrible finality, its edge finding the base of my wing in less than a second. I gasped, the sound strangled as agony shot through me, raw and primal. It felt as though my very soul was being torn apart. Fire licked through my veins, and my vision blurred.

Nelia's pleas became louder. "Stop it! Leave her alone!" Her voice was hoarse, broken. I could barely see her through the haze of pain, but the sight of her kept me grounded, kept me conscious when all I wanted was to slip into darkness.

The warrior steadied the blade at the base of my other wing. I trembled, fresh waves of nausea and agony flooding over me. This time, I couldn't hold back the choked, ragged sob that escaped as he drove the blade up, severing the remaining wing.

Blood pooled around my feet, staining the pristine steel floor with crimson. My vision dimmed at the edges, and my limbs weakened, every ounce of strength draining from my body. I sagged forward into the arms of the second warrior holding me upright.

The onyx blade dripped with blood, while my wings lay discarded, lifeless on the floor, their glow fading with each passing second. My heart twisted at the sight.

"Take the wings," the Magister said, her voice crisp and unfeeling.

One warrior righted me against the glass wall before letting go, while the other guard gripped the wings.

Nelia collapsed to the floor, her sobs muffled against her hands as she wept for me, her body shaking.

I twisted away, pressing my forehead against the cool glass wall, letting its surface support me as I fought to stay conscious, every inch of me drenched in pain. The world seemed distant, the voices around me muffled, but Nelia's cries grounded me, echoing in my ears like a heartbeat.

Then, the room spun, the floor tilting beneath me. Darkness crept at the edges of my vision. I let it come, slipping into its embrace.

THREE

The cold clung to me like a second skin, seeping into my bones and draining the life from my limbs. A single touch of warmth broke through it—a hand, firm yet gentle, pressing against my cheek. It tilted my head slightly, and I mumbled, instinctively leaning into the touch, desperate for the comfort it offered against the relentless chill.

"I told you not to return to Xavier's quarters," a deep, velvety voice whispered, laced with reproach.

My brow furrowed, confusion threading through the haze. Forcing my heavy eyelids open, I blinked against the blur. Slowly, his figure sharpened—a broad, imposing frame, his cognac hair catching the faint light, and his face etched with a mix of frustration and concern.

"Donovan," I croaked, my throat raw. I tried to push myself upright but my hands slipped uselessly. The warrior gripped my shoulders and eased me to sitting.

A sick, crawling sensation slicked over me, coiling tighter with each breath. Something was horribly wrong.

I hiccuped, memories crashing in like a tidal wave—the

vile woman who dared call herself my aunt, her cold smirk as she stole something vital from me. My hands flew over my shoulders, frantically searching my back, my fingers skimming across two shallow indentations nestled just inside my shoulder blades.

"What are you doing?" Donovan's concerned voice cut through the fog.

I turned to him, blinking through wet lashes. The black, backless shirt I'd been wearing since I woke up hung loose around me, exposing the hollow spaces where my wings should have been. Without a word, I twisted, showing him my back.

"They cut my wings off," I said, the words tasting of bile and despair. "I can't feel them anymore."

Silence fell like a heavy stone between us. Donovan's hand hovered for a beat before his fingers brushed against one of the depressions, tracing the emptiness where my wings had once been. His touch sent a shiver rippling down my spine.

I faced him again, my eyes narrowing. "You knew," I said. "You knew this already, didn't you?"

"No," he whispered. His stunned face stared back at me. As if I could believe him. Even though he stood inside my cell with me, he was clearly free—a free man with an open door at his back and two guards flanking the entrance.

I swung my legs over the edge. "What are you doing here?"

His throat bobbed. "I thought you were dead. Then I found out you were at the Northern Institute. I had to see for myself."

What?

"Well, now you have. You can leave," I said, my voice clipped.

"Arien..."

"You knew about the Fringe's attack on Invicta," I said,

my eyes boring into his. "That's why you said those words to me at the lake. How could you? You betrayed the Seraphs... the Earthbounders..."

Donovan winced at my words.

"I did what I had to do," he growled.

"For what? What's in this for you?"

He leaned in, his gaze heated. "Hafthor had to pay for his sins." His tone was as cold as the floor underneath my bare feet.

My brows furrowed. Hafthor was no saint—no doubt there. But Donovan's betrayal hadn't just punished the Magister. It had jeopardized the security of the entire institute.

"I don't understand," I said, my voice rising with frustration. "You can't seriously believe the ends justified the means. These are your people we're talking about!" My pulse quickened as I thought of the Seraphs and the other Earthbounders he put in danger—beings I'd only just discovered existed a few weeks ago but had already started to think of as my own people.

Donovan's jaw clenched. "My father was a true champion," he said. "A loyalist. He would never have sold out his people or eliminated his rivals for a power grab the way Hafthor has done his entire life."

The venom in his tone made my stomach twist.

I'd heard the whispers, the rumors that Hafthor had orchestrated the death of Donovan's father—a man who had once been a contender for the Magister seat. Was revenge all that drove Donovan's actions? What about the innocents caught in the crossfire?

A wave of disgust curled my lip. "You're ruining his legacy. Don't you see? You're nothing like your father. And those nymphs at the Invictus Lake? They will never judge you worthy. I'd stay away from the water, any lake really, if I were you..." The words kept spilling until a cough gripped me.

I peered at Donovan.

If words could wound, I'd just plunged a dagger straight into his heart. Pain flickered in his eyes, only to harden into a glare that burned like a brand.

"Enjoy your stay," he said, his voice low and icy.

He spun on his heel with unnerving composure and loped out of my cell. The guards moved swiftly, ready to seal the door the moment the stubborn warrior departed.

"Wait," I yelled. "They have Nelia. Take her back to Invicta. Please!"

Donovan halted just outside the entrance. My breath caught, my heart pounding so violently it felt as if it might shatter my ribs.

Turn around. Say something. Tell me you'll take her. Just...give me a sign.

Without a single word or look, Donovan resumed striding, his silhouette soon disappearing into a corridor beyond the main entrance.

FOUR

I glared at the girl in the white coat entering my cell as she clutched a small silver case filled with vials. More blood tests. *The almighty Magister Mariola orders, and her lackeys obey.* I'd had enough. Every day, they drained more of me, as if my blood alone would reveal the secrets they were so desperate to uncover.

The girl peered at me with wide, emotionless eyes as she prepared a needle. I flinched at the sight of it, not from fear but from exhaustion.

"Tell your boss she's wasting her time," I said, clenching my fists. "She already has everything she could want from me. There's nothing left."

She ignored me, snapping the syringe into place with clinical detachment.

The frosted entrance slid open again, revealing a tall figure behind it. The daily swarm of lab coats and guards had desensitized me to my surroundings. I didn't expect to see anyone worth my notice.

A chill swept over me when he entered, a presence that

sent the girl in the lab coat scrambling, her face paling as she rushed to leave.

"The canary bites," he drawled.

"Damian," I muttered, my jaw tightening.

He strolled in with that same indifferent arrogance, his eyes drifting over me, assessing, calculating. But there was something else, a flash of anger—or was it possession?—in the depths of his dark gaze. He approached slowly, hands clasped behind his back, his leather coat sweeping around his legs with each step.

"Angel," he said, his voice silk over steel, a feigned gentleness masking his true intentions. "Where are your wings?"

I straightened, resisting the urge to flinch under his scrutiny. "Ask your friend...Mariola."

A muscle in his jaw twitched, his mouth pressing into a thin line as he strolled around my bed. His gaze lingered on the deformed scars. When he came around again, I half-expected to see satisfaction in his expression, that cruel smirk he wore so well when others were suffering. But instead, a flicker of something far darker glinted in his eyes.

"Those wings were mine to take," he said finally, his voice low. "Mariola had no right. And yet..." He leaned closer, his lips curling into a sneer. "...you let her. Just like that."

I scowled. "As if I had a choice."

He laughed, a sound devoid of humor, and pivoted, studying the workers beyond the cell with disdain. "So loyal to her science, our Magister. But she doesn't understand the value of what she takes. Or what it will cost her." His voice had dropped to a near whisper.

"Cost?" I asked. "You're acting as if you didn't betray us all. Even your own accomplice, Hafthor."

He veered back at me, his expression unreadable. "Hafthor is dead." I blinked. The news of Hafthor's demise caught me off guard. *How is it possible?* I'd have accused

Damian of lying, but he never did. His only redeeming qualify —and even that was debatable—was that he always told the truth. Or omitted the truth.

Damian leaned in, delighting in stunning me. "Dead, and I'm still here. Strange, don't you think?"

I frowned, trying to parse his words.

An entertained grunt escaped him. "You really think I ever believed in Hafthor's grand plans? That I was content to be a mere soldier, a pawn, in his little war?" He shook his head, amusement glinting in his eyes. "No, nightshade. Hafthor's goals were...shortsighted. He was never capable of seeing beyond his own lust for power, his desire to disassemble the council and rule over all Earthbounders."

"Then why did you support him?" I asked. "Why fight against your own people?"

"Support him?" The Soaz chuckled, the sound cold and hollow. "Let's just say I allowed him to believe I was an ally. My father was useful, at times. He birthed the chaos, destabilized our system...paved the way for my own plans."

I shook my head, disgust pooling in my stomach. "So, what? You used him? You were manipulating all of us from the start?"

He tilted his head, feigning thoughtfulness. "Manipulation, loyalty...they're meaningless distinctions. What matters is purpose, power, and knowing where to apply pressure." His gaze darkened, the gleam of ownership in his eyes making my skin crawl. "And you are a remarkable weapon in my hands, even now."

I recoiled. "I am *not* your anything."

His hand shot out, fingers gripping my chin tightly, forcing me to look into his eyes. "Not yet," he whispered. His confident gaze held a promise, making me question what the future held and why our paths kept intertwining. One puzzle piece I'd gleaned from our interaction today was that Damian held no regard for Mariola. It was only a matter of time before he stabbed her in the back too.

I forced myself to hold his gaze, feeling a spark of defiance flare in me, even as fear twisted my insides. "What are you planning?"

His dark smirk widened. "If I were you, I wouldn't get too comfortable here."

With that, he turned and strode to the entrance, not bothering to look back as it slid open.

I curled up on the steel cot, squeezing my eyes shut. *He wasn't here. This was just a bad dream.*

But the cold bite of the steel beneath me said otherwise. I bit my trembling lip. I let images of Kole flood my mind—my new daily routine. His brooding demeanor softening each time he laid his eyes on me. Him carrying me to the bed with an uncommon gentleness for the powerful being he was. Him flying, his charcoal wings beating in rhythm with my heart. The shaking abated and I released a long exhale.

I promise I will return to you.

FIVE

The guards escorted me down a pristine corridor lined with soft lighting. We stopped at a door that slid open with a whisper, revealing a luxurious suite. Plush carpets, a gleaming bathroom, and even a set of clean clothes laid out neatly on the bed. It felt like a trap and yet I couldn't resist the relief that flooded through me. After the damp chill of the cell, a hot shower and clean clothes were nearly as tempting as freedom itself.

I took my time under the scalding water, feeling each stream wash away the residue of the transparent box I had been held in for how long now? I had lost track of days. Shutting the water off thrust me back into reality, and a quiet dread settled over me again.

Dressed in loose black pants, a snug shirt, and for the first time in days, sneakers, I drummed my fingers on the seat of the sofa, waiting. A guard reappeared, ushering me silently out of the elegant quarters and down more corridors. He halted at a dark wood door and motioned for me to enter alone. I crossed the threshold, feeling a wave of discomfort settle over me.

The Magister narrowed her eyes from behind a mammoth black stone desk. A small, almost welcoming smile curved her lips, but her cold, devious gaze betrayed her. Stark white walls framed the office, while white shelves held rows of ancient tomes, their cracked spines hinting at the weight of the history they carried.

"Arien," she said, motioning to the chair opposite her desk. "Please, sit."

Reluctantly, I lowered myself into the chair, my gaze never leaving her. I was painfully aware of how little power I held at that moment.

"You seem surprised," she observed, studying my reaction with a curious tilt of her head. "Did you think I would leave you in that cell forever?"

"I don't know what to think," I said, keeping my voice as steady as I could. "Every move you make feels like part of a game."

"Isn't it always?" She gave a slight shrug, almost playful, as if we were discussing nothing more than a casual disagreement. "But this is no game. What I do here...it's the culmination of decades of research. Research your mother helped me start."

I stiffened at the mention of her. "My mother had nothing to do with whatever twisted experiments you're running here."

"Oh, she had everything to do with it." Mariola leaned forward, her voice softening in a way that made my skin prickle. "Your mother was brilliant, you know. Driven, loyal. Until she learned she was pregnant. Then something changed. I blamed the hormones."

I clenched my fists, forcing myself to stay silent as Mariola's gaze grew distant, as if remembering a past life. When she glanced back at me, a hint of nostalgia flickered in her eyes before it was quickly replaced by resolve.

"She and I were pioneers," she said, her voice low but charged. Her fingers drummed against the edge of her desk, a faint rhythm underscoring her words. "We set out to unravel the secrets of the Earthbounder gene, to unlock our full potential—just as our predecessors once could. To push the boundaries of evolution."

She leaned forward, her eyes narrowing with intensity. "Imagine it: every Earthbounder able to travel through the allura as easily as you can. Demonic breaches dealt with in an instant. No need for trackers, no dependence on technology. We would gain the stamina and speed of our ancestors. We could stand as equals against the strongest of Archons."

Her hand curled into a fist, knuckles white. "But then she betrayed me. She stole everything we'd worked for—everything—and vanished, leaving only fragments behind. I've been forced to sift through the wreckage she left, piecing it back together clue by agonizing clue."

My stomach churned with every word she spoke, the unease twisting tighter and tighter inside me. The second-born women who had volunteered for this research never returned home. And what about the births they'd given? What had happened to the children? *This isn't about saving anyone. This is pure obsession.* My eyes darted to her clenched fist, the fury in her words bleeding into the rigid lines of her body. "You act like she destroyed everything," I said, my voice sharper than I intended, even as fear prickled along my skin. "But maybe she was trying to stop *you*."

Mariola tapped a button on her desk, and a holoscreen flickered to life between us. She scrolled through dozens of files, scans of handwritten notes, data sheets, formulas, blueprints... She paused on an image of a woman with soft eyes and wavy light-colored hair, standing beside her, both of them looking toward the camera with expressions of cautious hope. My mother?

My heart clenched, the familiar features of her face like a blade twisting in my chest.

"She left me," Mariola murmured, her gaze fixed on the image. "But she left something even more valuable behind. She left you."

"Me?" The word slipped from my mouth before I could contain it, confusion swelling within me.

"She took our research and integrated it into her own body. She created you as...a vessel of sorts. A being meant to bridge the power of the original Earthbounders and her secondborn blood. You are the key. The culmination of everything we worked to achieve."

Her words hit me like a blow, every syllable twisting my understanding of who I was. My mother...had she truly done this? Had she turned me into some experiment?

I shook my head, bile rising in my throat. "You're insane. My mother may have made mistakes, but she wouldn't have wanted this."

Mariola sighed, almost pitying. "I don't expect you to understand, not yet. But in time, you will see the necessity of what I'm doing here. Together, we can unlock the true potential of what you are. I'm giving you a chance to carry on her legacy." She pierced me with a warning glare.

I forced myself to breathe, steadying the fear that pulsed through my veins like a relentless drumbeat. "I will never help you," I said, my voice firm despite the trembling inside me. "And I know my mother wouldn't have wanted this either. She ran away for a reason." At least, I hoped she had. Maybe she had turned her life around when she found out she was pregnant. Maybe she was trying to protect me.

My gaze flicked to the gold bracelet on my wrist, a bitter mix of admiration and resentment knotting my stomach. The orphanage had kept it safe for me, but now it felt like both a keepsake and a curse.

A flicker of annoyance cracked Mariola's composed mask. "I had hoped you'd be more cooperative, given that we're family," she said. Leaning forward, she lowered her voice to a whisper laced with quiet menace. "But know this: whether you help me willingly or not, the outcome will be the same. I only offered you this chance out of respect for your mother."

I gripped the arms of the chair. She might have stolen my wings, might have revealed truths about my mother that shattered everything I thought I knew, but I wasn't broken. Not yet.

"I think my mother made the right choice," I said slowly, meeting her gaze with as much defiance as I could muster.

She leapt to her feet, brushing off her hands as if to rid herself of the entire conversation.

"Return her to her suite," she said to the guard, her voice cold and final. "She can consider her choices there."

The warrior's iron grip crushed my arms as he yanked me upright and shoved me toward the door. Gone was the eerie politeness from earlier.

"Move faster. I don't have all day," he growled, his breath hot and acrid against my neck.

I stumbled into the suite. The door slammed shut behind me, the sound reverberating through the room like a gunshot. Whirling around, I threw myself at it, my fists hammering against the wood with wild abandon. The dull thud of bone on plank merged with my ragged breaths, each strike releasing a wave of frustration and pain I had bottled up for far too long.

Needing to clear my head, I stomped into the bathroom and stared at my reflection—hollow eyes, hair still damp from the shower, and blotched cheeks. *Give me some answers.*

The burning sensation along my back hadn't stopped since leaving Mariola's office. The strange, dull ache had persisted ever since my wings were severed, but now it felt more intense, prickling just below the surface of my skin, like something trying to push through.

I shrugged off my shirt, craning my neck to get a better look. Bruises rimmed the scars, the flesh still raw and tender. But there was no hint of feathers, no sign of growth, just two indents where wings used to unfurl. I swallowed, willing something—anything—to emerge, but the only response was the lingering burn and an all-too-familiar emptiness.

"I take it the family reunion hasn't gone well..." a deep voice drawled.

SIX

I spun around, a gasp escaping my lips. The Soaz was leaning against the bathroom doorframe, leering. He looked completely at ease, as if he belonged there, his dark coat blending into the shadows of the room.

"What are you doing here?" I snapped, my voice a forced whisper as I grabbed my shirt and pulled it over my head. "How did you get in?"

A slow, unsettling smirk spread across his face. "I go where I please."

I took a step back, instinctively putting more distance between us. "Do you get some sort of thrill from sneaking up on people?" *Of course, he does.*

He chuckled, low and quiet, pushing off the doorframe and nodding toward the suite's sitting room. "Join me," he said, not bothering to check if I'd follow as he strolled away.

I trailed after him, keeping a careful distance. He sank into one of the plush armchairs. "You're gawking. I told you not to get used to the cell," he said. Huh. So the Soaz had arranged my new accommodations, not my lovely aunt. *What gives?* I rolled my eyes at his revelation.

With a flick of his wrist, Damian—as I preferred to call him—grabbed the remote and switched on the television mounted to the wall. The screen flickered to life, and a voice filled the room, dragging my attention away from the Soaz's unsettling presence.

The news anchor's grave expression matched the somber tone in her voice as images flickered across the screen—a blurred montage of familiar places. The footage revealed Invicta, the Seraphs' stronghold in the Northwest, before the camera locked onto Donovan's unmistakable silhouette.

"To address the escalating unrest in the region," the anchor intoned, "Donovan Graves has been appointed as the new Magister of Invicta, effective immediately. Following allegations of aiding the Fringe factions, Invicta's former commander, Xavier, and his loyalists—including the infamous P6 unit—stand accused of treason. Under the new Magister's command, anyone found guilty of conspiring against the institute or endangering its operations will face execution."

I slumped into the couch, my mind reeling. Kole and Xavier, my closest allies, now hunted like traitors. P6—the warriors I'd fought alongside—facing death if captured. And Donovan...Donovan taking Xavier's rightful place, the mantle of Magister now his.

I shook my head, my voice trembling. "This can't be true. Donovan—"

"He picked the right side," he cut in, his gaze piercing as he studied my reaction. "My brother and his men are fugitives now. Outlaws in a system they once served."

A strange numbness settled over me, heavy and suffocating. This news had stripped away the last shreds of hope I'd clung to. I was trapped here, helpless while my friends were hunted and turned enemy.

I would have tucked into a ball and wept if Damian hadn't been here. Why had he come? To revel in my misery?

"Tell me, nightshade." The Soaz's voice broke through the fog of despair clouding my mind. "What would you do for a chance to go out there and find them?"

I peered at him, catching the glint of something predatory in his gaze. He already knew I'd give anything for a chance to see Kole. I hoped my angels were safe. I pressed my lips tighter, refusing to play his games.

He leaned forward, a dark gleam in his eyes. "I could give you what you desire," he murmured, his voice rich with temptation. "Two days of freedom to do as you wish. But only if you're willing to exchange something in return."

Warning sirens went off like a chorus of screaming banshees in my head. *Don't bite, Arien. Don't you dare...*

"What do you want?" I blurted out.

"Your blood," he said, each word falling like a weight between us. "But it will be different this time—a mutual exchange. You drink from me, and I from you."

"I know what exchange means," I said with bite. My mind scrambled, recoiling at the idea. "Why? Why would you want that?"

A flicker of amusement crossed his face, as though he found my confusion endearing. "Let's just say I have my reasons. I could tell you...but it would ruin the surprise." He leaned back, letting the offer hang in the air, then sighed impatiently when I continued to stare ahead. "Think of it as a kind of bond. A blood pact. You would feel my power, and I yours. It might even give you a fighting chance out there."

The idea of tasting his blood left a bitter taste in my mouth. But if he was telling the truth...if this could buy me a chance to escape, to find Kole, Xavier, and the others before it was too late...

I swallowed. "Two days?" I asked, meeting his gaze with resolve. "And then?"

His smile sharpened into a blade, cold and merciless.

"You'll meet me at the Everlake, near the mouth of the cave overlooking New Seattle. If you don't..." His voice dropped, laced with quiet venom. "I'll hunt you to the ends of the earth, and I won't come alone. My army will tear through anyone foolish enough to stand between me and what's mine."

I didn't expect any less from this monster. Scowling, I asked, "What are you going to do during the two days?"

He quirked an eyebrow—the gesture reminded me of Xavier, and a tiny pang of something I'd buried deep squeezed my gut.

"They have this saying in the mundane world: If I tell you, I'm gonna have to kill you." Damian smirked, the scar pulling one side of his lip down. "And that'd be a shame." His tongue flicked out, wetting his lips.

I chewed on the inside of my cheek. What did I have to lose? The alternatives before me were bleak. Remain at Mariola's mercy? In two days, I could find a way to break this weird blood pact.

"I accept," I said.

Damian flashed from his spot to the cushion beside me, his coat brushing my leg. I winced. The closeness unnerved me. The sound of his incisors lowering drew my gaze to his face. He slashed a line across his exposed wrist. Blood welled up on the surface, brimming and overflowing.

"A sip will do," he said, bringing his wrist toward my lips.

With trembling hands, I grabbed it. The pulse beneath his skin beat steady and potent. I pressed my lips around the wound and slurped, making sure I swallowed enough. The rush of his blood, hot and intoxicating, flooded my senses. His hand slid to my neck, and with a quick prick his fangs punctured my skin, the sensation blurring the line between pleasure and pain.

I dropped his arm and placed my hands on his chest,

ready to shove him if he didn't stop soon. Sensing my aggra-
vation, the monster pulled back. His intoxicated gaze held a
mixture of triumph and satisfaction.

"Two days," he said softly, his thumb brushing against the
fresh mark on my neck. "Make the most of them."

"Why do you care?"

I touched the wound, feeling a strange rush of energy
surge through me. Nothing I'd ever felt when he drank from
me before. It was terrifyingly exhilarating, and it made me
feel...powerful, for the first time in days.

Damian shrugged and leapt to his feet. "I don't. Next
time we meet, none of it will matter."

I gasped as a heat wave brushed my spine. Damian rolled
his shoulders.

"You felt it too? That's our bond settling in. Faster than I
anticipated."

Another wave rushed up my spine and I fell to my knees,
my vision blurring. Damian's boots stepped into my line of
vision. He gripped my hair and made me look at him. But
something odd was happening to my eyes—they burned, and
my vision tinted red, on and off.

"Once the tracking link forms between us, there will be
no place for you to hide," he said. Tracking link?

He laughed cruelly, letting go of my hair and leaving me
alone with the searing pain rocking my body. This time I
rolled into a ball, hoping I hadn't made the worst mistake of
my life.

SEVEN

Ice-cold water splashed across my face, yanking me from the fog of restless sleep. I gasped, sputtering.

"What the—?" I scrambled upright, wiping my face with trembling hands. My heart hammered against my ribs, my skin slick with sweat. My vision blurred as I tried to make sense of the dark figure looming over me.

"Rise and shine," Damian drawled, his tone a cutting mix of mockery and impatience. "You're not dying...yet."

I blinked hard, my surroundings coming into focus. The couch legs were at my eye level and a cold surface bit into the palms of my hands. Great, I'd fallen asleep on the floor. I rubbed my shoulders. The remnants of the earlier burning sensation smoldered deep in my bones.

I peered up along black leather-clad legs. Damian stood over me, a glass in one hand, his maniacal smirk in full force.

"What the hell is wrong with you?" I asked, my voice hoarse as I tried to gather myself.

"Nothing you can fix," he shot back, setting the glass down with a deliberate clink before turning away.

The dim light of the suite caught the gleam of steel

strapped across his thighs and hips. Swords, blades, throwing knives—an arsenal, each piece meticulously arranged against the leather of his pants. He shrugged out of his coat and tossed it onto a nearby chair. His tactical shirt stretched over his back, the slits near the shoulder blades already parting to accommodate his wings.

The leathery black expanse emerged with a sickening crack, sending a shiver racing down my spine. The room seemed smaller with them out, their jagged edges brushing against a wall as Damian stretched and flexed, testing the full span.

Most warriors at the Northern Institute didn't know the truth about him. To them, Damian was just another Pure, lethal in his precision but otherwise a normal Earthbounder. Mariola knew, of course. But if Damian was willing to bare his wings now, here in plain sight, he was planning something big.

I opened my mouth to ask, but before I could speak, a short sword clattered into my lap.

"Get up," Damian said, his voice a whipcrack of authority. He raised an eyebrow and with a slight tilt of his head, dared me to argue. "Unless you'd rather stay here?"

I gritted my teeth and pushed myself to my feet, every muscle aching in protest.

"Look at us." He grunted, assessing my readiness with his no-nonsense glare. "I'm starting to think I've grown on you."

I winced. "Thanks, I prefer cancer."

"Hmm." A corner of his lips curled, a faint, wicked smile. "Are you ready to drown our enemy in rivers of their own blood?"

I gulped. Something was coming, all right. The question was whether I'd survive it.

The alarm shrilled through the halls, each wail a knife to my ears. Damian moved with brutal efficiency ahead of me, his blade a blur. He carved through the last of the warriors on this level. The metallic stench of blood filled the air, and crimson pooled beneath prone bodies. My stomach twisted.

Damian wiped his blade on his sleeve with a chilling calm, his gaze cutting to the lone warrior still writhing on the floor.

"You can't do this!" the man gasped, clutching at the gash splitting his side. "The Magister will—"

Damian's boot slammed down on the man's wrist, silencing him with a sickening crunch. "Speak again," he snarled, "and I'll make you regret I didn't finish you."

He kicked open the door to the alluron chamber, the heavy steel groaning as it crashed against the wall. The air inside hit me like a wave, thick with humming energy. The shimmering expanse of the alluron pulsed like a living thing. My skin prickled and giddiness squeezed my gut. I was getting out of this hellhole.

"Touch it," Damian barked, snapping me out of my frozen daze. "Now. Before they catch up."

Boots thundered against the floor behind us, and my pulse spiked. I whipped around as a dozen more guards poured into the chamber. Their weapons glowed faintly with enchantments, their edges sharp enough to cleave bone. I tripped on my feet and sprawled on the floor, giving them enough time to surround me. And Damian, who'd flashed himself to my side, acted like a protector. In reality, I'd always been his pawn. He yanked me up and wrapped his arm around my chest.

"Stop!" the lead guard roared. "Hand the girl over and surrender."

Damian didn't answer. Instead, he unfolded his wings with a grotesque crack, the leathery expanse unfurling like the shadow of death itself. His body rippled, muscles swelling, blackened veins snaking up his arms as his claws elongated. I peered at him—his grin turned savage, his pupils spilling over the whites in his eyes. *Oh, shit...*

The guards hesitated for a fraction of a second. It was all Damian needed.

He launched forward in a blur of claws and fury. His wing smashed into the nearest guard, sending him hurtling into the wall with a bone-crunching thud. Another charged, sword raised, but Damian's claws sliced through his chest, leaving a spray of blood that splattered across the floor.

I screamed, a plea for him to stop tearing from my throat.

Another guard lunged, and Damian caught the man's wrist mid-swing, twisting until the snap of bone cut through the chaos. He slammed the man into the ground with a force that made the floor quake.

Blood coated the walls. I turned in hopeless circles, trying to get away from the fray. But Damian somehow was always there, cutting me off and anyone coming after me. My hands trembled, one gripping the short sword.

He veered toward the last guard standing, his grin feral. The warrior charged with his blade raised, but Damian's claws tore through him in one fluid motion. He crumpled to the floor, moaning.

Panting, Damian stood amidst the devastation, his monstrous wings folding partially, though his eyes still burned with savage intent.

He seized my hand in an iron clasp. "Portal us. Now."

I stared at him, at the blood pooling beneath our feet, at the guards' lifeless bodies. My chest heaved as panic warred with the pull of the alluron behind me.

"Now," he snarled, yanking me toward the portal.

The barrier pulsed, its rhythm matching my frantic heartbeat. Swallowing the bile in my throat, I pressed my palm to its surface.

Light and shadow swirled around us. I concentrated on the location. Then the world steadied, and cold air bit at my skin. I staggered, falling to my knees in the grass. The scent of pine and damp earth filled my lungs.

Behind me, Damian landed with a dull thud. Slowly, his monstrous form shrank, his claws retracting, and the veins faded. Within moments, he faced me as his usual self, though his eyes still glinted with something feral.

He scanned the clearing with suspicion. "What is this place?"

I brushed dirt from my palms. "The only safe location I know. I used to come here with Pau—Kwanezerus," I fibbed. Xavier had brought me here once to meet the great druid. And I suspected it had only worked for me because of some connection I had with the mysterious creatures—Kole had said I was their familiar. "It holds enough druid magic to use it as a portal."

Damian sneered, his lip curling. "I despise lies. But it won't matter soon."

He stepped closer, his tone dropping to a cold whisper. "You have two days."

"And if I don't come?" I asked, my voice shaking despite the strength I tried to project.

His cruel grin widened. "Then I'll come after you. And trust me—it won't be pretty."

His words grated against my nerves. He reached out, brushing his knuckles lightly against my neck and the mark from our blood exchange began throbbing.

"I can feel you now, nightshade," he murmured. "No matter where you go, when the bond between us fully forms, I'll know. There's no hiding."

My breath hitched as loathing flared in my chest. "You're sick."

Damian laughed, the sound low and mocking. "And yet,

I'm the one giving you a gift. Two days. Isn't that generous?"
He stepped back, wings unfurling. "But don't fool yourself—
you won't care about your angels once you return to me."

What did he mean?

The monster launched into the air, his dark form disappearing into the sky.

His parting words echoed in my mind. My fists clenched as the storm inside me raged with fury and determination that burned hotter with each passing second.

Damian was delusional—I'd never stop caring about my angles, my family. And if severing the bond meant removing him out of the picture then that's what I'd have to do. I just had to do it quickly.

EIGHT

T he mountain stretched quiet and endless under the pale glow of moonlight, its ridges like the spine of some ancient, sleeping beast. The crisp night air stung my skin, carrying the tang of pine and the earthy scent of moss and damp underbrush. I stood motionless, arms wrapped tightly around myself as if I could block out the biting chill. My heart pounded, its rhythm weaving into the whispering winds that stirred the grass at my feet.

Would they hear me? Could I even call them?

The great druid had said we were connected—that they would answer me if I reached out. But standing here now, with nothing but the cold and silence pressing in, doubt gnawed at me.

I closed my eyes and forced my breath to steady, focusing on the memory of the druids as they had appeared that day in the clearing with Xavier and Kole. They had been radiant, glowing like living constellations cloaked in silver and green. Their movements had been fluid, like streams flowing through a forest, their voices resonant and rich, humming with the very essence of nature.

They had spoken to me as though I belonged to them—*with* them. That connection had felt so real then, like a thread binding us together.

I latched onto that thread now, gripping it with everything I had. *Please, hear me. Find me.*

The wind shifted, colder now, brushing against my face like a ghostly hand.

"Please," I whispered, my voice barely more than a breath, swept away by the restless wind. "I need your help." The words trembled as they left me. "I don't know where to start, but you said I was connected to you. If that's true—if there's even a shred of that connection left—show me. Let me know you're there."

For a moment, nothing. The silence pressed in. The night seemed to hold its breath.

Then, the air shifted.

A low hum rose from the earth beneath my feet, faint at first but building in intensity, vibrating through my bones. The wind turned, its icy edge softening as it carried a new scent—wildflowers and damp, ancient earth, rich and alive. A pale glow began to flicker at the edge of the field, like fireflies gathering in the distance.

The glow grew stronger, swirling and coalescing into shapes. One by one, the druids stepped forward, their forms solidifying in the moonlit haze.

The great druid, their leader, emerged first. He moved with quiet authority, his tall, lean figure draped in a silver cloak that shimmered like spun moonlight. His ageless face carried both wisdom and an otherworldly calm, framed by flowing hair that rippled as if touched by an invisible current.

Around him, the others gathered in a wide semicircle, their eyes radiant in the dusk. My legs threatened to buckle under the weight of their collective gaze. But I held my ground, heart racing as I waited for him to speak.

"Arien," he said, his tone rumbling like distant thunder. "You have called us, and we have come. What is it you seek?"

I swallowed hard, my throat dry and tight. "I seek your help," I said. "I need to find P6 warriors. Would you happen to know where they are now?"

His soulful eyes locked onto mine. He regarded me in silence.

"Your heart is troubled," he said at last as though he was tasting each word before releasing it. "The paths before you are shadowed, but the ties you share with us endure. We would give to you freely, should you choose to accept it."

My brows furrowed. "What do you mean?" I asked.

He neared me, his presence washing over me like an ocean —steady, calming, yet undeniably commanding. "A place among us. A refuge. You carry burdens that strain the very fabric of your being. Let us shoulder them with you," he said.

The offer stole the breath from my lungs. I glanced at the druids surrounding us; none even so much as blinked. They all agreed with their leader. The temptation to let someone else carry my burdens was there, but I couldn't. Not while Kole and the P6 members were out there fighting to survive. Not while Xavier and Nelia needed me.

"I appreciate your kindness," I said and dipped my head in show of respect. "But I can't stay. I need to find my friends."

His eyes softened. He held my gaze, the silence stretching until it felt like the entire mountain had stilled with us. Then he nodded.

"If that is your will, then we shall aid you in the way you desire. The one you seek...is not on the surface." He paused and a chill crept along my skin. "What you seek lies beneath," he said, his voice dipping into a near-whisper.

I lost the ability to speak. *Ohmagod, please tell me he's alive. The druid surely doesn't mean six feet under...?*

The great druid extended his hand, palm up. A soft glow shimmered to life above it, the light unfurling like liquid gold and casting faint shadows between us. "The Underground," he said, his voice reverent. "A hidden web beneath the world you know, veiled from those who walk only in the light. It is there you must go to find him. There, among the shadows, lies the path you seek."

The word Underground jolted something loose in my mind. A memory surged forward of the tunnels beneath New Seattle. The damp, suffocating air. The endless maze of darkness. Back then, I had chosen the Fringe tunnel, blissfully unaware of the secrets lurking just beyond my reach.

"How do I find it?" I asked, my voice taut with urgency.

He peered over his shoulder, casting his gaze on the druids behind him. With fluid grace, they moved as one, their steps synchronizing as if following the same silent rhythm. They formed a circle around me.

The glow surrounding them swelled, spilling over the field in waves of pale, ethereal light. The air thickened, vibrating with an energy that raised goosebumps along my arms. I fought the urge to leap out.

"We will open the way," the druid said in a reassuring tone.

I inhaled sharply.

The druids raised their hands. The light around them blazed brighter, searing against my eyes until I had to squint. It swirled, forming a portal that rippled like the surface of a restless lake.

The great druid stepped aside, gesturing toward the rippling mass. "This door will take you into the tunnels beneath your city. There, at the fork you once passed, lies an opening you have not seen before. Take that path, and it will bring you closer to what you seek."

I stared at the swirling energy. There was no turning back. Not now.

So, I shuffled my feet and stepped through without a second glance.

The light engulfed me, searing and infinite, until there was nothing but the blinding radiance and the sound of my heartbeat pounding in my ears.

NINE

When the light faded, the world around me shifted, plunging me into the familiar gloom of the city tunnels. The air pressed heavily against my skin, damp and rank. The faint drip of water echoed through the space.

I turned instinctively, half-hoping to see the druids standing behind me, but they were gone. The portal had vanished, leaving nothing but pitch-black darkness in its place.

Swallowing the knot in my throat, I pivoted toward the only source of light—a pale stream spilling from the vast open space ahead. I jogged, stomping in and out of puddles. The circular opening revealed a dome ceiling over a broad chamber that served as a maintenance station for the city's water supply. One of many and only accessed in emergencies. Water gushed and splashed in the corridors, the chaotic sound crashing in my ears like a waterfall.

My eyes locked onto the rusty metal bridge spanning the chasm. It hovered above the flooded passages, its skeletal frame slick with grime. The bridge led to the far side of the dome, where the muted light illuminated the entrances of four tunnels.

I knew this place.

Memories slammed into me with the force of a gale—the Archon's attack in the junkyard, my frantic escape, and stumbling upon the hidden passage that had led me here. From this chamber, I had traversed an ancient, beam-supported tunnel to the Fringe.

Steeling myself, I stepped onto the bridge. The worn metal groaned faintly under my weight. My boots slipped on the slick surface, the murky water below sloshing through the grating. Rust flaked off from the railing and bit into my palms as I righted myself. I stared at my blood mixing with the brown residue. *Oh, nice. Why does my every escape attempt have to involve bleeding?*

On the other side now, four tunnels yawned like black voids in the concrete wall. My eyes swept across the faint markings etched into the plaster near each entrance, their lettering crude but legible.

The first tunnel led to Central Station in the City Center. The second pointed west toward St. James's Abbey. The third marked the Queen's District in the southeast. My gaze lingered on the fourth marking—a single, jagged letter "F." The Fringe. Goosebumps erupted on my skin. Thank the angels I wasn't going there today.

I brushed my fingers over the rough, crusty wall, flakes of plaster crumbling beneath my fingertips and scattering to the ground. My boots echoed softly as I paced between the four openings, scanning the darkness for any sign of the Underground's entrance. It had to be here. Somewhere.

A subdued glimmer on the far-left side caught my eye. I froze, narrowing my gaze on a small, almost invisible opening tucked in the shadows. The glow surrounding it was easy to miss. What eventually gave it away was a soft pulse, the same ethereal light that had surrounded the druids earlier.

My stomach churned as I neared it. The light flickered, weak and unsteady, as though it might fade entirely if I hesitated too long. It hummed with a strange, electric energy that made the fine hairs on my arms stand on end. I pressed my palm to the jagged stone of the frame.

A powerful jolt shot through me like lightning exploding from the stone. The force knocked me backward, my body hitting the ground with a jarring thud. I lay there, blinking at the dome ceiling and wondering if the amplified white noise in my ears was a result of me banging my head pretty damn hard or the rushing water.

"What the—?" I croaked, sitting up. My head spun. For a moment, I just sat there, stunned, the charged air still prickling my skin.

Shaking it off, I pushed myself to my knees. The glow in the opening pulsed weakly, almost taunting me. I clenched my jaw, determination outweighing my fear, and reached out again—this time slower.

The instant my fingertips connected with the frame, the same surge of energy erupted. It slammed into me like a battering ram, throwing me back with an even greater force. My shoulder hit the ground hard, and pain radiated through me as I sprawled on the damp stone.

I glared at the faint light still flickering in the shadows. Whatever this was, it didn't want me to pass. But why? The great druid had sent me here. He wouldn't have done it, if I wasn't supposed to pass.

Unless...

My hand shot to my neck, trembling as my fingers brushed over the faint mark left by Damian's bite. The scar burned under my touch, a reminder of the tainted blood now coursing through me. How much time did I have before it changed me completely?

Ever since the exchange, I'd felt...different. It wasn't just the heat that had ripped through me like wildfire or the unnatural surge of energy that had left me reeling. No, this was deeper, darker. Something crawled beneath my skin, a constant whisper just beyond hearing, insidious and relentless.

I turned toward a small puddle nearby, the dreary surface catching faint reflections. I leaned closer, breathing slowly.

What?

My eyes were wrong.

At first, they looked normal—blue, just as they'd always been. But as I tilted my head, I caught sight of a rim of red that encircled my irises like a halo, so subtle it almost escaped notice.

I blinked rapidly and got to my feet.

Has Damian's blood twisted something inside me?

The thought sent an icy shiver down my spine. *Breathe. Focus.* Panicking wouldn't help.

"I'm still me," I whispered, my voice shaking. But as my gaze landed on the unrelenting passage, doubt slithered into my thoughts, coiling tighter with every passing second.

What if I'm not me anymore?

The memories crashed over me, dragging me under. Every loss, every failure, every part of me that felt shattered rushed in—stoking fury and a foreign craving for revenge. The passage seemed to sense the darkness within me.

"No," I said aloud, my voice trembling. "This isn't who I am. I'm not Damian's creation. I'm not my mother's mistake. I'm *me*."

I paced in front of the tunnels, hugging myself.

I'm Arien.

I'm still me.

I'm good.

I repeated the words like a mantra. They cut through the noise in my mind, carving out space to think. This wasn't about the changes in my body, the red in my eyes, or the power crawling beneath my skin. It was about the choices I'd made all my life, the lives I'd saved and fought for.

A strange calm washed over me. I sighed and faced the tunnel. The faint light that had flickered and faltered earlier glowed steadily, warm and inviting as if it had been there all along. Waiting for me to find *myself*.

This time, I didn't hesitate. I reached out, my hand steady as it brushed the jagged edge of the opening. A soft pulse greeted me. It wrapped around me like a gentle current, coaxing me forward. The air shifted from damp to earthy. The shimmer behind me dissolved, plunging me into darkness once again. I placed one foot in front of the other, trailing along the rough wall with my hand for balance. My boots scuffed against the uneven floor, and I began picking my feet up higher. I'd look like a total nutcase to an onlooker, but it was either that or kissing the ground, and I'd had enough of that today.

Thoughts of getting closer to Kole, the P6ers, and Xavier grounded me. If it weren't for the lack of any guiding light and the uneven terrain, I'd have run. Instead, I had to console myself with seeing them soon and the reminder: *You're still you.* It wasn't just a pep talk with me anymore; it was a promise.

TEN

The tunnel wound deeper into the earth, and the air, surprisingly, grew warmer with each step. A slight metallic tang mingled with something restless that prickled at the edge of my senses. It felt like walking into the heart of a beast.

At some point, clumps of bioluminescent moss appeared, clinging to the dirt walls. I studied them initially, wary they might be traps or some advanced technology. But as far as I could tell, they were just plants—natural, living, and oddly thriving in a place without sunlight. Still, their existence gnawed at the back of my mind. How?

The tunnel eventually widened, spilling into a massive cavern. My pulse quickened as I pressed myself to the rough wall, straining to peer into the space.

The Underground base sprawled before me like a hidden city carved out of the earth itself. Rough stone walls soared high above, studded with industrial lights that cast a warm, golden light over the space. Makeshift structures made of metal scraps and salvaged wood clustered together, their jagged edges softened by the draping of worn fabric or plant life that had somehow found a way to grow in here.

Pipes and cables snaked along the cavern walls, leading to generators that hummed with low, constant energy. The air buzzed with the sound of machinery and distant voices.

Earthbounders moved through the space in small groups. Some carried crates of supplies, while others sat around makeshift tables, deep in conversation. A few stood guard at key points, their weapons strapped to their backs and waists.

In the far corner, a workshop sent sparks flying as someone welded pieces of metal together. Another section appeared to be a communal gathering area, with rows of simple chairs and a central platform, as if they held meetings or gave speeches there.

It was nothing like the sleek, sterile halls of Invicta or the neat streets of the Fringe. This was a place built out of necessity, carved by hands that had nowhere else to go.

I edged farther into the cavern, keeping to the shadows as much as I could. Every step felt like a gamble. These were rebels—Earthbounders who had turned their backs on Invicta, on the Seraphs. If they saw me, would they recognize me? Or would they see me as an enemy?

I clung to the hope that Kole was here, that he'd vouch for me before anyone decided to shoot first and ask questions later.

I skirted past a pile of crates. The sharp smell of gasoline and metal wafted my way. My hand brushed against the rough surface of a support beam, and I winced as splinters bit into my palm. I sucked in a breath, glancing around to make sure no one had heard.

The cavern seemed too big, too open. I had no idea where to start. My pulse quickened as I scanned the faces of those nearby, searching desperately for Kole and the others.

I ducked behind another stack of supplies, stepping onto a piece of loose metal.

Clang!

The sound echoed through the cavern like a thunderclap.

I froze, panic clawing at my chest as heads whipped around in my direction. A moment later, a piercing alarm blared. The sound bounced off the walls in a deafening crescendo.

"Who's there?!" a voice boomed.

Guards appeared from every direction, surrounding me, their swords raised. Some transitioned into their true forms with their wings unfurled.

My muscles locked into place. My gaze darted between the drawn weapons and their faces—some wary, some openly hostile.

A man with broad shoulders and golden-flecked eyes stepped forward, his sword angled toward me. His long wings flexed behind him, brushing the edges of the cavern floor with their tips. He must have been older than Kole to have grown such magnificent wings. "You've got five seconds to explain what you're doing here," he said.

"I—" My words stuck, my mind racing for something—anything—to say that wouldn't get me killed or put my friends in danger if they were in hiding.

The guard's eyes narrowed, his sword shifting closer. Its edge caught the light, blinding me for a second. I scrunched my eyes shut.

"Is Roan here?" I blurted, the name escaping before I could second-guess myself. No one slit my throat, so I blinked my eyes open.

The warriors exchanged wary glances but gave no immediate reaction. The one closest to me frowned but didn't lower the sword.

"I'm looking for Roan," I said, my voice trembling but insistent. "He knows me."

Still nothing. No recognition. No easing the tension. Just the cold steel of their weapons and the weight of their scrutiny.

I'm screwed.

"I don't want to cause trouble. I just—"

"You've already caused trouble," the golden-eyed guard snapped, cutting me off. He gestured with his sword, motioning for the others to tighten their circle around me.

My throat bobbed as I braced for the worst.

Then a voice from the back of the group spoke up. "Roan?"

A lean woman with short-cropped silver hair and faint scars along her jawline stepped forward. Her dusty brown wings were clipped tightly behind her back. She studied me.

"You know Roan?" she asked, her tone cautious but less hostile than that of the others.

"Yes," I said quickly. "He rescued me from the Fringe."

The leader growled low in his throat, clearly unhappy with the idea, but the woman raised a hand, silencing him. "I'll take her to him," she said.

"But—"

"She said Roan knows her," she said, her sharp gaze cutting to him. "If it's a lie, he'll deal with her himself. Stand down."

The guard scowled but lowered his sword. The others followed suit, though their weapons remained close at hand, and their wings didn't fold away.

The woman wheeled back to me, her expression as hard as stone. "You try anything, and I'll put you down myself. Understand?"

I nodded, swallowing the lump in my throat.

"Good." She gestured for me to follow toward a path at

the far side of the cavern. I fell in step with her, keeping my hands at my sides and visible. My heart raced as we turned a corner, and the space opened into what looked like a large meeting chamber.

I recognized Roan's silhouette among dozens of others gathered here. The lean tall kind with room to fill more muscle—a rarity among the Pures. Maybe he preferred long-distance runs?

He whirled around as if I'd called his name, his expression shifting from guarded to surprised as his eyes landed on me. "Arien?"

The tension in my chest loosened, replaced by a rush of relief. "Hey," I said and nodded my head in a polite gesture. I'd only met the warrior once, if I didn't count the high school years, and although he'd been friendly then, I didn't know the norms and hierarchy the rebellion had in this place.

The woman stopped short, waiting for his signal.

"I've got her from here," Roan said, grinning. "Well, I'll be damned." He closed the distance between us in a few long strides, his arms wrapping around me in a firm but careful hug, as though afraid I might break. I squeaked anyway, more from surprise.

"You're alive," he said, pulling back just enough to look at me, his hands still resting on my shoulders. "Of course, you're alive. You're too damn stubborn not to be." He grinned again, his eyes gleaming.

I opened my mouth to respond, but he didn't give me a chance.

"You've got a knack for showing up in the most unexpected places, you know that?" His voice carried the same teasing lilt I remembered from the Fringe escape, though there was something deeper beneath it now—concern, maybe even relief.

"I didn't know if you'd even be here," I said.

"Where else would I be?" he said, watching me like he couldn't quite believe I was standing in front of him. "The Underground's been a little busy, you might've noticed. But enough about that—what the hell happened to you?"

I hesitated.

Roan's grin faltered, his sharp gaze catching the flicker of emotion on my face. His hand dropped from my shoulder, though his expression didn't lose its warmth. "Hey, we'll get to that. You're here now, and that's a win as far as I'm concerned," he said, his voice lighter now, the teasing edge back. "You look like hell."

A laugh bubbled up from my chest despite myself, shaky but real. "I've been through hell."

"Of course you have." He clapped his hands together and motioned toward a raised platform leading to a massive carved door. "Well, let's start untangling this mess. You've got that look again—the one that says trouble isn't far behind."

I stopped him with my hand on his arm. As much as I enjoyed Roan's company and owed him now twice for saving my life, there was one thing I needed to ask him more than anything else.

"Is the P6 unit here?"

ELEVEN

Roan led me into a vast chamber carved from rough stone, its industrial lights strung overhead like artificial stars casting a warm, uneven glow. The space balanced between a meeting hall and a lounge—one side dominated by a long, battered oval table, while the other held mismatched couches and chairs scattered haphazardly. The air carried a strange mix of coffee and leather, underscored by the faint tang of metal, and a low murmur of voices hummed through the room.

Within a few seconds of us stepping inside, the murmur ceased.

Dozens of eyes locked onto me. Earthbounders of every faction, gender, and status filled the room—some seated around the table, others sprawled on couches or leaning against the walls. Their faces told a shared story: hard lines carved by battles and exhaustion etched deep. But beneath it all, sharp curiosity burned in their gazes as they studied me, sizing me up, judging whether I belonged.

A man with a jagged scar slashing across his cheek squinted at me, his hand resting with deliberate ease on the hilt of a blade strapped to his thigh. Nearby, a tall, wiry woman with tightly braided hair and eyes like molten gold leaned back in her chair, her wings half-unfurled in a stance that was equal parts casual and poised for action. In the corner, a younger Earthbounder with messy black hair froze, his pen stilling mid-scratch against a notepad as he stared at me as if I'd grown two heads.

Whispers rippled through the room, a quiet current I couldn't fully catch but didn't need to. I knew what they were saying. *Who is she? What is she doing here?*

The weight of their scrutiny pressed against me, hot and heavy, setting every nerve on edge. My instinct told me to bolt, but I clenched my fists and forced myself to keep pace. Roan's presence steadied me, his easy grin slicing through the room's tension. He strode forward like he belonged.

"C'mon," he murmured, nudging me with a light elbow. "Ignore them."

Easy for him to say. I scowled in response to their intense stares, and some of them eventually looked away. Fighting power with power was the way of Earthbounders even when my chances were shit to nothing. And now with my wings absent, I didn't know where I ranked anymore—a Pure who could not fly? I gritted my teeth. What did it matter? I hadn't fit in before, so nothing's changed.

Roan veered right, weaving between couches with practiced ease and heading for a shadowed corner. My pulse quickened. I sped up, leaving him behind. The warrior chuckled softly.

Dark brown waves came into view, the head bowed slightly, with his back to me. Warriors surrounded him. A red-haired girl swiveled her head in my direction, her severe green eyes widening. Zaira!

A group of warriors rose and got in my way, their broad

frames forming a wall of muscle. I shoved through, ignoring their sneers and muttered protests.

"Kole!" I yelled, my voice cracking.

I broke free and froze as the Earth seemed to tilt under my feet. Time slowed; the noise of the room faded into a dull hum.

Kole stood a few feet away, facing me, mighty and scowling like a god of thunder. His piercing chocolate eyes locked onto mine, pulling me in and stealing my breath. His lips, sinful and unapologetically kissable, parted slightly in surprise. His square jaw was every bit a replica of a Greek god statue.

His charcoal gray wings snapped wide, commanding everyone's attention and sending a clear message: *Mine*.

I understood their language perfectly now and I only wished I could unfurl my wings in response and claim him in return.

My legs moved instinctually, carrying me toward him.

Kole loped, his long legs closing the distance between us in seconds. His formidable wings flexed again, their power and expanse warning anyone to stay back.

We collided in the middle, his arms wrapping around me with a strength that made my knees buckle. His scent—cedar and rain—washed over me. He swept his wings forward, cocooning us and shutting out the world.

I pressed my hands to his chest, my fingertips feeling the frantic rhythm of his heartbeat. My forehead dropped to his shoulder, and for a moment, nothing else existed.

"You're here," he murmured, his voice rough and raw with rare emotion. He tightened his hold, his fingers pressing into my back like he feared I'd disappear.

"I'm here," I whispered back.

He pulled back just enough to meet my gaze, his expression torn between relief and rage. I opened my mouth, but the words jammed in my throat, stuck behind the emotions crashing over me. He cupped my face, his thumb brushing across my cheekbone. His wings tightened their protective hold. His voice turned into something fierce. "Never again. Do you hear me? Never again."

He scrutinized my eyes, his lips pressed into a firm line. The red halo must have rooted itself in place.

My chest tightened, and I let myself lean into him for the first time in what felt like forever. His warmth, his strength, the sheer intensity of him—it pushed the chaos of the past days into the distance, even if just for this moment. I rested my hand over his, my fingers curled slightly, and nodded into his touch.

Kole withdrew his wings and the room surged back to life. He kept his hand firmly pressed to my lower back while stepping aside, revealing me to the others.

Zaira's eyes rounded, her fingers tightening on Rae's arm. The two female warriors gaped at me. Vex stood nearby with his arms crossed, his usual sardonic smirk absent, replaced by a rare flicker of shock. Mezzo and Anhelm stilled but their faces remained masks of careful neutrality.

And then there was Xavier.

His expression twisted into a storm of emotions, each fighting for control before giving way to the next. His sharp, commanding features faltered when his eyes met mine, disbelief striking first. A flood of guilt followed, so heavy it seemed to dim the air around him. For a fleeting moment, relief broke through, lifting something intangible from his shoulders—but just as quickly, guilt returned, tightening his jaw and hardening his mouth into a thin line.

He didn't move, his entire body wound tight, his hand clenched at his side like he was trying to control himself. His gaze flicked to Kole, something unreadable flashing in his eyes—acknowledgment, resignation, maybe both.

Kole's wings twitched with agitation and Xavier took half a step back, his shoulders stiffening. I scowled at Kole, not fully understanding what made him react that way. Perhaps he'd found out about the kiss? The former Invicta commander hadn't meant it; it was an act of desperation. He'd been hurting after discovering Nelia had been sent away. I shivered knowing I'd seen his sister but wasn't able to free her.

Xavier's eyes lingered on me for a moment longer, and though he guarded his feelings well, there was a flash of something raw in his eyes. Regret. Longing. Pain.

"Fine, I'll welcome her back," Vex muttered, breaking the charged silence. His exasperated tone did nothing to hide the smirk creeping onto his face. He proceeded to go around the female warriors, but Zaira and Rae darted ahead, nearly tripping him in their rush to reach me.

My grin broke wide as Rae tugged me toward a U-shaped couch and pulled me down onto the pliable cushions. Zaira stepped aside, letting Kole take the seat to my left, her scowl compelling Mezzo and Anhelm to scoot over. Mezzo rolled his eyes but complied, while Anhelm's eyes lit up. Vex plopped down beside Rae, his smirk firmly back in place, crowding her in his usual way. Across from us, Xavier sank into a chair with a heavy sigh, dragging a hand through his blond curls.

I leaned into Kole's side, prepping myself mentally for the inevitable interrogation. The P6-ers never let anyone off the hook, including me. But I had questions, too, especially about Invicta and the council.

I glanced at Xavier. He sat rigid, his curls tousled as though he'd run his hands through them a hundred times. The former commander might have despised his duties, but leadership ran deep in him, etched into his very core. Losing his position must have crushed him.

A new figure emerged from the far side of the room.

"Seth?" I said, my voice tainted with surprise. "I mean Exiousai." I corrected my blunder. The P6 leader and I hadn't exactly parted on good terms when he suspected I had enabled the Archon to return. Much had changed since I'd last seen him though. Kole had suspected the rebellion imprisoned him. Based on the ease with which he approached us now, Seth was no prisoner here. Maybe the Underground leaders had granted him refuge like they had my friends?

His easy presence brought me back to the day we first met. He'd combed his jet-black hair neatly, and his crisp shirt and tweed jacket remained pristine, even here. Roan trailed behind the P6 leader.

"Arien, welcome," Seth said.

"Thank you?" I said, rubbing my forehead. "What are you doing here?"

"Seth is our leader," Roan said, gesturing toward him with a small, almost proud smile.

"What?"

"I've been leading the Underground for years," Seth said. "P6, although successful in its mission, has always been the front for the rebellion."

"But..." I pinched my lips, trying to get a grip on the situation.

"We didn't know. None of us ever knew," Kole said.

"It was too risky." Seth shrugged. "The Underground doesn't recruit. Those tired of Invicta's regime usually find their way to us. We leave enough clues and informers on the ground. That's how Kole eventually tracked me down here, and the rest followed. We grabbed Xavier and his men from Invicta's cells following their arrests."

I raised a questioning eyebrow. Why would Seth want to save Xavier? He represented Invicta—the rebellion's numero uno enemy—after all.

"We figured, unlike Hafthor and the new Magister Donovan, Xavier can be reasoned with," Roan said. I glanced at the Seraph and his men, relief flooding me. The idea of losing him caused instant pain in my chest. Although he'd been arrogant and condescending, he'd also been caring and a patient teacher.

"Thank you...for saving the Seraphs. You can trust them. I trust them," I said. Whoa, where had that come from? Heat flushed up my neck. Roan grinned at me.

"But in case we don't trust them, there are always short swords, throwing stars, and those tiny slim knives Talen specializes in. What does he call them?" Vex asked. A small smile formed on my lips. Vex always knew how to lighten the mood. I peered around the chamber in search of the tall warrior.

"Where is Talen?" I asked.

"Patrol," Kole whispered.

"Oh."

"What happened to you?" Rae asked.

I took a deep breath and exhaled it forcefully. "The feather call was a trap. The girl worked for Damian. I fought him. I tried to get back...after he put me to sleep with some drug, I woke up at the Northern Institute as their newest lab rat."

Xavier straightened abruptly in his seat, his eyes narrowing. "Magister Mariola had you all this time? What does she want with you?"

"To study me, my genes," I said, the words bitter in my throat. I rubbed the gold bracelet on my wrist. "She's my aunt."

Rae gasped.

Seth's expression darkened, his brow furrowing as he leaned slightly forward. "I met her sister once, a long time ago. I can see the resemblance now."

"But your mother—" Rae said.

"Is dead. That remains true," I said. Glancing at Xavier, I added, "I saw Nelia. I begged Donovan to take her with him, but I don't know if he did. Have you seen her?"

"Donovan?" Xavier said with a hiss.

"He visited me once. I don't know why. I haven't seen him since."

The silence stretched unbearably long, broken only by the hum of the generators in the distance. Xavier's jaw clenched, and his fists tightened on the arms of his chair.

"No," he said finally, his voice like icicles.

His words sent a chill through me. If Donovan hadn't rescued Nelia, then what had happened to her? My heart ached at the thought.

Seth tilted his head, studying me. "Last question, for now... How did you escape one of the most secure compounds in Earthbounder possession?"

TWELVE

The room had gone still, every breath drawn but not released. The damp, earthen walls seemed to press inward as if even the Underground itself was waiting. The low whirr of distant machinery, the faint drip of water from the cavern ceiling—everything faded into silence.

Xavier stilled. Kole's fingers tapped once against his thigh, then stopped. The P6ers watched, their usual restless energy drained from them. Even Seth, whose patience had its limits, waited.

I exhaled, but the words caught in my throat. *Say it.*

The memory of Damian's mocking voice curled through my mind.

"Damian." The name tasted bitter.

Xavier's fingers twitched. I didn't dare to peer at Kole. I could feel his untamed hatred for the Soaz vibrating between us, barely contained beneath his skin.

"He offered a blood pact in exchange for my freedom," I said, my voice steady, though my stomach knotted at the memory. The sensation of his incisors piercing my skin. The way he watched me as the pact took hold. "Then he slaughtered his way to the alluron chamber with me in tow. He left bodies in every corridor. No one saw him coming."

Silence. I could sense them turning it over, making sense of it. Could feel the magnitude of his actions settling in their bones.

Xavier rose to his full height, his arms rigid at his sides. "What does he want from you?"

I hesitated. I knew what he wanted. He'd made it clear in every unspoken promise, every private moment between us. But saying it out loud would give it power.

I met Xavier's gaze. "He didn't say. He insisted that in two days, not much else will matter to me." I didn't mention the rest—the part I hadn't even allowed myself to process yet. That after two days, I would no longer care for my angels. I could still hear Damian's voice wrapping around those words, like a spell curling in my veins.

Roan muttered something under his breath.

Then Vex, ever the impatient one, let out a sharp exhale and lifted his hand, waving it between us. "Uh, okay, love all the doom and gloom, but are we just gonna ignore the giant flaming elephant in the room?"

I blinked at him. "What?"

He pointed at my face. "Your eyes. Nobody's gonna mention how they're doing that creepy red glow thing? Just me? Cool, guess I'm the crazy one."

My stomach dropped. Not now. Not here.

I blinked hard as if I could shake the red halo away. Then slowly, I turned to Kole. "Is it still there?"

He didn't answer immediately. His gaze flicked over my face, lingering at my eyes. His fingers twitched, just once. Whatever he saw there, he didn't like it. Something behind his eyes locked into place, a decision forming.

Xavier let out an abrupt venomous exhale. "*Fucking* Damian."

Vex flopped back, crossing his arms. "Yeah, no shit."

Seth studied me with the intensity of someone fitting the last piece of a puzzle into place.

I swallowed. "What does that mean?"

"It means you're changing," he said.

Cold slithered through my veins. I was hoping for something more like *"Oh, don't worry, that's normal. It happens to everyone."*

Seth's attention slid to Roan. "Double the patrols on the surface."

Roan nodded once, already turning to leave. "I'll handle it." As he strode out, the room remained heavy, weighted with everything left unsaid. I could feel their stares on me. Waiting. Expecting me to say something, to explain, to reassure them that I was still me.

But all I could hear was Damian's voice, saying those cursed words: *Two days.*

And I didn't know what would be left of me when the time ran out. I forced a breath, steadying myself. "It's not permanent," I said, though I had no evidence to back it up. "It's just...residual. From the blood pact. Right?"

No one answered right away.

Xavier ran a hand through his hair, his movements clipped and frustrated. "Residual from what? Damian's influence? That's not something you can just shake off."

I clenched my jaw. "I know."

"I don't think you do," he shot back. "You let him tie you to him in a blood pact—do you even know what that means? Do you feel him?"

I bristled at his rebuke of me. I hesitated. Did I feel Damian? I tuned in to my body. I could sense him, like the faintest tug on a thread wrapped around my ribs. Not words, not thoughts—just awareness. As if I reached out, I'd brush against his presence waiting for me in the dark.

"Arien," Xavier barked. "Does he have a hold on you?"

Don't touch your wrist. Don't let them see you hesitate. I forced an unwavering stare.

"I don't know yet," I lied. "The connection isn't that strong."

Kole made a noise low in his throat, the kind that meant he didn't believe a word of it. I hated this. I hated standing here, feeling like I was being dissected. Like I was becoming something I couldn't control.

Vex clicked his tongue. "Alright, well, that's not concerning at all."

I shot him a glare, but he just grinned.

Seth's brows furrowed. "It's a compulsion. A slow one. Blood pacts can be layered with commands." A sick feeling curled inside me. Was I that easy to manipulate? I'd just lied to Kole and we had promised to have no secrets between us. To me he said, "Fight it. We need time to reverse your condition."

Zaira gave me a reassuring nod.

Seth watched me a moment longer, then exhaled. "Until we know what this does to her, Arien can't leave the compound."

I stared at my clasped hands in my lap. I didn't argue. Because two days wasn't a lot of time. And I could already feel something shifting beneath my skin.

THIRTEEN

The cavern's ceiling soared high above, jagged with quartz crystals that refracted the warm light of sconces mounted along the walls. Their glow scattered in fragments, dappling the space with soft, shifting rainbows. At the far end, a lake stretched wide and clear, its surface reflecting the golden light like molten glass. A group of Earthbounders splashed in the water, their laughter and shouts bouncing off the stone walls.

The rich scents of food and spices wafted from the cavern's center, where a large table overflowed with steaming dishes. Secondborns bustled around it, serving and laughing with effortless ease. Some joined for the meal, while others leaned against the walls, chatting with the Pures.

Kole stayed close, his hand brushing mine every so often. We strolled toward the gathering. My former protector's presence grounded me, but it also carried an undercurrent of tension, like a string coiled too tight. He hadn't left my side since we collided in the communal chamber, and he showed no sign of pulling away now.

I gazed at the twinkling ceiling. "This is...breathtaking," I whispered.

"It's perfection," Kole said, his gaze lingering on me as if he were memorizing every detail.

A blush warmed my cheeks and I glanced away. "You don't have to...stay with me all the time, you know. I'll be fine," I said softly. I craved this winged brooding man but I understood he was a warrior first and foremost.

Kole grunted. With his callused fingertips, he swiveled my face toward him. "Let's make something clear. You're never a...burden, and I don't hover out of some obligation. I stay close because there is nowhere else I'd rather be. I am still the cold-blooded hunter you ran into at a fucking fast-food joint, out of all places." He shook his head, a playful smirk on his full lips. "But I am *your* hunter now. *Your* killer..."

His fingers slid deeper into my hair, awaking pleasure points along the way.

"I'd kill for you..." he said, lifting my hand and placing it on his heart. *Ohmygod*. He wasn't finished either. "I'd bleed for you..." I tried to pry my hand away. This was...too much. And insane. I glanced over his shoulder at the gathering around the table; they were close enough to hear every single word.

"Kole..." I whimpered, partly from appreciation and partly from embarrassment. Were all Earthbounder men this forward? And apparently, they didn't mind an audience.

He tugged me closer, lowering his mouth to my ear. "Do you feel my heart beating? It beats for you."

My lips parted. His strong heart thudded under my palm. Wild whistles broke out.

"That's the way to do it, my man. Leave her in no doubt of your feelings," Vex said, clapping Kole on his shoulder.

My warrior instantly growled. It had been a thing between them.

I stumbled on our way to the grand table. What had taken over Kole? Rae patted a spot beside her. I scanned the group. Except for P6 and Xavier with his men, I didn't recognize anyone. At least they'd stopped gawking at me. The rebels sharing our table chattered with ease.

To the side, Anhelm and Zaira lounged on a flat rock, their heads bent close. They spoke in low voices. Zaira's sharp features softened whenever she leaned toward him, and though Anhelm's usual stoic expression hadn't changed, his body language was relaxed in a way I hadn't seen before.

"Those two, huh?" Rae said as she sidled up beside me.

A smile tugged at my lips. "They look good together."

"Aye," Rae said, cracking a roguish grin.

Vex looped an arm around my friend's shoulders, pulling her close with an easy affection that made my heart ache in a way I couldn't name. "You gossiping about the lovebirds over there?" Vex asked, nosing her neck.

"Maybe," Rae said, smirking.

"You're worse than the secondborns," Vex teased, pressing a quick kiss to Rae's temple.

My gaze drifted back to the other side of the table where a few secondborns had finished setting the meal. They passed plates around, and laughter rippled through the group as someone spilled a ladle of stew, prompting a mock scolding from one of the cooks.

"This place feels different," I said softly, more to myself than anyone else.

"It is," Kole said, his tone thoughtful. "The secondborns are treated well here." He gestured toward the bustling group. "Better than Invicta ever dreamed of. They're allowed to choose their work—no one's assigned anything here. A lot of them still pick things like cooking or cleaning because it's what they know, but it's their choice."

"And the Pures?" I asked.

Rae grinned. "They pull their weight. Scrub dishes, clean the cavern, take turns in the kitchen. Everyone contributes here."

The thought made me smile, though the tightness in my chest hadn't fully eased. The camaraderie here was refreshing to see. But I couldn't help feeling like an outsider, a puzzle piece that didn't quite fit. Again.

Two days... Those cursed words worried me more than I was admitting. I needed to stop obsessing over Damian's cryptic message at least this once.

Kole's knuckles skimmed across my arm. I tilted my head toward him, questioning written on my face.

"Don't," he said quietly.

"Don't what?"

"Don't retreat." His eyes met mine, and the intensity in them made me gulp. He knew me too well. "I'm not wasting another second. Not after..." He trailed off, but I knew what he was thinking. The way we'd been ripped apart before.

"I'm not trying," I said, my voice barely above a whisper.

"Good," he said, then his wings unfurled and one appendage wrapped around me protectively. My safe haven.

I glimpsed Xavier perched on a rock farther down. His jaw remained clenched, and his gaze drilled into the ground. The tension in his posture radiated a simmering intensity just beneath the surface. The warmth of the room didn't seem to touch him. A quiet part of me wondered if it would ever reach me either.

The cavern settled into an uneasy stillness as the clatter of plates and muted voices dwindled, signaling the end of the meal—at least for now. Xavier and his men slipped away, gathering weapons propped against the wall. They had guard duty next.

"I need a word with X," I said, glancing at Kole. He gave a barely perceptible nod. Rising, I dusted off my pants, more to steady my nerves than for any real reason. What did I even want to say? The gnawing tension between Xavier and me felt like a widening chasm, and I hated it.

I followed after him, my boots crunching on the gravelly floor. He paused at the cavern's mouth, the flicker of sconce light throwing his shadow long and serrated against the walls. His posture stiffened, his broad shoulders squared, as if he sensed my approach before I said a word.

"X?" I said, halting within a few feet of him. "I'm really sorry about Nelia. I begged Donovan..." I bit my lip, unsure where to go from here.

"You're here." His whisper carried to me.

"What?"

He faced me, every inch of him radiating that infuriating, condescending magnificence. Tall and sneering, his voice dripped with disdain. "I said, and yet you're here, and she's not."

I gaped at him, unable to breathe. Xavier's eyes narrowed, studying me with an unsettling intensity, his icy lapis-lazuli gaze boring into mine. He didn't hold back, and though his words felt like a blade to my heart, they spoke the truth.

I couldn't fathom how fate could be so cruel. Nelia had been too pure, too kind, too undeserving of the mistreatment life had heaped upon her. Why her? Why not me?

The ache in my chest sharpened, but I stayed silent, refusing to let the storm of emotions spill.

I swallowed. "If I could, I'd give my life for hers."

He blinked, breaking some spell that kept him at the edge, and his expression softened. "That makes two of us." He leaned closer as if he was readying to shorten the distance between us, then he glanced over my shoulder and straightened.

My stomach knotted in response to the remnants of the broken mate bond. I knew without a doubt that Kole was heading in this direction.

"I'll see you around, little one," Xavier said with his usual pretentious tone. Then he whirled around and exited, with two swords crisscrossed tightly on his back.

Strong fingers glided from the small of my back to my hip, leaving a trail of goosebumps in their wake. His warmth enveloped me, his breath brushing my ear as his mouth hovered close.

"I sensed your distress," Kole whispered.

I whirled into his one-arm embrace, which brought our faces closer. My hand rose instinctively, brushing against the roughness of his jaw before settling on his cheek.

"Yeah, kinda, but it needed to be said. You can't protect me from everything."

He squeezed my hip, his chest rising as he drew a deep breath. "I can try."

A sheepish smile broke on my face and I lowered my eyes, blushing. Yeah, blushing as hell. No one had ever said anything near the things Kole had been proclaiming ever since I got here. No one had ever stood by me the way he did.

I touched my forehead to his collarbone, twisting my head from side to side.

"Not sure how to read all that, but I'll take it as though you approve," he whispered into my ear again, his head bent low.

I peered at him, still smiling. "I approve of you. I can't promise I'll always approve of your actions."

That delicious dimple of his cut into his cheek. The demon hunter was proving himself even more irresistible than I remembered.

"Ahem." Zaira cleared her throat loudly, strolling by us, with Anhelm in tow. "Get a room." She twisted her lips in mock disgust. I rolled my eyes at her, then cocked my head in Anhelm's direction. The man had blinders on his eyes and was determined not to let Zaira out of his sight.

"We have a patrol together," she grumbled, throwing a playful look over her shoulder at him. "Come on, *Captain Shadowpants*. You don't have to slink behind."

Anhelm's jaw tightened, and his voice took on an edge. "It's called vigilance. Maybe try it sometime."

Zaira grinned and winked at me. They disappeared down a side tunnel.

One by one, the others retired to their quarters, the laughter and chatter fading into the Underground's ever-present busy shuffle.

Rae lingered near the table with Vex, her shrewd eyes darting between me and Kole. A small, knowing smile curved her lips as she leaned casually against her mate.

"You must be terribly tired after your trek here," Rae said, her voice easy and light, but tainted with mischief. "You need to rest. Kole, since you don't have a roommate, I'm sure you wouldn't mind Arien sleeping there? With you?"

Kole stiffened beside me, his wings giving the faintest twitch. When he glanced at me it was all heat. "Rae..." he started, his tone low and warning.

She waved him off, grinning as if she didn't notice—or care—about his reaction. "It's settled. You've got the only single room among us, and she deserves some peace after what she's been through. Right, Vex?"

"Absolutely," Vex said, smirking. "Be a gentleman. Offer her the bed."

Kole shot him a death glare, his jaw tightening. Then he turned to me, and at the same time, the edge of his wing smacked Vex in his arm like a good ol' punch. Once Kole's eyes settled on me, they softened. "Would you like to get some rest?"

My heart skipped with a flutter of anticipation. For what, I wasn't precisely sure. "Uh...yes," I whispered.

Kole kept close, his wings tucked against his back. Each accidental touch—shoulders brushing, hands dancing around each other—sent a jolt of warmth through me.

He wasn't much better. I caught the way his eyes flicked toward me every few steps, his expression torn between restraint and something deeper, something raw. His fists clenched and unclenched at his sides like he was physically holding himself back.

"Rae did that on purpose," I said finally, my voice soft but teasing, trying to lighten the weird tension between us.

"She's always meddling," Kole muttered.

I laughed quietly, the sound echoing in the tunnel.

"Come on," he said, his tone gentler now as his hand skimmed the curve of my lower back. After a few more turns through the dimly lit corridors, we reached his quarters. The compact, unadorned room held a sturdy bed tucked against one wall and a single stool slid beneath a narrow wooden table. A lantern dangled from a wall hook, its golden glow casting soft light that tempered the harsh lines of the stone walls.

"This is cozy," I said, strolling in and taking note of simple furnishings.

"It's quiet," Kole said, lingering near the doorway. His eyes followed me intently, his wings shifting as though ready to stretch but held back by sheer will. I met his molten gaze.

"You should rest," he said, his voice rough.

"Right." My throat tightened as I forced the word out. Resting was the last thing on my mind.

He retreated a step, his wings shimmying in protest. "I'll... I'll be right outside if you need anything."

"Kole."

He froze, his dark chocolate eyes locking onto mine.

"Stay."

For a heartbeat, I thought he'd refuse. Then his wings snapped open with a resounding crack.

"Are you sure?" he asked, his voice hoarse.

I nodded, the ache in my chest blooming into something both exhilarating and primal. I needed him here, now. I didn't just want Kole—I chose him, every piece of me, no matter that the *Ashanti Rosa* bond had been severed. Bond or no bond, my heart and soul had already made their decision.

He joined me, shutting the door closed with his foot, and the room shrank in size. Or dissolved or something. My brooding angel filled my vision and overwhelmed all my senses with his presence. He closed the distance in two purposeful strides, heat burning in his eyes. All for me. I rose on my tiptoes, tilting my face to his, and welcomed his inferno on my lips.

FOURTEEN

The air grew warmer. The back of my knees hit the edge of his bed and I sank onto it, our lips breaking apart. Kole's gaze turned thunderous as he knelt before me, his fingers brushing mine. The touch was so gentle, so careful, that it sent a shiver racing up my spine.

"If I take you, there is no going back. You will be mine... Only *mine*," he rasped.

"I know," I whispered, my breath catching.

His hand slid to cradle my cheek, his palm warm against my skin. "Good," he said, his thumb drawing a delicate line along my jaw.

The space between us shrank to nothing. His lips found mine, soft and searching at first, but quickly growing more insistent, as though this moment had been his deepest craving. Sure, we'd kissed before, but this was different. Each caress felt like a promise, a vow made not with words but with our bodies. I melted into him, my fingers tangling in the fabric of his shirt, pulling him closer.

"Kole," I breathed against his lips, my heart hammering wildly.

He devoured my mouth with deep sweeping strokes of his tongue, his hands steadying me as though I might slip away. His touch shifted, trailing along my shoulders and brushing my back.

He froze, his hand hovering over the scars where my wings had once been, his fingers trembling. I winced.

"Love," he said softly. My warrior pulled back, his dark chocolate eyes wide, blazing with disbelief and something darker—rage. "What did they do to you?"

Shame twisted in my chest, and I dropped my gaze, unable to meet his burning stare.

Kole's jaw tightened, and his wings flared behind him, brushing the walls of the room in his barely contained fury. His entire body shuddered violently.

"Arien..." His voice was a storm threatening to break free. "*What did they do to you?*"

My tongue felt heavy, the words lodged in my throat. Finally, I whispered, "Mariola... She...cut them off."

Everything stilled. Then his wings beat violently, stirring the air and scraping the walls. The cords in his neck sprang taut as his chest heaved with the effort of holding back what looked like an eruption waiting to happen.

"I'll hunt her down," he snarled.

"Kole—" I began, but his rage surged like wildfire.

"I will rip out her feathers one by one," he said, each word dripping with venom. "She'll regret the day she ever thought of touching you."

Reaching for him, I grabbed his forearms with shaky hands. "Kole, please," I said, my voice breaking.

His ragged breathing slowed and his thunderous eyes met mine. "She mutilated you," he said, his voice cracking with anguish. "She—" His hand brushed my cheek, reverent, as if trying to replace what had been taken.

"She doesn't get to ruin this moment," I said softly. "You can't tell anyone. Not yet. I don't want pity."

His jaw flexed, the rage still simmering beneath the surface. "You're asking me not to protect you," he said. "You're asking me to let her get away with this."

"I'm asking you to give me time," I said, tightening my grip. "Please."

With a sharp exhale, his wings relaxed, and he sagged lower before me. His hands cradled my face. "Time," he said. "That's all I'll give her. No mercy. Anyone who lays a finger on you will know no mercy."

His thumb swept over a tear that had slipped free, his penetrating eyes softening. "You're the most beautiful thing I've ever seen," he said. "Nothing—*nothing*—will ever change that."

His words broke something inside me, and I threw my arms around him, burying my face in the crook of his neck.

When his lips found mine again, they were gentle, then he deepened the kiss with a hunger that matched the fire still smoldering in his chest. I welcomed it, pulling him closer as his hands kneaded my waist. My fingers tangled in his hair, anchoring him to me.

"I'll make you forget everything she took," he whispered against my lips.

I cupped his face, tilting his face toward mine. "You already have." My words cut through his simmering rage, leaving nothing but tenderness. He kissed my forehead, my cheeks, and finally my swollen lips with aching reverence.

When he lifted me into his arms, I clung to him. He laid me gently on the bed and followed, his wings fanning out, creating a cocoon that blocked out the rest of the world. Not that anything could've distracted me from my Grecian god.

Kole's skilled fingers gently traced the contours of my face and neck, admiration shining in his eyes. His touch grew bolder, slipping under the hem of my shirt. The sensation of his calloused fingers against my skin sent ripples of untamed desire through me. I tugged on the hem of his shirt, and he helped me remove it, exposing his sculpted body. I explored his broad shoulders and the expanse of his chest, his skin uneven at times, a remnant of old wounds.

His breathing quickened. He leaned down and pressed his lips to the sensitive curve of my neck, evoking a gasp from me. His kisses trailed down my collarbone, his hand slipping under the thin fabric of my bra and teasing the underside of my breast.

I heaved myself to my elbows, reluctantly breaking contact, and stripped the shirt and the bra in one go. Kole's eyes darkened with admiration. He opened his mouth, and I pressed my finger to his lips. I didn't want to talk anymore. Words were overrated.

Understanding shone in his hooded eyes. He dipped his head, lips trailing down my stomach in slow, deliberate passes. Kole explored every inch of my body, unraveling tension and teasing with pleasure until we were bare to each other, our bodies aligned and hearts pounding in tandem.

He intertwined our fingers above my head and flexed his hips. My head fell back, a cry of long-awaited pleasure escaping my lips.

FIFTEEN

D amian's voice came from everywhere and nowhere all at once, coiling around me like a dark, suffocating veil.

"Nightshade," he murmured, his tone smooth, laced with a chilling familiarity that made my skin crawl. "It's time."

I whirled, searching the dreamscape—a hollow, colorless expanse that felt unnervingly real. The space seemed to pulse around me, alive with his presence. His silhouette emerged in the distance, towering and ominous, his wings spread wide. Their leathery edges bled seamlessly into the darkness as if the void itself had birthed him.

"What do you want?" I asked.

"You," he said, the simple word slicing the silence with unnerving finality. "My timeline has moved up. I'm ready for you now. You know where to go."

The void rippled, and the air shifted. An image slammed into my mind—a jagged cliff, its pointy edges cutting into the stillness of the Everlake below. Mist clung to the landscape, shrouding a narrow cave mouth high on the ridge, barely visible through the haze.

"Get there before sunrise," Damian's voice hissed. The image burned itself into my memory. "Don't make me come looking for you. You won't like what happens if I do."

The darkness shattered, collapsing into nothingness, and I woke with a gasp.

Disorientation clouded my mind, the faint hum of the base grounding me as last evening's memories crept back. The weight of Kole's arm draped across my stomach confirmed it hadn't been a dream.

But how had Damian invaded my mind from a distance? His telepathy only worked when his victims were in the same room. Worse, how had he breached my thoughts while I slept?

The cursed blood pact—it had to be behind this.

His warning echoed in my mind, sending a chill down my spine. What if he could track me now too?

I bit my lip, forcing myself to stay silent. Kole's warmth radiated against me, his grip loose but protective. He faced me, his expression serene—a rare softness that made my chest ache. His dark hair lay tousled, and though his wings had retreated, I could still feel the memory of them, their powerful embrace cocooning me after we had climaxed and their strange thrumming. It was as if they'd sung a melody only I could hear.

Kole never truly slept—not like others did. His ancient blood rendered rest unnecessary, at least in the way mortals needed it. But now, he lay utterly still, his breathing deep and even, his body slack with a rare surrender to exhaustion. He hadn't rested at all while I'd been gone.

Guilt coiled tight in my chest.

My fingers slid through my hair, tugging lightly at the roots in a futile attempt to organize my scattered thoughts. It didn't help. Damian's voice still rang in my head, dripping dread, his words a festering warning I couldn't ignore.

I can't tell Kole.

If I did, he'd follow. He'd never let me go alone. And Damian... He would unleash hell—his twisted army of mutated Fringe soldiers—not just on the base but on everyone tied to me.

Carefully, I slipped from beneath Kole's arm. His fingers twitched, brushing against my skin for the briefest moment before falling still. My breath caught as I waited, motionless. He didn't stir. The steady rhythm of his breathing remained unchanged.

I'm sorry. The thought hit like a whispered plea as I eased off the bed.

Our clothes littered the floor, remnants of last night. I stooped to gather mine—what little there was. My aunt's generosity had supplied black training attire, simple but functional. At least it was clean.

As I pulled the shirt over my head, something flickered in the corner of my eye. My reflection glinted in a small, stained mirror glued haphazardly to the wall.

I stepped closer, narrowing my gaze as my left arm came into focus. Black, spidery lines snaked across my skin, branching upward in intricate patterns like the aftermath of a lightning strike.

My fingertips traced the marks. A foreign pulse thrummed beneath them like a heartbeat that wasn't mine. The lines shifted subtly under my touch, alive in a way that made my stomach twist.

That fae weapon—the one that had struck me. The wound had healed. At least, I'd thought it had. But now...this.

I yanked the sleeve down, covering the marks as a shiver raked over me. There wasn't time to dwell on it. Not now.

I turned back to the bed, my gaze tracing the lines of Kole's face. In sleep, the weight he carried seemed to lift. Without the tension that so often shadowed him, he looked younger, almost unburdened. I let the image sear into my memory, knowing it might be the last time I saw him like this —peaceful.

How can I leave him?

The question clawed at me, the battle inside threatening to rip me apart. I wanted to crawl back into his arms, to tell him everything, to let him fight for me like he always did.

Damian's voice slithered into my mind: *Don't make me come looking for you.*

A shudder rolled through me. With one last glance, I slipped out the door, leaving behind the man who had always protected me, who I knew without a doubt would die for me.

The very reason I had to leave.

I maneuvered to the main chamber, getting lost only once on my way there. Warriors weaved through the space with purpose. Some returned from patrol, dirt smudging their uniforms, while others prepared to depart, securing belts or murmuring over their assignments.

The air droned with activity until they spotted me. A ripple of silence spread through the room, like a stone plunging into still water.

Heads turned, eyes raking over me. Curiosity flickered in some gazes, wariness in others. Guarded expressions and tense postures told me I wasn't welcome by all. My legs threatened to give out, but I forced them to keep moving, my chin held high.

Roan's infectious laugh rose above the low murmur at the far end. I picked up my tempo, almost jogging in his direction. Mischief lit his eyes as he bantered with another warrior.

"Roan," I said.

His head snapped in my direction, his easy grin widening. "Couldn't sleep? Too much on your mind? Or is it me—?"

"I need to find Se—Exiousai," I cut in, my voice pleading.

His grin faltered, the shift in my tone not lost on him. He narrowed his eyes, studying me. "Alright," he said after a beat. "This way."

The Earthbounders parted instinctively to let us through. Their whispers trailed behind us. I kept my gaze fixed on Roan's back and slipped on a mask of composure, although I'd been freaking out on the inside ever since Damian's last contact.

After a few minutes in a desolate corridor, we reached a small, dimly lit office tucked away from the main activity. Seth was poring over an old-fashioned map spread over a single desk in the center of the room. The shelves along the walls held an eclectic mix—weathered tomes, ledgers, and odd artifacts whose purposes I couldn't guess. My gaze snagged on a display of glowing feathers encased in delicate glass.

Seth's shrewd eyes lifted from the map and focused on me with a precision that felt almost surgical.

"Something tells me this isn't a social visit," he said.

Was he expecting me? I shook my head and dispelled his comment as nothing.

Roan lingered near the door, his perceptive eyes darting between Seth and me. I thought he might stay, but then he stepped back, giving us space. The soft click of the door closing behind him felt louder than it should have as if sealing my fate.

I hesitated, my hands fidgeting as I tried to steady the whirl of thoughts. "I need to...leave," I said. I swallowed hard, forcing the next words out. "Without anyone knowing."

Seth's eyes darkened and he gestured to a chair across from him. "Sit."

I obeyed. The P6 leader lowered himself into his seat, that unreadable expression marring his face.

"There's something you need to know," he said, reaching

into a drawer and withdrawing a pencil-length polished wooden box. The delicate engraving of a feather adorned its lid.

"This was given to me by Xavier's mother. She had a gift of a prophetic sight and she shared her visions by encoding them into her feathers. The message could only be received one time when the box was first opened. After, the feather crumbles to dust. I've kept this box that once held such a feather all these years to honor her and to remember the message she entrusted to me. It concerned you."

"Me?" I asked. What could an Earthbounder who lived centuries ago have known about me?

"In the vision, I saw a young woman," Seth continued. "A Pure who would become a key to dismantling the tyrannical Earthbounder system and defeating a great threat to us and humanity. The woman's face resembled yours but since it's been centuries since it was shown to me, I wasn't certain."

I stared at the case now lying on the table and bit my lip. I'd seen a box like it before... Shelves filled with books flashed before my eyes—Xavier's library. He had a slim engraved case like this one resting among his books.

"I suspected it might be you," Seth admitted, his tone thoughtful. "Especially after witnessing the bond between you and Kole. But back then, you showed no signs of being Pure. And with no wings..." He trailed off. "When you transformed after the battle, there was no time to explain. I knew Hafthor would stop at nothing to have you. So I rushed back to P6 to coordinate a retrieval with the rebels."

My mind raced. "But...I didn't dismantle anything. I only made everything worse."

Seth cocked his head to one side. "Explain."

"Because of me, Invicta was attacked," I said, the words tumbling out before I could stop them. "Damian used my blood to weaken Invicta on the inside. He made it possible

for the Fringe to infiltrate and tear it apart." My voice
cracked, but I forced myself to meet Seth's eyes. "All of this
happened because of me."

His jaw tightened, the faint drumming of his fingers
against the desk the only break in his stillness. "Perhaps," he
said after a moment, his tone careful. "But your blood wasn't
the cause. It was a tool. The blame lies with those who chose
to wield it for destruction."

I shook my head. "You don't understand. Damian isn't
done. He has plans—something bigger, worse." Fear coiled in
my gut like a live wire, threatening to choke me. "What if he's
the threat in the prophecy?"

Seth leaned back, his narrowed eyes cutting through me.
"Do you know what he's planning?"

"No," I said. "But I need to stop him before he hurts
anyone else. I must go."

His frown deepened. "You're certain about this?"

I nodded, my throat tightening. "I think...our bond deepened somehow. He invaded my dreams. If I stay, he'll come
for me."

For a long, agonizing moment, Seth said nothing. His gaze
pinned me in place. My heart sank as silence stretched
between us.

"Please," I said softly. "I'm the only one who can get close
to him, the only one who can stop him."

Seth's expression shifted, the faintest crack in his composure. "She also forbade me from standing in your way," he
whispered.

I blinked, unsure I'd heard him correctly. "What?"

"The prophecy... She said I could guide you but never
obstruct you. That one day, you would come seeking my
help."

Hope flared in my chest. "So, you'll help me?"

Seth leaned forward, bracing his elbows on the desk. "I'll

do more than that. I'll make sure you get to the Everlake safe-ly." He turned his head. "Roan."

The door creaked open, and Roan stepped inside. His usual smirk was nowhere to be found.

"Take her through the secret tunnels to the gate," Seth said.

Gate? Did they have allura around here?

Rising, I peered at Seth one last time.

"Thank you," I said.

The leader gave a curt nod. His shoulders slumped ever so slightly, a hint of vulnerability breaking through his usual stoic demeanor.

Roan nudged me into the corridor, a sad smile curving his lips. "Come on. Let's sneak you out of here."

I forced a small smile. "Thanks."

He huffed, shaking his head. "Kole's gonna rip my throat out for this."

SIXTEEN

The tunnels grew colder, the flickering light casting long shadows that danced along the rough stone walls. Roan led the way with purposeful strides, but frequent glances over his shoulder betrayed his unease.

"You okay back there?" he asked.

"Just peachy," I drawled. We both knew I welcomed this situation like I would a root canal.

Roan didn't press further, though his shoulders tensed briefly at my deflection. The faint echo of our footsteps filled the silence. I didn't waver, forcing myself to march forward, unwilling to let the doubts clawing at my resolve slow me down.

Then, a scuffle. The sound snapped through the quiet. I froze mid-step, my pulse spiking.

Roan spun, his wings flaring halfway open. His hand flew to the hilt of his blade, his posture coiled and ready. A dark figure shifted at the edge of my vision, its movement too fluid, too deliberate. Before either of us could react, Xavier peeled away from the shadows.

"Xavier?" I whispered, my heart thudding against my ribs. This wasn't good. He'd want answers...

Roan's wings folded back, but his hand stayed firm on the hilt. "What the hell are you doing here?"

The Seraph's fierce eyes flicked between us, but his attention settled on me. "I'm not here to stop you," he said.

The conviction in his tone made me pause. What did he want then? I glanced at Roan, who frowned but gave me a small nod.

"I'll give you a minute," my guide said, his steps measured as he strode further into the corridor. The shadows swallowed him, leaving Xavier and me alone.

Silence stretched between us, taut and thick. Xavier watched me with an intensity that made my jaw clench. His usually composed demeanor was frayed tonight, his lapis-lazuli eyes darker, shadows lurking within.

"I had to see you," he whispered.

"I know," I said softly, though I wasn't sure how I knew. *Why did I say that?*

He inched closer and lifted my hand, his thumb gliding over the back of it in a slow stroke. My gaze dropped to our joined hands, my brow knitting as his strong, warm palm enveloped mine. His grip dwarfed my hand easily—too easily. He could snap my wrist with a flick if he wanted. When we'd first met, he had scared the living shit out of me on a few occasions. Yet, even then, I hadn't truly feared him. Not then. Not now.

"It's not easy to let you go..." he said.

I inhaled sharply, the sound catching in my throat. Was it the brush of his skin against mine or the raw honesty in his words? Whatever it was, it tugged at something buried deep in my chest. "Why are you here?" I asked.

"I need something from you before you leave."

My pulse quickened. "What?"

His piercing eyes locked onto mine, their intensity impossible to escape. They drew me in, dangerous and mesmerizing, like a flame luring a moth.

"A kiss," he said, the word rolling off his tongue like a dare meant to unravel me.

I blinked, caught off guard. "I can't," I said, wincing and shaking my head. "Kole..." His name stuck in my throat, the rest of my sentence trailing into the silence. Why couldn't I just say no? *Say no.*

"I know about you and Kolerean. I'm not asking you to choose me *instead* of him." He leaned closer, his eyes softening but still as piercing as ever. "I'm asking you to choose me *too*."

My lips parted, my mind racing as I searched his face. "What...?" Could I do that? Choose both? Xavier's fingers tilted my chin upward, forcing me to meet his unrelenting gaze.

"Why do you think my mother revealed prophecies about you to both of us?" His voice held a quiet urgency now, each word precise. "If Kolerean is your mate and protector, why would she make me swear to keep you close? To protect you too? Think about it, little one. That Power is an excellent warrior—but maybe he's not enough. Maybe you need more than one kind of protector."

I frowned, the words stirring something I didn't want to face.

His voice dropped low. "Kole would never let you go right now. But I am. I'm not stopping you, even though it kills me to see you walk away."

He saw the hesitation written on my face.

"One kiss," he whispered. "I'll take it even if you're thinking about him while you kiss me."

The vulnerability in his voice unraveled something deep inside me. I shook my head. "I can't."

Disappointment flickered in his eyes. His hold on my hand loosened and his fingers slid away. I tightened my grip in response.

"When I kiss you," I said, my voice trembling, "it will be because I'm thinking about you. Because I want *you*."

His mouth slackened. I reached up with my free hand, pressing a fingertip against his chin to nudge it closed. "You don't want to catch flies," I said, a faint smirk tugging at my lips.

His eyes didn't just twinkle—they erupted with light, recognition flaring as he caught the callback to the jab he'd made weeks ago. I'd been holding onto it, waiting for the perfect moment to strike.

His grin barely had time to form before he yanked me against him. The force of it stole my breath. My body molded to his, every inch of me brushing against him, and then his lips descended upon mine.

The tenderness of the kiss made my heart stutter. Then the dam broke. His hand cupped the back of my head, his fingers tangling in my hair with a possessive gentleness that sent a shiver through me. This wasn't just passion—it was pain, longing, and the bittersweet knowledge that this couldn't last...

Kole's thunderous gaze flashed in my mind and I wrenched myself away, my breaths coming fast and uneven. Xavier's forehead fell to mine.

"My little warrior," he murmured.

I said nothing, my throat too tight to form words.

Xavier pressed a red feather into my palm. I gawked at it.

"You know what this is?" he asked.

I nodded, my eyes stinging as they met his. The gift of a feather wasn't just rare—it was sacred. It would allow me to summon him, no matter where or when. But it was more than that. The feather was his promise to me.

Without a word, I spun on my heel and strode down the tunnel. I couldn't stay with him any longer or I'd risk abandoning my plan and falling into pieces. And that wasn't an option.

The shadows deepened around me and the silence pressed in until Roan's familiar whistle broke through. He appeared from around a corner, hands in his pockets, his smirk ominous as ever.

"If Kole's gonna rip my throat out, he's gonna skin that Seraph alive. Bright side? You survive..."

SEVENTEEN

We reached a dead end. The air thrummed with a foreign charge. A shimmering barrier stretched across the rock wall, translucent yet alive with twisting threads of light that pulsed and flickered like veins. An allura—small, ancient, and unlike any I'd seen before. Most alluras formed protective perimeters around entire compounds, their sprawling barriers humming with defensive strength. This one was different. Smaller, self-contained.

"This gate's unpassable for us," Roan said, his tone matter-of-fact. "We hit a wall every time. It's not tethered to any other barrier like the ones around the compounds are. Seth thinks it's the oldest allura on the planet." He gestured toward the shimmering field. "Warped over time, like it's out of sync with everything else."

My stood transfixed the twisting light. "Will it work for me?"

Roan shrugged. "It should. Just do your thing."

I nodded, my throat tightening. There was no turning back now.

Roan shifted, awkwardness flickering across his face.

Without warning, he wrapped me in a tight embrace, his arms firm but warm, like a brother's.

"If our paths don't cross again..." His voice was soft. "At least I can say I gave you your last hug. Guess that makes me a historical figure."

I shoved him with a snort, rolling my eyes. "You're ridiculous." The warrior reminded me of Vex but I couldn't think about any of the P6-ers right now because then I'd fall into a spiral of guilt again.

He stepped back, his smirk returning, though the glint in his eyes had dulled.

I stretched out my arm, hesitation clawing at me as the barrier's threads crackled and danced. My fingers hovered, the energy prickling the air around them. With a ragged inhale, I pressed my hand to the surface.

The barrier rippled under my touch, its warmth startlingly alive. A strange pull surged through me, like it recognized me, like it had been waiting. The twisting veins of light coalesced, folding inward to form a swirling portal. The center churned, a dark void that seemed to whisper my name, pulling me closer with an almost magnetic force.

Before I could step through, a blaring alarm pierced the air.

I whipped my head back. Roan's eyes rounded. The sound was coming from the direction of the rebellion base. Were they being invaded?

"What...?" The question barely left my lips before the portal flared, the pull becoming inescapable.

"Wait!" Roan lunged toward me, his voice swallowed by the allura's surge. The barrier yanked me in, the world fracturing into a kaleidoscope of light and sound.

Water struck me like a fist. The icy spray drenched me, stealing my breath as I stumbled forward, coughing and gasping. Behind me, the barrier shimmered with its last breath—then winked out of existence.

"No!" My boots splashed in a shallow puddle as I turned in circles, the walls of the small, damp cave pressing in. Slick stone surrounded me, the sound of dripping water echoing in the tight space.

This cave—it was the same one the Invictus Lake had led me to before.

My fists clenched. "Take me back!" I shouted, leaping into the now-quiet puddle and slamming my hands against the wet rock. But the portal was gone, the allura sealed.

It had closed? It'd never done that before. I growled, stomping my feet as if the furious splash could undo it. Known for granting wishes to Earthbounders, the Everlake had turned its back on me. Today, it wasn't a miracle—it was a curse.

If you grant wishes, grant mine! That was it—I needed to reach the main body of the lake and make my plea there. Or swim to its depths, where the allura pulsed beneath the water —a suicidal idea, but one that tightened in my mind with every second of silence. Not knowing what was happening at the rebellion base was already eating me alive.

"*Arien...*" An ominous whisper drifted to me. Damian...

I stumbled toward the cave's entrance, the cold mountain air biting through my soaked clothes. The jagged peaks of the range loomed ahead in a semicircle, their sharp edges cutting into the fading night sky. Dawn crept over the horizon, painting it in hues of deep orange and pale lavender. One by one, the stars disappeared into the growing light.

The crisp air burned in my lungs, sharpening my thoughts. If I couldn't get back to the Underground in time, I'd deal with the threat here then. I'd find out if this monster had sent his army into the rebellion base after all, when he'd promised he wouldn't track me if I came on my own. He'd never lied to me, but there was always a first time.

I closed my eyes, reaching for the vision Damian had etched into my mind. The image of a massive cave system high up the cliff face flickered sharply into view, its shadowed entrance yawning like a warning.

My eyes snapped open, scanning the ridge above until I spotted it—a dark hollow tucked against the towering rock.

Slick patches of dew and frost turned the rocky slope into a treacherous ascent. My muscles burned as I hauled myself higher, fingers gripping notched surface for purchase. The sun's rays crested over the horizon. Light spilled across the peaks, turning them to molten gold, while long shadows stretched down the cliffs and across the lake below.

I groaned as my foot slipped, leaving me dangling. A moment later, boots crusted with dirt appeared above the cave's lip. Brawny arms gripped mine, hauling me upward in one powerful motion.

The man's black long-sleeve shirt clung to his broad torso, every line of muscle apparent beneath the fabric. Suit pants and polished dress shoes completed his attire. I blinked. He looked more like a CEO than the brute enforcer I knew him to be.

"You're just in time," he said, his voice smooth and low, like velvet draped over steel.

My pulse thundered in my ears as he let go of me. He strolled to the cave's edge, where rock gave way to open air, and looked out with unnerving calm. His sly gaze swept over the sprawling expanse of mountains and valleys, and past them to the faint outline of New Seattle on the horizon.

I hung back a few steps. Standing too close to Damian felt like brushing against a serrated knife. Dangerous. I tried to read him, to anticipate what he wanted, but he'd put on a mask, his thoughts a void that swallowed any attempt to gauge him. My mind spun with possibilities, each one darker than the last.

The ground trembled, a low, hissing rumble that built into a deafening *boom*.

I stumbled, throwing out a hand to steady myself against the cave wall. My breath caught as I glanced north—a fiery plume erupted into the sky, a twisting column of smoke and flame clawing upward like a living thing.

"That's—" I choked out.

"The Fringe," Damian said, his tone gruff.

I inched closer, my chest tightening. "But why?"

His lips curled into a sneer. "They're useless," he said, his voice cold. "You saw them when they attacked Invicta—hideous creatures, barely more than animals. Their mutations have gone too far. They're loyal to no one, incapable of following precise order."

He folded his arms, his icy glare swiveling back to me. "For now, I'm content to work from the shadows, controlling things through Donovan. But the time will come when I build an army of my own—one tied to me by blood."

His words hit like a blow, and I fought to keep my composure.

"I'll know their thoughts," he continued, his tone matter-of-fact. "Their inner desires, their weaknesses, their strengths. I will imprint my will onto them, and they will do my bidding. Perfectly loyal. Perfectly obedient."

He cocked his head, staring at my profile.

I couldn't bring myself to meet his stare. My throat tightened as the implications sank deeper. The blood we'd exchanged—it had already given him some power over me. I could feel it in the dreams, in the way his voice crawled in my mind, unbidden. Was this what he meant? Was I becoming his number-one soldier?

His voice dropped to a soft, mocking tone. "You're quiet, nightshade. What are you thinking?"

I forced myself to glance at him, his haughty features illuminated by the distant fire's flickering glow.

"That you've been planning this for a long time," I said, my voice steadier than I felt.

His lips curved into a calculated smile. "More like I was predestined to do this. I didn't understand what *she* meant until now." She? Who was he referring to?

I shifted my gaze to the horizon. Flames tore through the distance, consuming everything they touched. The Fringe burned, and I couldn't summon any sympathy for what I knew roamed within those infernos. I thought of the possessed creatures that had attacked Invicta. Of the mutated shifter children. Of my best friend, Brie, and her newborn, nearly stolen for experimentation. She was safe now, thanks to my friends at Invicta. But knowing how close she'd come to losing everything ignited fury within me.

There was a strange beauty in the fire's relentless destruction, its hunger carving a path across the land. The horizon turned fiery orange but all I saw was red. A strange glee awakened within me. My lips lifted at the corners. I didn't know when I started smiling, and when I thought about it, I found that I didn't care.

EIGHTEEN

Damian's dark chuckle filled the cavern.

"You don't pity them, do you?" he asked.

My frown deepened as the red haze at the edges of my vision faded. I *should* have cared. The scourge hid innocents among them—humans like my best friend Brie, who had once been captive there. I *should* have screamed at him, called him the monster he was. But a part of me craved chaos and suffering.

"Come with me," he said, his voice brooking no argument.

We descended deeper into the cavern. My arm prickled, faintly at first, then it turned into an insistent itch. The tattoo-like marks from the fae weapon seared my skin. I clawed at the spot, my nails raking the surface in search of relief, but the burning only spread, spiraling outward.

"Stop," Damian snapped, his tone cutting through my frustration.

I froze mid-scratch, my teeth grinding together as I fought the urge to keep clawing. The marks writhed beneath my skin relentlessly.

Damian scowled. He seized my arm, his fingers digging

into the tender flesh. Heat flared beneath his grip, and I flinched, hissing through my teeth.

"Burns," I whispered, voice tight with restraint.

His jaw tightened as he studied the marks, his dark eyes shadowed with thought. For a moment, his lips pressed together, as though weighing words that never came. Without comment, he released my arm and resumed walking. My fingers curled at my sides, twitching with the urge to scratch, but I forced myself to follow instead.

The path opened into a massive chamber. Stalactites loomed overhead, jagged and dripping into a still reservoir below. The water mirrored the stone ceiling, its surface unnaturally smooth, corralled by a weathered half wall. The soft rhythm of drops hitting the surface bounced off the walls.

Damian strode toward the half wall. There he paused and gestured me forward with a single, curling finger.

"What now?" I asked.

"Now I complete your transformation."

My mouth formed an *o*.

His lips curved into a cold smile. "My tainted blood has taken root. I can see *it*, growing inside you, spreading. You've already begun to change."

I clasped my hands together. There had been moments I couldn't explain, flashes of something dark stirring inside me, but surely that didn't mean—

"Come closer. Look." He pointed at the water.

The force in his voice left no room for hesitation. My legs felt leaden as I stepped forward. I peered over the wall, staring into the reservoir's surface.

My gawk back at me, wary and pale. Damian's fingers combed through my hair, eliciting repulsive shivers along the way.

"What do you see?" he asked.

I glanced at him from the corner of my eye, uneasy with the shift in his tone. I looked back at the water. "Me," I said, studying my face, lips tightening.

His fingers stilled and flexed.

"Look again," he growled.

I exhaled slowly, leaning closer. My eyes darted over my features—cheekbones, lips, nose—all unchanged. But when I examined my irises, the streak of crimson surrounding them flared, threatening to spill over the blue. I jerked back, my heart pounding.

Damian's fingers resumed their crawl through my hair.

"Now you understand. She's there, waiting to be unleashed."

My grip tightened on the half wall, knuckles blanching. Another drop struck the water, shattering the surface into ripples that radiated outward before fading into stillness.

Damian's laugh sliced through the quiet, his voice curling with triumph.

"You're not going to ask me how? Smart girl."

I braced, shifting my stance. The threat in his tone coiled around me like a snake, ready to strike.

Damian swept my hair aside to expose my ear. He leaned in, his lips just an inch away.

"The answer is...death."

A squeak escaped my lips. Then his hands slammed down, shoving my head into the reservoir.

The icy water swallowed me. My arms thrashed, fingers clawing at his iron grip. My legs kicked uselessly against the wall, searching for purchase.

The marks on my arm ignited, the searing heat slicing through the cold and blinding me with its intensity.

This isn't how it ends.

A pulse surged through my body, discharging from the tattoo and rippling into the water. The reservoir churned violently, a force yanking me downward and wrenching me from Damian's grasp.

He dove after me, his weight crashing and dragging me further into the depths. Our eyes met, rage twisting his features as he struggled to overpower the pull. My lungs screamed for air. I convulsed, water pressing against my lips. Each second stretched into eternity, the invisible force wrenching me deeper while Damian's iron grip fought to drag us upward. The end was coming for me. Whatever Damian had planned wouldn't happen on his watch. The Everlake had decided my tomb lay within this cavern.

Damian's roar reverberated through the water, vibrating in my skull.

You don't get to escape me again, he hissed in my head.

Fuck you, I snarled back at him in my thoughts.

He recoiled as if he'd heard me. Then his features twisted into fury. With one last cry, he let go of me, propelling himself to the surface while the cursed force towed me away.

NINETEEN

I cy water seeped into my body, numbing every inch, and the last gasp of air slipped from my lungs. *This is it.* Cold resignation settled over me.

Soft touches coaxed my eyes open. Fingers, delicate as silk, skimmed my arms and face. My chest heaved as if air had been forced into me—smooth, steady breaths that filled the void where panic had lingered.

Slim figures surrounded me, their forms wrapped in gossamer fabric that flowed like water. Their hair drifted in long, fluid strands, moving in sync with their shifting shapes. Their wide, luminous eyes glowed like orbs of moonlight, fixed on me with a strange intensity.

Nymphs.

They circled, their hands cradling me as they pulled me deeper. A bubble of oxygen encased me. I gulped the air. I didn't know the otherwordly creatures had such powers. They sure hadn't created oxygen bubbles for me in our past encounters. Mercurial—was what Donovan had called them once. The word described them well.

Below, a pulsing light drew my attention, its brilliance intensifying with my descent. *Allura.*

"Wait," I croaked, a garbled whisper in the water. I didn't know where to go. I wasn't ready. But the nymphs ignored me. They flung me forward until the light swallowed me whole.

The world was ripped apart.

The void consumed me—an endless expanse of chaos where winds howled with unrelenting force. They tore at me, flinging my body in every direction, spinning me helplessly. My screams vanished into the roar, lost to the cacophony.

Then the eyes appeared.

Dozens of crimson orbs blinked open in the darkness, each one seething with malevolent hunger.

They lunged.

Claws raked my skin. Teeth snapped inches from my face. I thrashed, arms cutting through the void, pushing them back as they swarmed like predators scenting blood. The marks on my arm burned, their black lines igniting in a blinding blue flare. The pulse exploded, hurling me backward and engulfing the nearest creatures in a searing fire. They shriveled into nothing.

The others hesitated, prowling in the distance. But there were too many. Even if I unleashed another burst, they would overwhelm me.

A lightning bolt tore through the void.

The creatures recoiled, their screeches piercing the gale. A figure emerged from the light storm.

He didn't struggle like I did, tossed by the chaos. He flew with controlled grace. Wings stretched wide, silver-white with golden undertones, their feathers sleek and radiant. Light shimmered along their edges.

Built like Adonis with sculpted muscles and a striking

face, his jawline softened, curving his ripe lips. But what captivated me the most were his eyes—their glacial blue depths drew me in.

"Sylvan," I whispered.

He didn't speak, his expression calm but focused as he reached for me. His arms wrapped around me with surprising gentleness, and the warmth of his touch spread through my cold, aching body.

Sylvan's wings beat steadily, the void bending and rippling with each powerful stroke. A corridor of light appeared ahead, and he propelled us toward it without hesitation.

The light surged, stabbing my eyes and pain shot through my skull. I buried my face against the enigmatic warrior's chest, shielding myself from the numbing brightness.

My limbs hung limp and useless. Blinking against the haze clouding my vision, I stared at the scene above me.

The ceiling soared—a vast dome adorned with frescoes. Painted battles raged across the expanse, gods and mortals intertwined in intricate, vivid detail. Gold and sapphire hues shimmered in the soft light, the craftsmanship so lifelike it seemed to breathe.

Columns flanked the room, their marble surfaces streaked with veins of silver and bronze. The architecture mirrored the grandeur of a Greek temple, overwhelming in its beauty.

I turned my head, catching Sylvan's profile as he lowered me onto a four-poster bed. The mattress cradled me while the cool sheets soothed my skin.

Sylvan's expression was hard to read as he carefully tucked the soft white covers around me, making sure I was snug and warm. My eyelids grew heavy, fluttering shut as exhaustion pulled me deeper. Fighting it was pointless. *Just a quick nap*, I told myself. Maybe when I woke, this would all dissolve into another fleeting dream.

Warm fingers brushed against my temple, the touch gentle and lingering. The sensation melted away every worry, every hesitation, leaving nothing but quiet stillness in its wake. I exhaled a soft sigh, my body fully relaxing as I surrendered to the pull.

I jolted awake, linens rustling against my skin. The bed beneath me sprawled massive and luxurious, easily large enough for five. I scanned the room, brain fog dulling my thinking.

The air smelled unnaturally clean, tinged with something floral that teased my senses. I pushed up, every muscle protesting with a weight that clung to me like chains.

My astonished gaze dropped to the unfamiliar gown draping my body. The fabric hugged me, soft as silk, rippling over my legs as I swung them over the edge of the bed. The shimmering white material clung like a second skin, dipping low in the front, and the hem brushed my ankles.

I rose, unsteady at first, my toes curling against the cold stone. A warm breeze drifted through an arched balcony, stretching two stories high. I stepped outside, my breath catching at the view unfolding before me. It was breathtaking, yet so alien it sent a jolt of unease through me. The vast expanse stretched endlessly, the sky painted in muted hues of lavender and soft gold. It wasn't night or day, but something in between—a perpetual twilight bathed in the faint glow of the celestial body that loomed above the horizon.

At first, I thought it must be a moon. It hung low and massive, its luminescent surface etched with swirling patterns that pulsed softly like the rhythm of a heartbeat. But the light it cast wasn't cold or distant—it was warm, diffused, like a sun veiled behind an eternal haze or a dying star. It lacked the heat of home but radiated enough warmth for a mild summery weather.

A strange stillness enveloped the landscape, broken only by the occasional whisper of the wind. Hills rolled gently into the distance, dotted with gleaming crystalline structures. I examined the architecture of this building next. The tall columns, arches, and domes spoke ancient and grand. And the patterns on the marble nearly replicated those of the star shining above.

Where am I?

The answer dropped in my mind like a hammer, loud and clear: *Sylvan's domain.*

I flexed my fingers, pressing my lips into a thin line. *I should wait for someone to get me...* I paced the length of the balcony one time before I huffed and said, "Oh, hell in the fucking no."

I spun back into the room, the gown fluttering behind me like a restless ghost. Spotting a gigantic white door, I stormed toward it and flung it open. The sound boomed through the hallway beyond, reverberating off the walls like a declaration. I stomped down the curved hall and descended a wide marble staircase with angel statues guarding the bottom. My bare feet slapped against the polished surface.

Did anyone live in this gargantuan palace? I'd made enough ruckus to wake a sleeping giant.

Around a corner, a cavernous common area opened. The room teemed with figures, some engaged in quiet conversation, while others stood still, their postures rigid. Warriors. But none I'd ever seen, except for Sylvan. All had silver-white wings, and many wore white tunics under gold chest plates, shoulder covers, or a simple golden belt, their gladiator-like legs exposed from mid-thigh down.

I blinked, unsure if I was hallucinating, but there they

were, still present. And now all eyes glared at me, the intruder.

A single warrior strolled over, a thick eyebrow raised in challenge. "Follow me," he said. Then he swiveled on his heel, marching toward the double doors at the very end. Past all the warriors gawking in my direction.

Oh, fun. Heat crawled up my neck. I forced myself forward, chin high and steps steady.

My guide stepped behind the half-open door before opening it for me. I entered without hesitation.

Sylvan stood near a towering window, the opening stretching five times his height. His wings partially unfurled, framing his seven feet as he stared out at the sepia world beyond.

The light poured through the feathers, highlighting their golden undertones and sleek edges. They reflected the light in fractals, repelling every shadow that dared creep close.

His hair gleamed, silver streaked with platinum, each strand catching the light as if spun from starlight. His silhouette, perfectly still, radiated both grace and an almost unbearable power.

He turned leisurely, taking his sweet time. His piercing gaze locked onto mine, and the force of his ethereal beauty hit me like a blow.

High cheekbones, a sharp jawline, and perfectly sculpted lips that could deliver either sharp commands or tender smiles. But it was his eyes—icy blue, cold and luminous, pulling me into their depths—that left me momentarily breathless.

The sight of him stole my momentum, and I hated it.

Get it together, Arien.

"Sylvan," I said, my voice louder than I intended.

"Arien," he said, his voice smooth, like the first note of a symphony that resonated in my chest.

The sound of my name on his lips sent an involuntary shiver down my spine. I frowned, perplexed by his effect on me.

"Why did you bring me here? What is this place?" I said, my tone accusing, though my voice wavered slightly under his scrutiny.

A faint smile curved his lips, more knowing than warm, as though he'd anticipated my anger and found it amusing.

"Welcome," he said, gesturing to the vast expanse of the room, "to the place where your destiny begins. Or perhaps—" His smile deepened. "—it already has begun?"

The silk of the gown brushed against my skin as I shifted my weight. With a deep scowl, I said: "I don't know what you're talking about. Stop with the cryptic nonsense and answer me. Please."

He tilted his head, his wings shifting as if responding to an unseen breeze. "I will answer your questions. You have my promise," he said, his gaze unwavering. "But first, there are things you must remember."

"Remember?" My brow furrowed.

"Yes," he said, sauntering closer. The golden shimmer of his wings rippled with every step, a hypnotic glow that made the room feel smaller.

I stepped back instinctively, unnerved by his proximity. The force he exuded sent my heart racing and I needed to think. I rubbed my forehead. Maybe this was yet another dream?

"I can't stay here. My friends need me. Their lives are in danger."

Damian's face flashed in my mind, his cruel grin twisting my stomach. If he attacked the Underground in retaliation for my escape, their blood would be on my hands. And the sirens that had gone off—I had yet to figure out what they meant for my angels.

Sylvan leaned closer, his voice a whisper that seemed to echo in the vast room. "You're afraid for them, but you should be afraid for yourself."

My breath hitched. "Why?"

His unblinking stare rattled my nerves.

"Because you're running out of time."

TWENTY

I backed away, shaking my head. "No...this doesn't make any sense. I don't belong here."

Sylvan's smile widened, though it carried no humor. The expression that unsettled me more than any glower could. "Do you truly believe Earth is where you belong? After everything you've seen, everything you've endured?"

"Yes," I said, although doubt began creeping in. "My friends are there. Everyone I care about..." I whispered.

His expression shifted, a flicker of something darker passing through his eyes. "And yet, you came to me."

"You *took* me," I said, my eyes narrowing.

His head tilted, his wings shifting as if brushing off my accusation. "I answered a call," he said. "A call you don't even realize you made."

I blinked, his words throwing me off balance. "What are you talking about?"

Sylvan turned back to the towering window, the light caught the golden undertones of his silver hair. He motioned for me to join him. "Look," he said softly.

I traipsed closer.

Below us, the world stretched out in haunting, other-worldly beauty. Rolling hills of emerald shimmered faintly as if dusted with crushed gemstones, while rivers wove through them like silver threads, their surfaces gleaming under the pale dandelion sun. Cities of alabaster rose in elegant spirals, their towers crowned with light that pulsed in harmony with the gentle breeze. Golden shimmer veiled the horizon, blurring the lines where land met the sky.

"This is Ariada," he said, his tone reverent, his voice brushing against my ears like a soft hymn. "A world of peace and balance. A world free from chaos."

"It's beautiful," I whispered. "But this isn't my world."

"Are you sure?" he asked, glancing my way. His icy-blue eyes searched mine, unrelenting and disarming. "You've felt it, haven't you? The pull? The connection? Ariada isn't just a place. It's a part of you."

I opened my mouth to argue, but his words stirred something in my chest, an echo I couldn't quite reach. The sense of familiarity unsettled me.

"You belong here," he said, his tone placating. "You always have."

His conviction struck something raw inside me, cutting through the stubborn resolve I tried to hold onto.

"I don't belong anywhere," I whispered before I could stop myself, the admission slipping free like a wound torn open.

Sorrow flitted across his features before his mask of calm slipped back on. "Then let me show you that Ariada is your home."

The word home clawed at a memory. Sylvan had called this place my home before—when he appeared in the Everlake. I'd rejected the notion then, clinging to the belief that Earth was it for me, that Kole was my only home. But standing here, taking in Ariada's mystical beauty, something deep inside me stirred, a fragment of a truth I didn't want to confront.

My chest tightened. The pull of Ariada was undeniable, but so was the urgency to return to Earth.

Home? This place wasn't my home.

Without facing him, I asked, "What did you mean earlier? When you said I'm running out of time?"

"Our sun is...dying. It appears our mission on Ariada is coming to an end and we'll soon reunite with our Creator."

I stilled, my breath catching. Thin clouds drifted lazily over the sun, their gauzy forms exposing its surface—dull and dim, like a flashlight smothered by fabric.

"How soon?" I whispered.

"Time lost its meaning here long ago," he said. "We don't sleep. The nights no longer come."

I whipped my head around, giving him my full attention. "What about the mortals? You still have people here, don't you?"

A corner of his mouth lifted. "Yes. But the mortals no longer need us. They are ascending to a new dimension themselves, barren from all evil." He strolled back to the window, his fingers grazing the marble sill.

I frowned. "I still don't see how I'm part of your world. I'm not from here."

His gaze darkened, the humor fading from his features. "You were a priestess once, blessed with foresight," he said, his voice serene yet gritty. "You saw darkness swallowing our world and left on a solo mission without telling anyone. Something you have done in the past. But this time...you didn't return. I've searched for you ever since."

I gawked at him, my heart pounding.

"The day you appeared in your ethereal form, I didn't recognize you at first. This body—your new form—is weaker than ours. But your Sky Ice recognized you, didn't it? It healed you."

The mention of the stone jolted something inside me. Goosebumps prickled along my arms.

"Sky Ice..." I whispered, my throat tightening. "It's here?"

"Of course," Sylvan said, watching me closely. "It is a part of Ariada, just as you are."

I wrapped my arms around myself.

"You weren't meant to live another life. Ariada still needs you. I can feel the energy shifting—the darkness you warned me about draws near." His intense stare bore into me. "I need you to remember what you saw. Without you, the mortals won't ascend. And instead of paradise, the Earthbounders will face annihilation."

I exhaled shakily, torn between two worlds. I cared about Ariada's future, but Earth clung to my heart like an anchor. Kole's thunderous eyes flashed in my mind, followed by Xavier's ocean-blue ones.

My life on Earth had felt so real. Was it all a lie?

"What was my name?" I asked.

"Lirael," Sylvan said with reverence.

I tested the name on my tongue, but no memories surfaced. It was hollow, foreign. Quite unlike the reaction Sky Ice had stirred in me.

I tightened my arms around myself, rocking back and forth on the balls of my feet. Uncovering that Ariada was my origin and I had somehow gotten lost in the universe was messing with my head. It was too much to process.

I faced the beautiful angel leaning casually against a marble pillar that dwarfed him in height but not presence. The towering structure and the grandeur of the building faded beneath the weight of his piercing gaze. Words failed me for this place—for him.

"Send me back," I said, forcing the tremor out of my voice. "There's a civil war brewing between the Earthbounders, and I'm part of it. Let me finish what I started there. When it's over, we can meet again and figure out...whatever this is."

Shadow fell over his face, and the steel in his tone made my chest tighten. "*Whatever this is?*"

He pushed off the pillar, his broad shoulders rising as he stalked toward me. Each step carried an intensity that made the air feel heavier, tighter, until he loomed above me. The pale light of the dying sun framed his wings, washing his harsh features in haunting yellow.

A deep groove appeared between his brows, his jaw tightening as he stopped a breath away. "No one leaves Ariada."

I flinched, but he didn't stop. His wings arched behind him.

"Perhaps," he continued, his eyes narrowing, "once you remember who you are—a priestess with boundless power— you'll be able to send yourself away again. But know this: once you become her, the people you left behind will mean nothing to you. Their faces, their voices, their lives—just fleeting blips in the eternity that was your life. The life you've shared...with me."

His fingers grazed the side of my forehead and slid into my hair, tracing the strands to their ends before pausing. His gaze dropped to the exposed curve of my collarbone, then lower to the bare skin above my gown's neckline. His eyes glazed with desire.

"My *Ashanti Rosa,*" he murmured.

TWENTY-ONE

I knocked his hand away, heat rising in my chest. "What did you call me?" I hissed through clenched teeth.

It couldn't be true. It wouldn't... Nothing tethered me to this overgrown warrior. Not even close to the raw pull I felt for Kole—or, well, even Xavier.

Sylvan's lip curled. "You heard me."

I backtracked until my butt hit the smooth edge of a massive desk fit for this titan. The warrior tensed, his scowling eyes trailing my movements.

He cleared his throat, wings twitching as though restraining some instinct to close the distance. "Perhaps a walk in the gardens will help clear your head?" he said, his tone softening, though the steel beneath it remained. "It wasn't my intent to upset you." He sounded sincere.

I bobbed my head once.

"Corin. Ash," Sylvan called out.

Two warriors entered the room. The taller one had amber eyes and caramel-colored hair cropped short on one side. Beside him stood a leaner figure with a face pale as snow, marred by jagged scars crisscrossing from brow to chin. His eyes, silver and clear, seemed to pierce me as though weighing my worth.

They flanked me, taking an order from Sylvan to accompany me to the gardens and remain by my side.

My guards led me through the winding halls in silence, their strides in sync. The faint hum of Ariada's energy buzzed in the air, soft but constant, a pulse that seemed to come from the walls themselves.

When we reached the towering double doors at the end of the corridor, the taller one, Corin, pushed them open, the heavy wood groaning. Warm air rushed in, carrying the scent of something sweet and green.

Vines laden with tiny golden flowers draped over archways carved from ivory-colored stone. Colossal trees with leaves the color of copper stretched toward the pale sky, their branches intertwining like veins through the air. Some bore fruit that shimmered like glass, hues of deep crimson and pale lavender glinting among the leaves.

At the center of the garden, a massive fountain carved from pearly stone bubbled softly. Depictions of winged figures decorated its base, their hands reaching upward as water spilled over their open palms. The liquid shimmered with an iridescent glow, catching the dull light and scattering it like a prism.

I paused there, stealing a glance at my reflection. Sylvan hadn't mentioned the red halo that surrounded my irises, and I hadn't felt the demonic presence since I'd woken here. I pinched my lips, twisting my head from side to side. No matter what angle I inspected my reflection from, my eyes remained blue. Was it possible that coming to Ariada severed the blood pact?

Tiny, luminous insects flitted between flowers, their wings a blur of light. The soft chirp of unseen birds echoed from the canopy above, their song lilting and ethereal. Pathways paved with smooth, silver-gray stones meandered through the garden, lined with bushes that bore roses in every shade imaginable—some glowing, others trailing faint mists that gave the impression of smoke rising from their petals.

A gentle breeze carried the scent of jasmine and something richer, like honey warmed under the sun.

Ash lingered at the entrance, his posture stiff, while Corin stepped further into the garden with me, his gaze scanning the space like a sentinel on duty.

I leaned over to smell what looked like roses. But I got a scent similar to violets instead. I rolled my neck to stir the marbles in my head. I had to stay focused. After meandering between the confines of the garden, I requested a tour of the palace.

Corin glanced at Ash, who shrugged. "We can show you the main floor," he said.

I wandered through at least a dozen ornate halls filled with mesmerizing art pieces—from oil paintings to marble busts. The warriors probably thought I was a nutcase, but I had a plan. I was searching for the stone. And finally, ahead, an ornate cabinet loomed at the far end of the hall, carved from rich, dark wood that gleamed as though freshly polished. Its intricate patterns wove together like an ancient story told in grain and shadow, but it wasn't the craftsmanship that held me captive.

Inside the glass, resting on a velvet pedestal, lay the sapphire crystal—Sky Ice.

The pull was immediate, a visceral tug that left no room for doubt. The translucent stone shimmered with life, its blue core swirling like trapped lightning. Smaller than I remembered, but unmistakable.

I picked up my pace, the world around me narrowing to the glow of the stone. My fingers hovered near the glass, the delicate warmth emanating from the crystal brushing against my skin like an old friend.

Memories hit me in fragments. The last time I touched this stone, I wasn't...human. I had been a ghost, an ethereal fragment of myself, and I'd reached through matter as if it didn't exist. My spectral hand had closed around Sky Ice, and the connection had jolted through me like a second heartbeat. It healed me.

I tapped the glass lightly, testing the boundary that now stood between us. Impenetrable. Frustration coiled hot in my chest, my fingers curling into fists. It was mine. Everything in me screamed that the stone belonged to me.

Breaking the glass crossed my mind—a single strike, and it would be in my hands again. My gaze flicked toward Corin, who stood nearby, his amber eyes narrowing slightly as if sensing my intentions. The short sword strapped at his side caught my attention. One quick motion and—

Footsteps approached, breaking my spiraling thoughts.

"Drawn to it, are you?" Sylvan's smooth voice slid over me.

I stiffened. His eyes gleamed as if I sat him on edge somehow. He approached with calculated calm.

"You keep a close eye on me," I said.

"You're worth watching," he replied, the faintest trace of a smile curving his lips. Was he flirting?

He stepped beside me, his gaze settling on Sky Ice. Silence stretched between us, the crystal casting blue shadows across his face.

"It's more than a stone," he said. "It's alive, in its own way. A tether to something greater than yourself."

I frowned, my fingers still hovering near the glass. "What does that even mean?"

"The Sky Ice is a familiar," he said simply. "And it chose you."

The words sent a shiver rippling through me. "Why?"

His eyes shifted to mine. "Because it recognizes what you don't yet see in yourself."

My attention returned to the stone, the swirling light mesmerizing. "It healed me once," I said, more to myself than to him.

"It will always answer your call," Sylvan murmured.

I turned to him, my brows knitting together. "Then let me have it."

For the briefest moment, something flickered in his eyes —a storm held at bay, dark and fleeting. It vanished almost immediately, his expression smoothing into practiced neutrality.

He smiled, but it lacked warmth. "The Sky Ice responds to those who understand its purpose. And for now, you don't remember how to wield it."

I narrowed my eyes at him. He was holding something back—I could sense it. But no matter how hard I tried to read him, he gave nothing away but the blips of simmering anger.

"I don't get it," I whispered. The crystal had acted on its own before—healing me when I was dying, obliterating the Archon that had nearly destroyed me. But there had been a woman once on the battlefield, manipulating the stone, and it had answered to her. Maybe Sylvan was telling the truth after all.

I pinched my lips to the side in contemplation. "I can't leave. I can't have the stone. I've already toured your grand palace, stoking no memories... What else you got?"

Sylvan straightened to his full height of over seven feet of sheer presence, and stretched his wings wide. "How about we fly?"

TWENTY-TWO

We stepped onto a wide balcony, one of many that encircled the sprawling palace. The balustrade, carved from the same pale stone as the rest of the structure, seamlessly merged with its design. Every four feet, an onyx predator perched atop the handrail—birds with razor-sharp talons, sleek big cats poised mid-leap, or coiled serpents with fangs bared. Their predatory stillness felt alive, as though they might lunge at any moment.

"It's time you saw Ariada in its full glory—from above," Sylvan said.

Blood drained from my face. He watched me closely, scrutinizing my reaction.

"You're quiet," he said.

I forced a small shrug. "Maybe flying just isn't my thing," I said lightly, but the tremor in my voice betrayed me.

He cocked his head, his icy blue eyes narrowing as he studied me, dissecting me without a word.

My throat constricted, panic clawing its way up my spine as memories from the Northern Institute surfaced—flashes of steel, pain, and Mariola's cold smile. I focused on the distant mountains, desperate to bury the rising fear.

"Besides," I added, my voice quieter now, "I couldn't flap my wings even before..." The words slipped free before I could stop them.

"Before what?" he asked, his tone low and unyielding.

I froze. I considered brushing it off, but his heavy gaze demanded honesty. With a shaky sigh, I turned to face him fully. "Before I lost them."

Sylvan stilled. His expression didn't falter, but the tension in his frame betrayed him. Slowly, his wings unfolded, the golden undertones catching the light as he straightened, his posture rigid.

"Lost," he repeated, his voice dangerously soft.

"Sheared off," I corrected, the words scraping against my throat like shards of glass. "Magister Mariola wanted them for her research."

Sylvan's eyes darkened, the glacial blue turning stormy as the calm mask he wore cracked just enough to reveal the fury beneath. "She dared," he said, his tone cold, "to maim one of her own kind..." His jaw clenched, his gaze fixed past me as if Mariola herself stood before him. "If I ever travel to your planet," he said, his tone low and deadly, "I'll pay her a visit."

A grin tugged at my lips, spreading despite myself. "That'd be a sight," I said.

His glanced away, pain flitting across his face. Had he fought my battles for me in the past, back when we were... together? There was no doubt in my mind he'd destroy anyone who dared harm his mate. But I wasn't her, and I needed to stop letting that idea creep in. I shook my head, silently scolding myself.

Still, his mention of visiting Earth reignited something—a flicker of hope, or maybe suspicion. If he could get to Earth, that meant there had to be a way. A portal. An allura. Something. After all, he'd made it into the void to find me.

I peered at my feet, hiding my thoughts from the warriors.

"Do wings ever...grow back?" I asked. "On Ariada, with all your knowledge and technology...is there a cure? Something that could..." I trailed off, unable to finish.

Sylvan's wings twitched as if they were commiserating with me.

"I'm afraid not. Even here, we grow only one pair of wings in a lifetime. They are tied to our essence, our very soul. Once severed..." He paused, his jaw tightening again. "They are gone forever."

The finality of his words struck like a blow, knocking the air from my lungs. I turned my head, blinking rapidly, willing the sting in my eyes to fade.

With a flick of his wrist, Sylvan dismissed the guards. Corin and Ash bowed slightly before retreating, their heavy steps fading into the distance.

"There is a story about an angel, long before Ariada. He defied his purpose, and as punishment, his wings were taken from him. Stripped of his power and his connection to the divine, he fell into the depths of hell."

A bitter laugh escaped me. "So, what? I'm a fallen now?"

Sylvan's frown deepened, a spark of rage flaring in his eyes. "You are nothing like him. Your wings were taken by cruelty, not justice. The one who harmed you will pay the price."

The conviction in his tone twisted something inside me, painfully tight. I didn't know if it was the weight of his belief in my worth or the way his anger burned so brightly on my behalf.

I turned back toward the horizon, the warm wind pulling at my hair and teasing loose strands across my face. The marigold light bathed the landscape in soft radiance, but it did little to soothe the hollow ache growing inside me.

"It feels like a part of me is missing," I said, my voice barely above the breeze. "Like I'll never be whole again."

Sylvan's wings settled behind him. "You are more than your wings," he said, his voice growing darker.

I glanced at him, startled by the intensity in his expression. His eyes churned with something fierce, like a storm trapped within.

"Why do you even care?" I asked, the question slipping out before I could stop myself.

His jaw slackened, though the fire in his eyes didn't fade entirely. "Because *you* matter," he said.

I squinted. Sylvan had a way of delivering his declarations with unwavering confidence as if his devotion to me were a universal truth. The problem was, it wasn't mutual. He wasn't my mate. His words didn't strike the chords he hoped to play. What I felt for him was...appreciation, I supposed. And frustration—anger, even—for keeping me here against my will. But deeper feelings? No. No matter how much he tried, I wouldn't fall for him. I couldn't.

I could see it in the way his shoulders tensed, in the hesitation that flickered across his face when he looked at me. He was testing the waters, feeling for something that wasn't there. And maybe he was beginning to realize that too.

He extended his hand toward me, palm up, his fingers steady. "Let me show you Ariada," he said, his voice quieter now, but no less insistent.

His wings flared open, their sheer size commanding the space around him. They beat once, a powerful motion that stirred the air and sent a faint cloud of dust rising from the stone floor. I hesitated, my heart thudding in my chest. But curiosity won out. If I could win Sylvan's trust, maybe he'd let his guard down. Maybe I could find a way home. Because although something deep within me stirred at the connection to Ariada, nothing—nothing—would stop me from returning to my true home. To *Kole*.

I stepped toward him, slipping my hand into his. His fingers curled gently around mine, and for a moment, I caught the faintest flicker of hope in his eyes.

The sky, bathed in honeyed tones, reached far and wide, streaked with amber and pale lavender that glistened like fading embers in twilight. Below, emerald hills rolled into the horizon, their soft curves broken by shimmering rivers that snaked through the valleys like liquid silver. Cities of marble and crystals rose from the landscape, their spires catching the light and gleaming like freshly polished gemstones.

Sylvan's powerful wings sliced through the air, the golden undertones of his feathers gleaming with every stroke. The wind shifted around him, bending to his strength, and the currents rippled in his wake as though even the skies obeyed him.

But it wasn't the views or his glorious wings that held my attention.

Sylvan's gaze kept drifting—not toward the horizon, but to my face. My lips.

I tried not to notice, keeping my eyes on the stunning landscape below, but the heat of his scrutiny was difficult to ignore. Our bodies, close by necessity, didn't help his control. His arm braced me firmly against his chest to keep me steady. Yet I wasn't the woman he wanted, and that knowledge burned in his eyes like a lingering ache he couldn't hide.

A pang of sadness for him gripped my chest. He carried himself like a warrior—graceful, composed—but this was a man who was not entirely whole. *Ashanti Rosa* was the most powerful mate bond Earthbounders experienced, and it was rare too. Losing a mate felt like an essential part of you was missing. Forever. A void worse than the one filled with goblins.

When Sylvan landed on the balcony, his wings folded neatly behind him, his feet touching the stone with quiet authority. He released me gently, as if afraid I might shatter.

"I've arranged for some food to be brought to your room," he said, his voice steady but distant, his gaze averted now.

"Thank you."

He hesitated, his lips parting as if wrestling with a thought. "We didn't start on the best note," he said finally. "Let me make it up to you. Is there anything you wish for at this moment?"

My eyes rounded, the obvious answer forming on my tongue: *Return me to Earth*. But even I knew that was beyond his willingness—if not his power. I exhaled, the tension in my chest softening, and forced myself to think of something else. Something simple.

A smile tugged at my lips as I glanced down at the velvety gown clinging to me. The material was luxurious, soft as a whisper against my skin, but far too extravagant for my taste. I squinted into the building. A group of female warriors gathered in the sitting room nearby. They wore plain linen dresses under gold leather belts and bandoliers that crossed their chests. Practical. Unassuming.

"That," I said, nodding toward the women. "I'd like a new set of clothes. What they're wearing will do."

Sylvan grimaced. "Priestesses don't wear—"

I interrupted him with a slow double blink of my lashes, my best impression of innocent persistence.

He blinked, his lips twitching as though caught between amusement and resignation. "Ah, yes," he said. "A new set will be waiting for you when you return to your quarters."

We entered the palace. The tallest of the warriors observed us, her lips pinching into a thin line as if she'd bitten something sour.

Sylvan's tone shifted back to business, his hands clasping behind his back. "I believe you still require sleep. Whenever you're rested, come down and ask for Callista. She's my best female warrior. She'll take you to the nearest city."

Without waiting for my response, he walked me to the bottom of the grand staircase. The marble steps stretched wide before me, their polished surface gleaming under the soft light spilling in from the balcony. Angelic statues flanked the base, their carved wings arched protectively as if standing guard over all who passed.

Sylvan's presence lingered behind me as I ascended, his gaze heavy on my back. I could feel it counting every step.

At the top, I hesitated, glancing toward a hallway branching off to the right. The temptation to explore this place on my own was strong. My stare snagged on the figure standing at the far end of the hall—a guard stationed outside what Sylvan had called *my room*.

Of course. I rolled my eyes. Sylvan wasn't taking any chances. He didn't trust me. Touché.

Plastering an over-the-top smile onto my face, I strode past the guard, my chin lifted in exaggerated confidence. His stony expression didn't waver, but I caught the faintest flicker of suspicion in his eyes as I slipped inside the room.

The heavy door clicked shut behind me, and I exhaled sharply, leaning back against the smooth wood. My stared at the luxurious space once again, its opulence doing little to soothe the unease stirring in my chest.

Rest? I snorted quietly, pushing off the door. *I'll rest when I'm dead.*

TWENTY-THREE

I kept pace beside Callista who had been tasked with showing me the human residences. This time, boots on the ground.

My guide stood tall and commanding, her silver hair pulled into a long braid that swayed with each purposeful step. Light and fitted armor hugged her frame, gleaming with a faint luminescence. Its intricate, fluid design resembled a masterpiece of craftsmanship more than simple protection. Each stride carried calm confidence, yet an unmistakable darkness lingered in her aura, keeping me on guard. A leather skirt layered over a white robe paired with gleaming gold shin plates gave her the appearance of an ancient warrior forged with the fierce elegance of a goddess.

Unlike the ethereal grace of Sylvan, Callista's beauty had an edge to it, her sharp cheekbones softened only slightly by the fullness of her lips. Her nickel eyes held an intensity that pinned you in place, daring you to hold her gaze too long. And she stood a foot taller than me which was already intimidating.

"Sylvan said there is no more demonic activity here," I said, attempting to break the silence between us.

Her lips quirked into a humorless smile. I didn't know what to make of it. Of her.

We entered the city, and my eyes rounded. The layout unfolded like a scene from a dream, a harmonious fusion of design and nature. Sweeping arches and towering domes stretched high, blending seamlessly into the surrounding landscape. Waterfalls spilled gracefully from elevated platforms, their streams caught and channeled into glistening canals that wound through streets paved with crystal-like stones. The air carried the rich scent of blooming flowers, an intoxicating sweetness that lingered on my skin. The glass-like buildings, in hues of gold, emerald, and amethyst, pulsed faintly with energy, their surfaces alive with ripples of light.

The people moved through the streets with serene elegance, their white linen robes and flowing dresses catching the pale, rusty light of the dying sun. They looked human in every way, yet there was something different about them—an unshakable calm, an unhurried grace—that set them apart.

"This is what perfect harmony and peace look like," Callista said, gesturing to the tranquil scene before us. The pride in her tone was unmistakable, but a subtle note of something else lingered beneath it—bitterness, perhaps, or regret.

I glanced toward a pair of warriors crossing the square, their silver-white wings tucked neatly against their backs. They moved with purpose, their armor polished to a mirror shine, but there was no tension in their steps, no readiness for battle.

I nodded toward them. "If there's no need for protection, what do they do?"

Callista followed my gaze. "Some of us have adapted," she said. "We've found new roles to fill—teachers, healers, scholars." She motioned for me to follow her down a quiet path, away from the main thoroughfare, where the hum of activity faded into a tranquil stillness.

"Earthbounders were created to protect, to fight, to destroy, if necessary," she continued, her voice lower now, as though sharing a secret. "But here, on Ariada, that purpose has been stripped from us. People don't need us anymore."

She halted and turned to face me, her eyes lively. "They have achieved spiritual evolution. They've found balance and enlightenment. That's why this world thrives while Earth crumbles."

How much did she know about the events on Earth?

Her smile returned. "Some of us remember the thrill of the fight, the purpose it gave us. There are factions among the Ariada Earthbounders—those who dream of settling in places like Earth."

"And Sylvan?" I asked. "Where does he stand in all this?"

Callista glanced my way. "Sylvan believes in Ariada's peace. He's committed to seeing it through. But even he can't control everyone."

I chewed on my lip, her words raising subtle red flags. There was only one reason she'd open up to me like this—she wanted something. Maybe she thought I could get her to Earth. Unfortunately for her, I was as trapped here as everyone else.

We emerged onto a high terrace overlooking the city. From this vantage point, the glowing canals wove through the streets like threads of light, their brilliance mirrored in the crystalline structures. The celestial body above cast its pale brass glow over everything, illuminating the intricate symbols etched into the buildings and streets. From up here, the markings formed a complex web of patterns that seemed to hum with meaning.

Callista leaned casually against the balustrade. "Ariada is a haven. But it's also a cage for those who can't let go of what they were."

I joined her, my hands gripping the cool stone. "And you?" I asked, glancing at her. "Do you feel caged?"

"My duty is here," she said.

I frowned, sensing there was more she wasn't saying, but I let it go. My thoughts churned as I took in the peaceful city below. Ariada seemed to embody everything humanity aspired to, yet a quiet restlessness lingered in the air, a tension threatening to crack the perfect facade.

"You're an enigma," Callista said, her voice pulling me from my thoughts.

I cocked my head, brows furrowing. "Why?"

She studied me for a moment with unnerving intensity. "You don't fit neatly into this world or the one you came from. You're something else entirely. And that makes you... dangerous."

I raised a brow. Me? A wingless Pure, smaller and weaker than the Pures of Ariada—dangerous? The idea was laughable. "Dangerous to who?"

"Everyone. No one," she said as if she was musing to herself.

My muscles tensed, my instincts kicking in. Was this the part where she tried to slit my throat? I wouldn't put it past her.

Callista's lips curved. "Don't worry. You have nothing to fear as long as you're under Sylvan's protection."

"Why are you telling me all this?" I asked, suspicion creeping into my tone.

"I wouldn't want him to get hurt. That's all."

My lips parted, trying to decipher the meaning of her words. She cared about him, in a personal way, not like a soldier protecting their commander.

"Come on. Priestesses are sticklers for being on time," the warrior said.

Priestesses?

TWENTY-FOUR

A chill brushed against my skin like a warning. I hugged myself as we descended into the tunnels beneath the palace. Brass sconces lined the curved walls. Callista strode ahead, her braid swinging like a pendulum with each step.

"Where are we?" I asked.

"The sacred chambers," she said with a clipped tone. I frowned at her back. She didn't elaborate, and I didn't press further. The firmness in her voice didn't invite questions anyway.

A vast, circular space opened before us. Crystals jutted from the walls and ceiling in irregular formations, each glowing with a kaleidoscope of colors that pulsed in some invisible rhythm. Threads of light wove through the air, alive and twisting like translucent ribbons.

Two women waited by a small pool of luminous blue water in the heart of the space.

The priestesses' pale, iridescent skin shimmered under the crystalline light, catching hints of violet and silver with every subtle movement. The taller of the two wore a gown of sheer, gauzy fabric that deepened into amethyst at the hem before fading into a shimmering pearl white at her shoulders. The high neckline gave her an air of authority while flowing sleeves pooled elegantly around her wrists. Tiny gemstones adorned the fabric, scattering light like stars caught in a twilight sky.

The second priestess, smaller but no less striking, wore a gown of deep coral, the fabric hugging her frame as though sculpted for her. Emerald beads draped over her shoulders and spilled down her back, catching the chamber's light in a cascade of radiant green. Pale blond hair tumbled in loose waves, crowned by a delicate circlet of braided silver.

The taller priestess stepped forward, her wide, iridescent eyes locking onto mine with an intensity that made my pulse stutter. Her full lips parted as though she couldn't quite believe what she was seeing.

"It's true," she whispered. "She looks just like her."

The second priestess inched closer, studying me with a mixture of awe and curiosity. She reached out, taking my hands in hers, her smile blooming like a flower.

"Oh, this is wonderful," she said, her voice almost trembling. "Thank the gods for such a gift. We've missed our sister and now you can wake her."

My spine stiffened. "What did you say?"

Callista jerked upright from where she had been leaning casually against a pillar, her features tightening. "Ossana," she said, her voice scolding.

The priestess in coral flinched, her face paling. "I-I'm sorry. I thought—"

"What did she mean by 'wake her'?" I demanded, my breath catching in my throat.

"Nothing," Callista interjected, stepping closer. Her hand brushed my arm as if to steer me away. "We need to go. Sylvan—"

I tore my arm from her grasp, spinning to face her. "No. I'm not going anywhere until someone tells me what's going on."

Callista's jaw clenched, her eyes narrowing. "Sylvan will explain everything—"

"I don't care what that self-righteous wannabe demigod has to say," I said, cutting her off.

The priestesses gasped audibly, their wide eyes darting between Callista and me. One of them hissed, "We don't disrespect our warriors."

"I do," I shot back, rolling my eyes.

They recoiled, their hands flying to their mouths. "She looks like her, but she doesn't sound like her," they whispered, their hushed voices thick with disapproval.

Callista remained stone-faced, her expression betraying nothing, though her crossed arms and raised eyebrow radiated smug superiority. She wasn't going to make this easy.

I chewed on the inside of my cheek, glaring up at her. I wasn't going to win this standoff. "Fine," I said with finality in my tone. "I'll ask Sylvan myself."

I turned to leave, but before I could take another step, Callista's arm shot out, her hand pressing firmly against my chest.

Teeth gritting, she said, "Priestesses, open the Celestial Volt."

The two women exchanged uneasy glances before inclining their heads. Moving in unison, they stepped toward the pool and pressed their hands to a ruby gemstone embedded in its base.

The edges of the pool lit up, tendrils of light rising like fog as the water began to drain through narrow slits lining the stone. The hum of energy thickened, vibrating through my bones. A moment later, a section of the pool slid open, revealing a spiral staircase of smooth stone leading into darkness.

"After you," Callista said, her voice devoid of emotion, though something flickered in her eyes—satisfaction, maybe.

I descended, each step drawing me deeper into the strange resonance, while Callista's heavy footsteps followed close behind.

The walls pulsed with intricate carvings, alive with the rhythm of the glowing crystals embedded in their surface. Above, the domed ceiling glittered with constellations of light, the stones shimmering as if capturing fragments of the stars themselves. Laser-like beams shot from crystal to crystal, converging in the center.

There, suspended in midair and encased in a cocoon of golden light, hovered a woman.

I halted, marveling at the resemble. Her silvery-blond hair floated weightlessly, a halo framing her face. The soft glow of the cocoon outlined her delicate cheekbones, the gentle curve of her lips, and the faint crease between her brows. Her gossamer white gown rippled around her legs as if caught in a breeze that didn't exist.

My pulse thundered in my ears. I knew her.

It was her—the woman from my dreams.

Callista watched me closely, her arms crossed. "You've seen her before, haven't you?"

I nodded, unable to tear my eyes away from the suspended figure. My voice came out a whisper. "In dreams... But I don't understand. Who is she?"

"She is everything."

A deep, resonant voice broke the silence, making me spin around.

Sylvan strode into the chamber, his presence as commanding as ever. His wings stretched partially open, their silver-white feathers catching and reflecting the glow. His expression was calm, controlled, but his eyes burned with an intensity that made my chest constrict.

He halted a few steps from me, his glowering eyes flicking to Callista. His dark eyes narrowed to dangerous slits, and for the first time since I'd met the stoic warrior, her unshakable mask faltered.

"She deserves to know," she said, her voice trembling with suppressed intensity.

His tone cut like a blade. "Leave."

Callista straightened, her jaw tightening as she inclined her head. Without another word, she jogged up the staircase.

Sylvan stepped beside me, his gaze fixed on the woman encased in light. His voice softened, almost reverent. "This is my *Ashanti Rosa*," he said. "My love."

I gaped at him, my mind racing. "Your mate?" I asked. "But she's—"

"Sleeping," he interrupted, his tone firm but laced with something that sounded like pain. "When she foresaw the darkness that would threaten not just Ariada but the universe itself, she believed she could stop it. I argued against it— begged her not to. The Celestial Volt was never meant for this. But she ignored me, as she often did when her conviction outweighed reason."

He neared the glowing cocoon, his hand reaching out to brush its edge. The honey-like light rippled at his touch, faint waves radiating outward like water disturbed by a stone. A pained look marred his features.

"So foolish," he murmured. "So reckless..." His jaw clenched, and bitterness edged his voice. "A local shaman said she sent a fragment of her soul to another dimension, to a distant realm. She believed that was where the answer lay."

His words landed like stones, sinking into my chest. "Another dimension? Another...life?"

His piercing gaze snapped to mine. "You."

I staggered back a step, shaking my head. "You said she left. As in she wasn't here anymore. How is this possible? How am I possible?" My voice rose, trembling with a mix of confusion and anger. "If she's me—or I'm her—shouldn't time collapse or something? That's how it works in every sci-fi movie I've ever seen."

Sylvan didn't react to my sarcasm. His expression tightened, a flicker of expectation in his eyes. "You can awaken her. You can become whole again."

The room seemed to close in, the hum of the carvings growing louder. I clenched my fists, struggling to keep the panic at bay. "I don't know how," I said, my voice breaking. "Even if what you're saying is true, I wouldn't know where to start."

Sylvan's calm façade shattered. His wings snapped wide; his eyes bore into me. "You can," he boomed. "And you will."

My gaze darted back to the cocoon, my chest tightening as a dozen questions pressed on me. "Why would she do this?" I asked. "Why send part of her soul to Earth, of all places? What does that have to do with Ariada?"

Sylvan's lips pressed into a thin line. "That is the one thing I do not understand. Why Earth? Why you?"

He loomed over me, his towering form casting a shadow. "She did this without my knowledge. Without my consent. One day, she was here, guiding our people, and the next..." He trailed off, his jaw tightening. "She was gone. Left this behind." He gestured toward the cocoon, his wings vibrating.

"I've spent centuries searching for the fragment of her she gave away. For you."

"I'm not her," I said, my voice firm despite the tremor in my chest. "Even if this is true—even if part of her soul is inside me—I'm not Lirael. I'm not your priestess. She chose this faith. I chose mine. And it has nothing to do with Ariada."

His cruel laugh sent a jolt through me, forcing me to recoil. A flicker of madness ignited in his eyes, unveiling the true Sylvan—a being far more menacing than I had ever imagined. My pulse quickened as the realization hit: he'd been hiding something all along. I just hadn't expected it to be a still-living mate he'd go feral for.

"You don't have a choice in this," his voice echoes around the volt. "I suppose I should thank Callista for bringing you here after all. Now I can stop pretending. You hold no meaning to me beyond this—you're nothing but a vessel. A means to an end." He sidled closer again, breathing down my neck. "You're a *nobody*."

Before I could react, his hand shot out, gripping my throat. The pressure wasn't enough to choke me, but it forced tears to well up in my eyes.

"Figure this out," he snarled, his breath hot against my face, "before I lose my patience with your existence."

He released me, and I crumpled to the floor, stunned and shaking.

TWENTY-FIVE

Swaths of floating fabric rushed me.

"What on the angels—?" The priestesses hauled me upright, their graceful faces tight with concern. "This is quite a predicament—"

"You don't say," I muttered, squinting against the fuzz clouding my mind.

The taller priestess frowned. "There is no need for insolence."

I gaped at her. Insolence? Who even talked like that? Then it hit me—it was a different realm. At least the Earthbounders here spoke English.

I exhaled, letting go of the frustration twisting inside me. My anger wasn't meant for them. "You're right." My gaze drifted back to Lirael, her serene expression a cruel contrast to the chaos she'd unleashed.

"Is there any way to communicate with her?" I asked.

The priestesses exchanged weary looks and shook their heads. "We've tried rituals, divination, runes... She blocks us every time. She's stronger than all of us combined."

"What about Sky Ice?" I asked. The stone had healed me —surely it could heal Lirael as well?

Another shake of their heads. "She did this to herself. The stone can't interfere."

"There must be a way," I said, more to myself than them.

"I wish there were—" one priestess began, but I cut her off.

"She came to me once in spirit form. She used Sky Ice to annihilate Bezekah," I said, my mind spinning through the memory aloud, ignoring their interruptions.

The priestess in coral leaned forward. "You saw her?"

I nodded. "She was me...but she wasn't." Seeing their puzzled expressions, I explained how Lirael's spirit had blended with my body, locking my limbs in place.

"Then she...poofed," I added, mimicking the sound with my lips.

"Did she say anything?" the shorter priestess asked, eyes wide.

I shrugged. "Her only words were 'Remember how to shine.' I haven't figured out what she meant."

The shorter priestess hiccupped. "So like her to speak in beautiful riddles."

I frowned, studying Lirael again. She'd sacrificed everything—her life, her mate—for what? To stop the darkness no one seemed to know anything about?

"Sylvan said Lirael spoke of a coming darkness. But Ariada is free from evil, so what could she have meant?" The question swirled in my head.

The priestesses exchanged uneasy glances.

"This confuses us as well," the taller one said. "Ariada has been sealed from demonic activity for longer than I've lived—and I've lived a long time. It would take a catastrophic event, like stars colliding, to break that seal."

I began pacing, the heels of my boots echoing against the

marble. What if the darkness wasn't coming here? What if it affected Ariada indirectly?

I froze mid-step as a memory clawed its way to the surface. The Exiousai, Seth, had said Xavier's mother gave him a prophecy about a girl destined to defeat a great evil. Lirael wasn't trying to stop a threat aimed at Ariada—she'd been fighting to stop a threat targeting Earth.

"The Earthbounders in my realm are battling for control. One, in particular—the Soaz, Invicta's enforcer—is a Pure with a demonic mutation. He's determined to rule them all." I turned to the priestesses. "I think she was trying to stop him."

The taller priestess tilted her head. "But how would his actions impact Ariada?"

I turned in a slow circle, my eyes drifting to the star-like crystals embedded in the walls as if they might hold the answer. "Your realm is unreachable by demons, yes. But what about a Pure with a demonic mutation?"

The priestesses exchanged wary glances.

"It's possible," the taller one said slowly. "But for someone from your planet to invade Ariada, one of our own would have to open the gate. And that would never happen."

My head snapped toward her, my pulse racing. "Are you saying...there's an allura gate here?" Sylvan had to have access to one. That was how he traveled to the void.

Their widened eyes betrayed them. They'd said too much.

"It's volatile," the taller priestess said. "When the spiritual revolution took hold, the need for alluras vanished, and most collapsed. Only one remains today—but its use is forbidden."

"Forbidden," I parroted, raising an eyebrow. "Funny. Sylvan doesn't seem to care about that."

The priestesses stiffened but didn't respond.

"It's dangerous," the taller one finally said. "Not just for the traveler but for Ariada itself. Frequent use could destabilize the region—earthquakes, tremors, rockslides..."

I filed the information away. "But a Pure with the ability to portal could breach Ariada, right?"

She nodded. "In theory. But they would still need someone on this side to open the gate, and no one here would risk Sylvan's wrath."

Callista's words echoed in my mind. A faction of Ariada's Earthbounders wanted to leave and rediscover their purpose.

I peered at the priestesses. "You're attuned to Ariada's energy, the constant hum—"

"You hear it?" the shorter one interrupted, startled.

I nodded. "It's under my skin, soothing me. But sometimes it jolts me like the realm itself is trying to warn me something isn't right..."

Their faces fell, confirming my suspicion.

"How confident are you in your warriors' allegiance to Sylvan?" I asked.

The taller priestess pressed her lips together, refusing to answer. That said enough.

Boots stomped against the stone steps. My chest tightened, fists curling as I braced for another confrontation with Sylvan.

Corin's amber eyes fixed on mine as he appeared in the doorway. "The commander requests your presence."

TWENTY-SIX

ole. His name was a lifeline. His face sharpened in my mind—the intensity in his eyes, the way his wings snapped open when he was furious or protective.

And *Xavier*—my chest tightened. His raw honesty. His reckless courage.

I rolled my wrists, shaking the tension loose, forcing my focus back to the present.

Corin and Ash flanked me, silent and stoic. We traversed past the grand lounge area that led to Sylvan's office. My brows pulled together when we veered away from it. The warriors, towering two feet above me and broad as the red pines at the P6 headquarters, blocked most of my view, but I glimpsed Callista with a group of warriors in the distance. Swords slashed through the air as they sparred, cheeks flushed with exertion. The gleam in her eyes dimmed when she saw me, her lips pressing into a thin line.

Yeah, Callista definitely wasn't my biggest fan.

Ahead, guards shoved open a pair of ivory and gold double doors. The chamber beyond stretched half the length of a football field. A long, light-wood table dominated the space, one side open to the breeze through arched cutout windows, the other wall covered in intricate brushstrokes.

A map.

I strolled over, drawn to the detailed landscape. Cyan-hued water swirled around uneven coastlines and vast sandy, gray, and forest-green lands. It had to be Ariada, though its edges were scorched and blackened as if burned by fire.

"This map was drawn after the last battle," Corin said, following my gaze. He pointed to the charred contours. "The land we lost fell into the void, the people and Earthbounders alike consumed by hell-stricken realms forever."

My throat tightened. I scanned the map's vast expanse, marveling at the masterpiece. Ariada resembled Earth in some ways, such as its icy polar caps.

A door creaked open at the far end. Sylvan marched in, silver hair catching the light, composure plastered on his face. That calm no longer fooled me; the tension beneath the surface set me on edge.

I stiffened. I hadn't gotten any closer to waking Lirael in the last hour, and if my guess was right, she wouldn't wake until her mission on Earth was finished.

Sylvan's eyes softened, as they always did when he first saw me. My presence reminded him of her, though the soft-ening didn't last. The underlying hatred I'd come to expect burned through soon enough. His emotions clashed—grief and rage warring with each other—and his fraying patience ensured the rage won lately.

He halted in front of me, grabbed my hand, and shoved something onto my finger. A teardrop diamond encased in pink light sat on a gold band.

I jerked my hand back, flexing my fingers, ready to rip it off.

"Don't," he growled. "It belonged to her."

I glared at him, but he leaned back, unbothered.

"The ring marks you as mine. Corin and Ash won't always be by your side. This will grant you access to the archives—and Lirael's chambers. Use it to get closer to finding an answer."

My jaw clenched. His fixation on waking his mate bordered on obsession. He wasn't interested in what Lirael wanted—just his own needs.

"What about what she wants?" I asked.

Sylvan's eyes flashed. "She wants to be with me."

"But she can't be if Ariada falls. Can't you see it?"

"That's why we need her back *now*, so we can prepare for the threat she foresaw."

"No! The threat is on Earth. She went there—she sent me there—to stop it. If the allura here is opened and the darkness enters, there's no stopping it."

His eyes narrowed dangerously. "How do you know about the allura?"

The priestesses chose that moment to glide into the chamber.

The taller one curtsied low, her round eyes flicking between us. "I had a vision, commander. Arien must complete Lirael's work on Earth. That's the only way to bring our sister—your *Ashanti Rosa*—back."

The other priestess's eyelids trembled and he struggled to hold anyone's gaze. Hold on—were they lying? Sylvan wouldn't have listened to me alone. They knew that and apparently, saw merit in my argument.

A small, relieved smile tugged at my lips. Sylvan scowled and I wiped the smirk off.

He raked a hand through his long silver-streaked hair, a flicker of uncertainty breaking through his stoic exterior.

"Are you sure?" he asked the taller priestess.

"Yes," she said. "This is the only way."

TWENTY-SEVEN

The room Sylvan had given me radiated the same pristine serenity as the rest of Ariada, but its stillness pressed in on me now, suffocating. I rifled through the clothes on the bed, stopping when I spotted the black tactical pants and fitted top I'd worn when I arrived.

The fabric was clean, the faint floral scent of whatever Ariadans used clinging to it. I slipped into the outfit quickly, grateful for the familiarity, even if it carried its ghosts.

Ariadan warriors dressed like ancient Greek soldiers—tunics, fitted armor, and sandals laced to their knees. Beautiful, yes, but useless for Earth. I sighed, pulling my hair into a loose ponytail and lacing up my boots, the familiar routine grounding me.

I joined the priestesses waiting on me in the hall. They recoiled at my sight, their lips twitching as if I'd stepped out in rags. I bit my lip to stop a chuff of laughter bubbling inside.

We descended into sacred chambers. Passing by the shallow pool, I couldn't help but hesitate.

"Can I...see her again?" I asked.

The taller priestess inclined her head, her face softening with understanding. "Of course. We will wait here and call you when it's time."

They released the locking mechanism. Taking a deep inhale, I took the steps down one by one. When I reached the bottom, I stopped cold. Lirael floated, suspended in an oblong sphere of golden light. But seeing her again pulled at something inside me—a blend of unease and uncertainty that wouldn't settle. Was I making the right choice? My heart tugged in two directions—this world, which felt inexplicably tied to me, and mine, where people I loved waited.

The hum grew louder as I shuffled forward, my boots scuffing against the stone. Her face was serene, almost unnaturally perfect, as if sculpted from marble. Yet something familiar lingered in her cheekbones and the gentle arch of her brow.

"Who are you?" I whispered, my voice cracking.

The connection I felt with her was undeniable, an invisible thread that had tugged at me since the moment I saw her. But it wasn't based on the memory of her alone. It was deeper than that—existential even.

"I don't know what to do," I said, barely audible. "Sylvan thinks I can save you, but I don't even know how to save myself. You sacrificed yourself to stop evil, but I'm not you. I'm not a priestess or a savior. I'm just...me."

The silence pressed more heavily, broken only by the faint hum of the volt.

I reached out, my hand trembling as my fingers hovered above the glowing cocoon. "What would you do? How would you fix this? Because I—"

The words stuck in my throat as a voice whispered in my mind—the same voice I'd heard after the battle with Bezekah.

Remember how to shine.

I stumbled back, heart hammering. The words crackled through me like lightning, biting and electric. But their meaning slipped through my fingers, as elusive as smoke.

I stared at her for a long moment, my hands curling into fists at my sides. "I'll do everything I can," I said. "I promise. I'll try to stop whatever this is—for your people and my family."

I choked when a vision took hold. In it, Lirael hid in a passage leading away from the chamber above. A figure fully cloaked in white rushed across, a silver braid peeking out. Lirael etched Roman numerals on the wall. She was keeping a tally—no dates. I squinted in the vision to read the years but I got pulled back to reality before I could make sense of them when footsteps thudded above.

I jogged up the stairs, my heart still racing. At the top, I found Sylvan. He scowled, whirled, and strode into a connecting chamber.

The taller priestess caught my eye and mouthed, "Go." I hesitated as the other priestess sealed the Celestial Volt behind me, then hurried after him.

The narrow passage twisted before opening into a vast space. I skidded to a halt, gasping as the path dropped off into a bottomless pit. My boots scraped against the stone, arms flailing. I caught the wall just in time.

Wheezing, I scanned the area. A semicircular platform jutted from the opposite wall several stories below. The rotund made my head spin. Sylvan glowered up at me, Corin and Ash by his side.

Yep, still a wingless Pure here.

His wings snapped open, and in one powerful motion, he shot across the pit, then yanked me into his arms and carried me to the platform.

A metal circle cut off at the base pulsed with dark,

whistling energy that swirled at its center. I shivered. The allura gate. But something about it felt...wrong.

Corin and Ash's outfits caught my eye, the modern tactical designs eerily like what Kole and Xavier wore on their scouting missions. Their expressions betrayed their discomfort in this new attire.

I gestured to them, my brow furrowing. "Why are you dressed like that?"

Sylvan's lips quirked with rare amusement. "A priestess suggested it would suit Earth's current timeline."

My lips parted. "They're coming...?"

"I won't risk anything happening to you," Sylvan said firmly. "They're my most skilled warriors. You need only ask, and they'll assist."

"Why not send an entire army? Or better yet, come yourself?" I crossed my arms over my chest.

"The gate can't relocate an army. Overloading it would destabilize the land further. As for me—" His brows knitted. "—I want to be here when Lirael awakens. I won't miss that moment."

His devotion to her softened my frustration with him by a sliver.

Sylvan turned to the gate, raising his arms. The carvings framing the metal circle flared with light, pulsing rhythmically, like an engine stirring to life.

The air thickened, buzzing with invisible energy. The hum grew into a deafening roar.

With a flash, the allura burst to life. The swirling darkness coalesced into a shimmering portal of silver and blue, crackling with arcs of lightning.

"This will take you to the Everlake—where I last saw you," Sylvan said over the howling winds.

I stiffened. "Wait, I can't set my coordinates?" I'd planned to travel to the hill where I'd met the great druid and seek his assistance. No other place seemed safe at this moment. Not even the Everlake.

"The destination must be preset from this side. Otherwise, the gate will hurl you into the void." His voice rose over the howling. The roaring grew louder, sending an unpleasant ripple through me.

Sylvan motioned for us to proceed, but I halted the men, needing to know more. "How much time has passed on Earth?" *Please don't say a year or a crazy number like that.*

His frown deepened. "I can control the temporal drift, but there's always some variance. You should arrive shortly after you entered the void."

Panic flared. *Damian.* He could still be there.

Corin and Ash seized my arms, their grips ironclad as they hauled me off the ground.

"Wait!"

My protest was swallowed by the maelstrom.

The gate dragged us in, winds screaming as we tumbled through a spinning vortex. My stomach twisted with nausea. Ariada's allura was nothing like the others I'd traveled through.

Corin and Ash fought against the chaotic currents, their statue-like bodies clamping around me. Arms intertwined, they encased me in a protective cocoon, shielding me from the worst of it.

We spun endlessly, weightless, until a glistening light pierced the darkness ahead. We broke through the barrier with a splash.

TWENTY-EIGHT

The water churned violently before spitting us out onto the unforgiving floor of the cave. The allura's pull released its grip with a final shudder as the portal flickered and died. I slammed onto my knees, coughing up air that burned with the cavern's icy dampness.

"Are you alright?" Corin asked, his amber eyes assessing, his voice more professional than concerned.

"Perfect. The rocks broke my fall. How about you?" I rasped, brushing off his outstretched hand as I staggered to my feet. Damp clothes clung to my skin, uncomfortable and cold, but the familiar chill of Earth's air cut through the disorientation like a balm.

Cave loomed around us, its jagged walls slick with moisture seeping from the Everlake. Dusky light seeped through the cavern's mouth, painting the rocks in molten hues of smoky orange and red, like the dying embers of a fire.

I staggered forward, my boots squelching and I peered outside. Smoke rose in thick plumes from the charred remains of the Fringe, now a sprawling wasteland of rubble and ash. Fires smoldered in scattered patches, their faint crackle carried on the wind. Hours must have passed—long enough for the sun to sink lower on the horizon. The fear of running into Damian eased its hold on me.

"He killed them all," I whispered to myself.

Corin tilted his head, peering at the damage.

Ash crossed his bulky arms. "Now what?"

I didn't answer right away. My tattoo throbbed, the black lines on my arm pulsing in time with my heartbeat.

Where are you?

The question hadn't fully formed when my vision tunneled. The cavern blurred and I gripped Corin's sleeve to steady myself.

The world shifted, pulling me incorporeal and weightless into shadowed hallways and towering corridors. Massive doors loomed ahead, etched with intricate patterns of wings and celestial symbols. I passed through them like a ghost, slipping effortlessly into the council's meeting chamber.

It was exactly as I remembered: vast and oppressive, with soaring columns and a dome ceiling. Red throne-like chairs stood on a raised platform, their gilded frames gleaming under muted light. Most were occupied by Magisters draped in formal regalia, their expressions carved in stone.

Mariola's seat sat empty.

Donovan, perched in Hafthor's chair, scowled as if the world itself had wronged him.

The Oath Keeper slumped forward in his seat; his otherworldly aura had dimmed to something painfully mortal. His hands gripped the armrests like they were the only thing keeping him upright. One eye glimmered, the other clouded and lifeless.

Before him, Damian stood, his posture rigid as he addressed them. I couldn't hear what he was saying, but his tight features signaled importance..

The audience sat in strained silence—advisers, Magisters' children, and a handful of high-ranking Pures. Among them, I recognized

Thalassa, Galadon, and Caelum, but Elyon's heirs, Zephyr and Seraphina, were absent.

The Oath Keeper stirred, his head whipping around as though something unseen yanked his attention. His clouded eye locked onto me, piercing through the veil of my poltergeist form.

My heart stuttered. He rose, the motion dragging the attention of everyone in the room.

"She's alive," he said, his rough voice cutting through the chamber.

Everyone stilled. Damian's head snapped in my direction, his gaze narrowing with unsettling precision. A smile tugged at his lips—a small, eerie curve that chilled my blood. He couldn't see me, not fully, but I felt the tether between us tighten.

Then he let it go.

A jolt surged through our connection, slamming into me like a battering ram. The vision shattered.

I gasped, air rushing into my lungs as I slumped against Corin's chest.

"What was that?" he growled.

I blinked, my vision swimming at the edges. "Damian," I managed, my voice hoarse. "He knows I'm alive."

Ash's pale features twisted into a scowl. "Great. Five minutes here, and we're already compromised."

If Damian had sensed my presence, he'd seen enough to guess my location. It wouldn't take him long to send a team to the Everlake. The thought sent a shiver through me, but another realization struck—I could learn to wield the tether. If he could track me, maybe I could block him. I tested the connection between us but was met with an invisible wall. Damian had blocked me from tracking him for good.

The warriors exchanged wary glances.

"We fly from here," I said, my stomach tightening at the thought. I missed my wings more than I wanted to admit—and now, one of these brooding giants would have to carry me. Ugh.

Two pairs of wings swept wide. In perfect unison, the warriors stomped forward and then upped their speed.

"Uh..." My eyes darted between them, trying to guess who would grab me before they bulldozed me off the cliff. I squealed as Corin surged ahead, scooping me into his arms like I was a feather. We shot into the air, Ash trailing behind before leveling with us. The wind lashed at my face. Once we ascended above the clouds, the sky stretched bright and boundless. Ash tapped the screen of a smartwatch strapped to his wrist. A hologram map flickered to life, floating above the display. With a flick of his finger, the map spun to show the terrain directly ahead.

"Where to?" Corin asked.

I bit my lip, pinching the map between my thumb and forefinger to zoom in on the P6 territory. If Kole had left clues behind, they'd be in the places he knew I'd search for him. Seth had likely moved his underground base to evade Damian, and consulting the great druid was too risky now that Damian knew I'd returned.

"I'm going to introduce you to my family," I said, tapping the image of the P6 cabin.

TWENTY-NINE

Corin's grip crushed my back, keeping me secure in his hold. I wouldn't have slipped if he'd slowed his insane pace. Kole sailed this fast only during battles. Earth's Earthbounders always conserved their Pure energy, but these advanced warriors were a different breed. They didn't sleep, and they could stay in their Pure forms indefinitely. No wonder they wiped out any demon foolish enough to invade Ariada.

Corin's wings cut sharply through the smoky twilight air. Being carried like this was a cruel reminder of the wings I'd once had. Wings Mariola had stolen from me. The thought twisted like a blade, but I shoved it aside and focused on the horizon.

"Land there," I said, pointing to the overgrown clearing in front of the P6 gates.

With a crisp maneuver, Corin descended, landing with the precision of a hawk. Ash followed a beat later, his pale, scarred face surveying the area.

I drew in a shaky breath. The gargantuan stretched high and wide, iron bars rusted in patches. The once-proud emblem etched into the center had faded. Or had it always been that way?

"This is it?" Corin asked, his tone skeptical.

"Yeah," I said, forcing confidence into my voice. "This is P6."

I squinted at the iron fence stretching into the shadows on either side. Something was missing—the hum of the magical barrier.

Corin cleared his throat and kicked the gate. It swung open with a groan. "It's unlocked."

My stomach churned. "All institutes have allura barriers around their perimeters. Someone deactivated this one." I stepped through the opening, Corin and Ash flanking me. My brows knitted. Had Hafthor ordered the allura taken down after I disappeared following the battle with Bezekah?

The gate creaked as Ash closed it behind us, the only sound the eerie stillness around us. Our boots crunched against loose gravel. I strained my senses for any movement, sounds—any sign of life.

But the grounds remained deathly silent.

A rustle came from the bushes to our left. Before I could blink, both angels had their swords drawn. Their expressions taut.

"It's just a deer," I said, my voice breaking the tension.

The animal froze, wide-eyed, then bolted into the brush.

We pressed on, sticking to the road. The hidden garage entrance came into view, though it was no longer hidden. The massive rock that once shielded the passage sat raised, revealing the tunnel below.

"That's not a good sign," I muttered.

I crouched at the edge and tossed a stone inside. The motion-activated lights flickered on, casting harsh white light over the corridor. It didn't reach far, the shadows beyond swallowing everything.

Corin proceeded to enter, but I caught his arm.

"This doesn't feel right," I said.

He studied me, considering, then gave a curt nod.

"Check the cabin," I said to Ash, jerking my chin upward. "See if there's any activity."

Ash launched into the air, his wings slicing through the heavy haze.

Corin's amber gaze darted between the tunnel and the surrounding grounds. "Why do you think it's open?"

"I don't know," I said honestly, my pulse thudding in my ears. "But it feels like a trap. The question is...who set it?"

Ash landed moments later, his boots hitting the ground with a thud. "The cabin's dark," he reported. "No movement. No bodies."

The tension in my chest didn't ease. "Let's go," I said, backtracking. "If they're here, the courtyard cameras will alert them."

Corin set me down near the firepit. The bricks around it were dark and cold, untouched for weeks, maybe longer. I scanned the roofline, searching for the telltale glint of a camera.

As if on cue, floodlights blazed to life. I yelped and threw up a hand to shield my eyes.

The unmistakable sound of weapons being drawn cut through the air.

"Stop! It's me—Arien."

The lights dimmed just enough for two figures to emerge from the shadows.

Vex and Mezzo.

Relief swept through me, but their guarded stances made me uneasy.

Vex reacted first. His lips twitched into a disbelieving smirk. "I'll be damned," he drawled, sarcasm thick in his voice. "But who the hell are these overgrown ogres?"

I pressed a hand against Corin's arm, lowering his raised sword. "They're with me," I said. Turning to the Ariadans, I added, "This is part of the family I told you about."

Vex raised a brow, his smirk deepening. "Family, huh?"

I ignored his comment, rushing and pulling him into a tight hug. He stiffened, then returned the embrace with a firmness that said more than words.

"Where's Kole?" I asked, pulling back. The name left a lump in my throat. I almost asked about Xavier too but stopped myself.

Vex sobered.

"In the city," he said in a grim tone. "The demon breaches have gotten worse. It's like the barriers between worlds are... collapsing. I've never seen anything like it."

A chill rippled through me, and the tattoo on my arm pulsed faintly.

"But the council—" I started, only for Vex to cut me off.

"Donovan brokered a truce between Invicta and the Underground. Temporary. We're working together to fight the breaches, but..." He trailed off, glancing at Corin and Ash. "There's still a bounty on our heads. We can't let our guard down."

His attention turned to the Ariadans, eyes narrowing. "I don't recognize these guys," he said pointedly.

"They look different, too," Mezzo added, his usual straightforward cadence carrying a hint of suspicion. "Where'd you get your escorts from?"

I rubbed the back of my neck, tension twisting in my shoulders. "What if I said...from a different realm?"

THIRTY

Vex chuckled, the sound incredulous. "Different realm, huh?" He glanced back at Corin and Ash. "Good one."

I raised an eyebrow, staying silent and waiting for it to settle.

His smirk wavered when he noticed I wasn't joking. "Wait. You're serious?"

Static crackled from his comm. Then Rae's unmistakable, giddy voice burst through. "Arien? She's there? Take her down to the mission center, Vex! Now!"

The sheer joy in her tone made something in my chest tighten.

Vex groaned dramatically into the comm. "Alright, alright," he muttered, waving for us to follow. "Let's get moving."

An awkward silence fell upon us inside the elevator. Vex stood casually to my left, but his fingers twitched against the hilt of his sword, a subtle tell of his unease. Corin flanked my right, shrewd eyes sweeping every corner, his posture rigid and ready. Behind us, Ash leaned against the wall, arms crossed, his icy gaze bouncing between Mezzo—who kept his vigil on the newcomers—and the reflective steel walls.

Mezzo didn't trust them, and I couldn't blame him. Two towering warriors from a realm never seen or heard of here on Earth weren't easy to explain away or accept as true.

"Relax," I said, glancing over my shoulder at the Seraph.

He scowled. "I want to know what they're after." His tone low and clipped.

"They're here to help us," I said.

Corin's lips twitched, but he said nothing, keeping his gaze forward.

The elevator doors slid open, and we marched into the mission center. It buzzed with activity. Monitors glowed with real-time feeds of P6 territory and sections of the city. Earth-bounders shuffled between workstations, their faces a blend of exhaustion and determination. But all of it blurred when Rae darted across the room, arms wide and smile brighter than the monitors behind her.

She threw herself at me, pulling me into a fierce hug, her ringing laughter like sunlight piercing through clouds.

"You absolute idiot!" she said, pulling back just enough to glare at me with mock anger. "Do you know how many times I wanted to strangle you for disappearing like that again?"

I laughed, though the sound came out shaky. "Missed you too, Rae."

Her glare melted into another wide grin, and she hugged me again, tighter this time. "Don't you ever pull that crap again, or I swear, I'll—"

"I get it," I said, cutting her off. "I tried to stop him," I whispered.

She let me go reluctantly and motioned toward the monitors. "Come on. You need to see what's been happening while you've been gallivanting across the void." She eyed the Ariadans behind me with a raised eyebrow.

The screens displayed live feeds from across the territory —the charred remains of the Fringe, the outskirts of P6, and parts of the city where small-scale breaches shimmered like cracks in reality.

But my attention zeroed in on the screen displaying vitals. Names blinked beside the pulsing lines: Kole, Xavier, Zaira, Anhelm. My heartbeat spiked, hammering at least twice as fast as Kole's.

"They're in the city," Rae said, noticing where my gaze had landed. "Trying to contain the breaches before they spread any further."

Then my eyes shifted to another set of names on the monitor, and my brows knitted. Zephyr—along with two warriors I recognized as his guards.

"What is he doing here?" I asked, pointing at his name.

Her smile dimmed. "A lot's changed in the past few hours," she said. "Zephyr refuses to recognize Donovan as the new Magister of Invicta. His father had no choice but to banish him—Elyon couldn't risk more regional instability."

"That doesn't sound like Elyon," I said.

"It's not," Rae said. "But with Mariola and the Northern region already cut off..."

"Cut off?" I echoed.

Rae nodded, crossing her arms. "The Soaz accused her of unsanctioned experimentation—said she collaborated with the Fringe. This morning, she tried to cover her tracks by setting the Fringe on fire."

My stomach churned. "That wasn't her," I said, shaking my head. "Damian caused the explosions."

Rae's brow lifted, curiosity flickering in her eyes. "Damian?"

I met her stunned expression. "He told me himself. I don't know how deeply he was involved in the experiments at the Fringe, but I'm certain Mariola's research didn't extend beyond her lab."

Rae turned fully toward me, her arms tightening over her chest. "What happened after you met with him?"

I recounted the events of that night: my conversation with Seth, Damian's attempt to drown me, and the nymphs' intervention. I left Xavier out of the story—it felt too raw, too...undefined. The memory of him left heat prickling at my face. I caught myself and glanced at the warriors listening, hoping they assigned my fluttering to something else.

"But the nymphs guided me to the void instead," I continued. "Sylvan was waiting there. He pulled me through to his realm, Ariada."

I gestured toward Corin and Ash, who stood silently behind me like stone sentinels. "That's where these guys are from."

Rae regarded the warriors, assessing them with quick precision before she exhaled and returned her attention to me. "We're definitely going to need more details."

The kitchen radiated warmth, the scent of biscuits and fresh eggs wafting through the air as Rae and I worked side by side. She hummed softly, her movements precise and confident, like someone who'd fed armies of hungry warriors countless times.

I, on the other hand, was a mess. My hands shook as I cracked eggs into a bowl, my heart pounding erratically.

Kole and Xavier would return soon.

It had been days for me, mere hours for them—days since I'd last seen them, hours since I'd disappeared without so much as a goodbye. Xavier had known I was leaving but hadn't stopped me, and now they would walk through those doors, and I had no idea how to face them.

"You're sweating," Rae teased, nudging me with her elbow.

"It's hot in here," I mumbled, wiping my brow with the back of my hand.

She raised an eyebrow, clearly unconvinced. "Uh-huh. Sure it is."

Across the room, Corin and Ash perched like statues, their vigilant eyes fixed on the windows, surveying for potential threats. They hadn't left my side since we'd arrived, and their silent vigilance was both comforting and unnerving.

I focused on whisking the eggs, trying to drown out the storm of anxious thoughts swirling in my head.

Then the sound of boots stomping on floorboards broke through the last of my composure. A heavy bang followed when someone slammed doors shut.

My heart leaped into my throat.

Kole emerged in the doorway, his stormy eyes locking onto mine with a murderous intensity that froze me in place. His broad shoulders filled the frame, his wings twitching like they might snap open at any moment.

Xavier nudged the Power to the side and entered the kitchen, his expression equally fierce, though something else lingered in his eyes too—relief, maybe?

Corin sidled closer to me, his scowl deepening.

Kole's nostrils flared.

"Corin," I said quickly, my voice unsteady as I placed a hand on his arm. "It's fine. That's my...my..." I stumbled, my face heating. My what? Mate? Lover? Everything? "Kole," I finished lamely.

Zaira snorted, her hand half-covering her mouth as she tried—and failed—to smother her snicker.

I shot her a glare before rounding the counter. I brushed past Rae, who shot me an exaggerated look of pity, and grabbed Kole and Xavier by their wrists, tugging them toward the adjacent library. They followed without resistance or hesitation.

Once inside, I shut the door, knowing full well the others could hear every word. Enhanced hearing was a cruel curse when privacy was on the line.

"I know there's nothing I can say," I began, my voice trembling slightly. "You have every right to be mad—"

Kole flashed to my side and lifted me off the ground. I yipped, surprised by his action. He buried his face in the crook of my neck, and I slid my fingers into his hair, laying my head atop his and closing my eyes.

This wasn't the usual protective, unyielding embrace I was used to. His body trembled, his rage barely restrained. He held me like I might disappear again if he let go.

"I'm learning to trust you," he said, his voice a low timbre. "But it's not easy when you vanish without a word."

"What are hours, days, or weeks in comparison to our long lives?" Xavier said, his tone as smooth as ever.

I glanced at him over Kole's head, a small smile tugging at my lips. I'd missed his wit, teasing, the way he always knew exactly what to say to reassure or torment me.

Kole's head tilted slightly, his gaze flicking to Xavier. "I never cared for the passage of time before her."

I blinked, startled by the sincerity in his voice. They weren't arguing, weren't bickering or posturing like usual.

"You two are getting along," I said, my eyes dancing between their cordial faces.

"It was either that or killing him for letting you go... alone." Kole sighed, releasing me. "I'll give you a minute with him."

My eyes widened. "Alone?"

Kole's voice turned brooding again, his default style. "Don't make me come back for you. I'm still processing this."

"This?" I asked, frowning.

He inspected my face, my eyes. The red halo didn't reappear with my return to Earth. I hoped Ariada cured me of it.

"You and Xavier," Kole said.

My throat tightened, but before I could respond, he leaned down, his lips brushing against my ear.

"I get you all to myself in my bed tonight," he whispered, his tone laced with possessive heat.

My cheeks flamed as he strode away, shutting the door behind him.

I swiveled toward Xavier, embarrassment flooding through me. "I...um..."

He didn't wait for me to stumble over an excuse. He invaded my personal space, his hand cupping my chin, and pressed his lips to mine. The kiss started slow, almost tentative, then deepened, his grip tightening as a surge of warmth spread through me.

When he pulled back, his thumb brushed my cheek, his eyes holding mine hostage. "Soon, you'll blush for me like that too," he said, his voice soft and confident.

I stared after him as he strolled to the door, pausing just long enough to smirk before slipping out. I pressed my fingers to my lips, blood rushing to my face. The two Pures were going to be the death of me.

The realization that everyone in the kitchen had probably heard everything made me groan, the sound echoing softly in the empty library.

With a deep breath, I straightened my shoulders. The warriors needed their eggs and biscuits, and I wasn't about to let this duo ruin me.

At least not completely.

THIRTY-ONE

The sitting area near the kitchen purred with warmth, the soft crackle of the hearth flames filling the silence between bites of food and stolen glances. Empty plates and glasses cluttered the coffee table. For the first time in weeks, I felt a flicker of something close to comfort—a fragile, fleeting thing, but comfort none-theless.

I perched on the couch, Rae on one side and Corin on the other. Ash stood behind me, his watchful eyes scouring the room like he expected an ambush. Across from me, Kole and Xavier occupied the chairs, their faces tense as they leaned forward, elbows on their knees. I preferred the two of them by my sides, but they'd either decided Corin and Ash weren't a threat or wanted to keep the Ariadans in their sights.

I still couldn't get over them working together—or just *getting along*.

Familiar faces crowded the room: Kole, Vex, Talen, Rae, Zaira, Xavier and his men, and even Zephyr, who leaned casu-ally against the wall, arms crossed and a playful smirk teasing his lips. Firelight caught in his golden hair, creating a halo-like glow around this playboy's head.

Rae jabbed me in the ribs with her elbow. "Tell us again."

All eyes turned to me, and the fragile comfort shattered.

I took a steadying breath. "I ended up on Ariada," I said, keeping my voice steady despite the nerves. "It's a long story, but it wasn't by choice. After Damian tried to drown me, the nymphs pulled me into the void. They...saved me, in their way."

Zaira choked on her drink, then muttered, "Fucking nymphs."

"Sylvan—the warrior from my dreams—appeared out of nowhere and brought me to Ariada. Somehow. I blacked out, and the next thing I remember is waking up in his realm."

"Did you see the crystal?" Kole asked.

"Yes, and the woman. She's Sylvan's *Ashanti Rosa* and a seeress. She placed herself in stasis to stop the threat to Earth and chose me as her...vessel, sort of. Sylvan believes defeating the threat will wake her." I gestured toward the Ariadans with us, who remained still and alert. "He sent Corin and Ash to help us."

Corin shifted, his amber eyes narrowing slightly as if questioning why I omitted how I'd been treated on Ariada. If he didn't want Kole and Xavier to rip him and Ash apart, he'd better keep his mouth shut too.

"So why didn't this almighty commander come himself—or send more soldier?" Vex asked, breaking the quiet.

"Ariada needs a leader," Corin said, his tone clipped. "And our only allura is damaged. Sending an army would destroy what's left of the planet."

"And how are we supposed to defeat this threat?" Xavier's voice cut through.

I hesitated, my stomach twisting. "I don't know."

Corin's jaw tightened. "She will know when the time

comes. Until then, we're her guardians. While we're on Earth, we answer only to her."

"That's reassuring," Vex muttered, earning a glare from Ash.

"That explains some things, but not everything. Why did Damian try to drown you in the first place?" Rae asked.

I twisted my hands in my lap. "To trigger full transformation. With my body on the brink of death, the demon would have easily taken over..." I shuddered at the memory, the moment replaying vividly in my mind.

"Can you control the bond now?" Kole asked.

"I think so," I said, meeting his gaze. "I accidentally tracked him to a council meeting when I returned. He sensed me and blocked me. I... I felt how he did it and managed to create a block of my own."

Kole and Xavier exchanged a dark, dangerous glance.

"If we are done here, I'd like to take Arien to the med unit and collect blood samples," Rae said.

"What about the demonic breaches?" I asked, desperate to shift focus away from myself.

Rae's expression brightened slightly, the spark of her geeky enthusiasm breaking through. She tapped her smartwatch, pulling up a holographic map of the region in front of her.

"The original fissure site never closed," she explained, gesturing to a glowing red marker on the map. "Its frequency has been fluctuating for weeks, but now? Its readings are almost identical to those from when the Great Archon tried to invade Earth."

My stomach dropped.

"Bezekah?" I whispered.

Rae nodded, her fingers flying across the hologram. "The energy signatures are too similar to ignore. Whatever's happening, it's big—bigger than anything we've faced before."

"How is Damian connected to this?" Xavier asked, his fingers curling into tight fists.

"I don't know," Rae said.

I leaned back against the couch, my mind racing. "He arranged for Bezekah's soleil to be stolen and brought to Earth, forcing Bezekah to breach the veil. But that was child's play. With demon blood in his veins, Pure genes, and now my blood…He may be capable of portal travel like I am. What if he's opening pathways between the demon realms and Earth?"

"Then we send the demons back," Ash said, his voice calm and matter-of-fact. "I brought a gadget that will handle it."

Corin rolled his shoulders, restrained tension rippling off him in waves.

Vex shot to his feet. "Hell yeah! Let's blow things up!" He threw me a grin, his expression equal parts excitement and mischief. "I knew having you back would bring this place back to life."

THIRTY-TWO

"We leave for the fissure site now," Corin said, rising to his full height. His cold stare swept over the room, daring anyone to argue.

"They don't eat. And they don't sleep," Vex muttered, shaking his head in disbelief. "Figures."

Corin either didn't hear him or didn't care. The warriors looked visibly drained, exhaustion etched into their faces after what must have been a sleepless twenty-four hours.

I set my coffee mug down with a clink. "If someone hands me a smartwatch, I'll take Corin and Ash to the fissure myself."

Kole crossed his arms over his broad chest, his jaw tightening as his scowl darted between Corin and Ash. Xavier lounged casually in his chair, but the fire in his eyes betrayed his thoughts.

"We're coming," Kole said, his voice like steel.

"Agreed," Xavier added, standing smoothly. "If you're going, we're going too."

Corin's jaw tightened. "Don't slow us down."

Vex and Mezzo joined us in the armory. The warriors unsheathed and checked their weapons and tightened straps with swift, practiced efficiency. I secured the blade to my thigh, my fingers fumbling under the weight of Kole's and Xavier's intense stares.

The seven of us filed onto the courtyard. Corin had insisted we get there by flying.

"Come," Xavier said, his low voice startling me. He flashed before me and was now reaching for my waist. "I'll carry you," he murmured, his voice rich with something that made my stomach flutter.

A low growl rumbled behind me.

Kole swept me off my feet in one swift motion, his possessive glare fixed on Xavier. "I've got her," he said, his voice a dangerous warning.

The Seraph raised an eyebrow, a smirk tugging at the corner of his mouth. "As you wish."

The forest edge loomed in unnerving silence, broken only by the rustle of leaves and the sensation of unnatural energy prickling against my skin. Ahead, the ground split open like a festering wound—jagged, raw, and pulsing with tendrils of shimmering energy that twisted through the air like ghostly vines. A low, ominous vibration thrummed around us, crawling up my spine and settling uneasily in my stomach.

"Invicta's guards patrol this site. If they're not receptive, we may have to subdue them," Xavier said, his sword drawn.

Mezzo fell into step beside him. He possessed the gift of telesomnia which induced a sleep state in any person he touched.

A figure emerged from the shadows, his red mohawk unmistakable even in the dim light. Mattias landed smoothly in front before us, his wings folding neatly against his back as he regarded us with irritation and unease.

"You're not supposed to be here," he said. "I have orders to keep you away."

"Not so long ago, you followed my orders," Xavier shot back.

Mattias's jaw clenched, his expression conflicted. "You'll always be my commander. But Donovan is Invicta's leader now, and I have my orders. You're lucky it's me on patrol. Anyone else wouldn't hesitate to take your head."

"Even with demons breaching our barriers?" Xavier asked, raising an eyebrow.

Mattias shrugged. "You know how we crave distinction. But this..." He gestured toward the fissure. "This is bigger than all of us."

I tugged on Kole's sleeve, making my way out of his protective cage behind his back. "What about doing a favor for an old friend?" I asked, my voice steady.

Mattias's gaze sharpened, a reluctant grin tugging at his lips. "Perhaps," he said, rubbing his chin. "I was about to send my team to scour the homeless encampment nearby." He shot into the air toward the fissure where he barked orders at his subordinates. Moments later, they vanished into the haze, their wings disappearing in the smoky twilight.

Mattias waved us forward. While the Ariadans studied the fissure, the red-haired Pure strolled to my side.

"I'm still deciding whether it's bravery or naivety driving your actions," he said with what sounded like fondness in his voice.

I tilted my head toward him. "Make sure you let me know your verdict."

A chuff of laughter escaped him. "Many of Invicta's warriors will be pleased to hear you're well," he said before striding to Xavier's side.

Corin extracted a small metallic orb from his pocket. The

device shimmered, vibrating as he tapped his smartwatch to activate it.

"What's that?" I asked, eyeing the sphere warily.

"A quasar," Corin said without looking at me. I glanced at Kole, my lips pressing into a thin line. He met my gaze with a barely perceptible shake of his head—he didn't know what a quasar was either.

The orb floated upward, hovering for a moment before diving into the fissure.

We waited in tense silence, the ominous hum growing louder with each passing second. The orb finally returned, its metallic surface glowing and a holographic projection flickering to life above it.

Obsidian rocks loomed in the background, their edges illuminated by erratic flashes of light. Hordes of demons clawed and thrashed in a violent frenzy, their sheer numbers making me nauseous. A sudden burst of lightning lit up the scene allowing us to see farther into the distance, and I flinched, the magnitude of the horde sinking in like a lead weight.

"What the fuck is that?" Vex asked.

"Demons," Corin said.

"No, I mean what kind of tech is this? I need one. Stat." Vex jabbed a finger at the floating orb.

"You don't have them?" Ash asked, his expression genuinely perplexed.

"Clearly not," Mezzo drawled.

"How long do we have before they breach?" Xavier asked.

Corin's jaw tightened, brows pulling together. "Hard to say. These are some of the most primitive demons out there. They're not strong enough to open a ley line on their own. They're waiting for something—or someone—to let them in."

"Primitive or not, their numbers are staggering," Mattias said. "I need to alert our new Magister and the council."

"They're still at Invicta?" Xavier asked.

Mattias nodded. "Everyone is."

"And my brother?"

The mention of Damian sent shivers along my body, and I wrapped my arms around myself. I scowled. What I had felt just now wasn't repulsive. A part of me, the part under his influence, was awakening.

"I saw him leaving the Institute earlier," Mattias said.

Xavier cast a quick glare my way, his expression darkening. "You're taking me in."

"What?" I asked, my voice rising. I ran up to him, forcing him to meet my eyes. "Didn't you hear? The council is still there. They'll kill you on sight."

"I'm not concerned with them. I have to speak with Donovan. And I'm sure Mattias can arrange it." He hiked an eyebrow in challenge.

Mattias smirked. "It'd be my pleasure."

"You're delusional." I glared at Xavier. "Donovan wants you dead. When he came to see me, the only thing on his mind was avenging his father. Do you really think he'll set that aside for a warning from *you*?"

Xavier's hands pressed down on my shoulders, his intense blue eyes brimming with conflict. "I'm the true leader of Invicta. That's my purpose. Even if my welcome is hostile, I have to warn my people."

I opened my mouth to argue, but before I could say a word, he shoved me away—straight into Kole's waiting arms.

"Let go!" I pleaded, my eyes fixed on Xavier as he veered away from me.

Kole's arms tightened around my chest, his voice low and soothing against my ear. "It's his duty. Would you have him lose his honor?"

The words struck me, quieting the whirlwind inside me.

No, of course, I didn't want Xavier to sacrifice his beliefs and duties for me. My body trembled, but I stopped fighting.

Xavier glanced over his shoulder, the corner of his mouth quirking into his signature cocky smirk. Then, without another word, he turned and shot into the sky, Mattias following close behind.

THIRTY-THREE

I stared, unblinking, at the space where Xavier had stood moments ago, dread clawing its way into my head. *That might have been the last time I'll ever see him.*

Donovan's thirst for vengeance, his obsession with punishing the former Magister and his family, loomed in my thoughts. I understood those emotions—too well—but they terrified me. Revenge burned hotter than reason, and Xavier had just flown into a blasting fire.

"Come." Kole's whisper broke into my spiraling thoughts, his lips brushing the shell of my ear.

I rounded on him, my fists clenched. "You could've stopped him."

Kole's brows furrowed, his expression caught between frustration and calm restraint.

"Ash and I need access to your lab and weapons," Corin said. "If our theory is correct, we can create a counter-frequency to neutralize the energy bleeding from the fissure and seal it permanently."

Kole's jaw tightened as he shifted his gaze to the Ariadan.

Vex's eyes darted between them before stepping in. "Just say the word," Vex said, ready as ever.

After a tense beat, Kole nodded. "Fine. Go back with them and wait. Rae and I will assist and see what they come up with." His tone carried an edge.

Corin inclined his head. "Good. Time is of the essence."

The warriors launched into the sky. I faced Kole. "What are you thinking?"

His chocolate eyes narrowed as he cupped my face. His thumb grazed the bridge of my nose before planting a gentle kiss there. "I don't trust them. That's why I'm going with them. P6's cameras monitor their every move. We'll see if their actions match their words."

"Oh." I swallowed a lump of unease. Taking a deep breath, I braced myself. "Don't freak out," I said, knowing full well what reaction that would provoke.

Kole's expression darkened instantly, his features darkening like the incoming thunderclouds.

"I couldn't be completely honest earlier. Sylvan didn't intend to let me return to Earth at all. He's obsessed with waking his mate, and I was a prisoner to him. The only reason I'm here is because his priestesses convinced him I needed to complete Lirael's mission."

Kole ground his jaw, his voice turning menacing. "I'll kill them."

"No." I gripped his arm. "You can't. We need them. You saw what they're capable of. We need their tech. But I don't know what they'll do once we stop Damian."

"They'll stay the hell away from you, or we'll throw them into the underground cells. Mezzo's gift makes it easy enough," Kole said.

Relief washed over me. "Good. At least we have a plan B."

Kole scooped me up, and we soared through the air before landing in the P6 courtyard.

"I need a moment," I said, gesturing to the forest behind the training facility. "A short walk. Just some air."

"I'll find you," Kole said before disappearing into the building.

The cool midday breeze carried the scent of pine and damp earth, calming my nerves as I wandered beneath the canopy of trees. Paulie's face flashed in my mind, unbidden. What would he say if he were here? He always balanced impossible choices with unshakable logic.

"What are Corin and Ash really up to?" I whispered, pacing.

Then I halted, ears straining as a high-pitched squeal broke the quiet.

"*Kwin, kwin.*"

I turned toward the sound and spotted a small, furry creature stepping out from the underbrush. Its tiny nose twitched as its beady eyes fixed on mine.

A smile broke across my face. "Well, hello there. It's been a while."

The chikaka sniffed the air before hopping closer. I crouched, extending my hand. Its soft fur brushed my palm as it nuzzled against my fingers, its tiny ears flicking back and forth.

"Been busy, huh?" I asked softly.

As if on cue, another chikaka waddled into view, its round belly dragging slightly, with a dozen tiny offspring clinging to its back.

I gasped, laughter bubbling up in my chest. "No way."

The male chikaka rubbed against my hand one last time before retreating with his mate and their brood, disappearing into the forest.

I resumed pacing, my thoughts returning to Sylvan.

"If Corin and Ash succeed, will she wake from her slumber?" I murmured aloud.

"There is a way to ensure she does."

The cold, steady voice behind me sent a jolt through my body. I spun around to find Corin stepping out of the shadows.

"What are you doing here? I thought you were in the lab with Kole," I said.

He didn't answer. Instead, he reached over his shoulder, drawing a gleaming crystal blade. The edge caught the light, glowing fierce yellow as he leveled it at me.

"There is a gate near the lab," he said simply as if that explained everything.

He'd used the P6 alluron to get to me before anyone else could. But how did he transfer himself to this exact place? There were no portals here. I gulped, backing away.

"You've been holding out on me about your barrier manipulation skills," I said, trying to stall him. "You don't want to kill me. You *need* me, remember?"

"We were given two orders," he said, his voice devoid of emotion. "Remove the threat to Earth and return her soul piece. There is only one way to separate a soul from a body *permanently*."

My back hit a tree. I ducked when he swung. His blade sank into the trunk inches from my head.

"Corin, wait!" I scrambled out of his reach.

He hesitated, his eyes narrowing.

"The fissure isn't the real threat," I said quickly, desperation gripping my voice. "It's a sign of something bigger— something worse. If you kill me now, you'll lose your chance to stop it."

His grip on the blade tightened, but he stopped pursuing me.

"Blow the fissure first," I said, my voice steady despite the pounding in my chest. "If the demonic activity stops, I'll willingly return with you to Ariada to wake her."

A shadow descended between us, landing with a heavy thud.

Kole stood tall, his onyx blade drawn, his charcoal wings flaring wide.

"I've got a better idea," he said, his voice rumbling like thunder. "I'll rip your shiny wings off and send them back to your realm with a thank-you note."

Vex and Mezzo appeared at my sides. Corin's expression twisted with fury.

"Where's Ash?" he asked, his head tilting as if listening for something.

Kole sneered. "Is a whopper right hook in your Ariadan vocabulary? Don't worry, we will behead him as soon as I'm done with you."

Corin's nostrils flared. "Our commander will never stop coming for her."

"He's right," I said, jumping between them. "We need him."

Kole shot me a dubious look.

I spun toward Corin. "This was a misunderstanding, wasn't it?" I said, forcing calm into my voice. "We don't even know if your jammer will work yet."

Kole hovered at my back, ready to strike. I placed a hand on his, lowering his blade. "Trust me, we need the Ariadans to finish this. Then..." I let the sentence hang.

Pain suddenly lanced through my skull. I staggered, clutching my head.

Where are you? The familiar voice slithered into my mind.

"Damian," I croaked.

Kole was beside me instantly, his hands gripping my shoulders. "What is it?"

"He's trying to track me," I managed through gritted teeth. "But I'm blocking him." The pressure shifted to the back of my eyes, and I pressed the heels of my palms against my temples, trying to push it away.

"Talk to me," Kole urged.

I sucked in a ragged breath. "I think he wants to see through my eyes."

"Then let him see," he whispered through gritted teeth.

Huh? Slowly, I opened my eyes.

My gaze zeroed in on Corin. His impressive wings spread wide, the faint glow of the crystal blade catching the light. He looked every bit the angel of justice.

Through the bond, I sensed Damian's confusion and rage swelling like a storm.

Who is this? he roared in my mind.

I took a shaky breath, forcing my thoughts into a single command. *Get out of my head. Now!*

THIRTY-FOUR

The pressure lifted, and I gasped in relief, Damian's presence finally gone from my mind. My breaths came unevenly, but a small smile tugged at my lips as I squinted at Kole.

"I blocked him," I whispered, the words quiet but triumphant.

Pride flared in Kole's eyes. That look sent a wave of warmth rushing through me. "You're one of the strongest Earthbounders I've ever met," he said.

I doubted his words—I always doubted my strength—but the heat that crept into my cheeks betrayed me. It wasn't the compliment but the fact that he said it. Kole never wasted words, never dressed them in empty flattery or meaningless reassurances. Everything he said came from the depths of who he was—no gimmicks, no games, just truth.

"Zephyr reports the other Ariadan is stirring," Vex said, tapping his smartwatch.

Corin's scowl deepened.

"Let's bring him out. And the jammer he built," Kole said.

Vex wasted no time stripping Corin of his sword and scanning him for hidden weapons with a handheld device.

"Do we even need this one?" Mezzo asked, his condescending stare sizing up Corin. "I'm itching to try my gift on one of these sleep-never warriors."

Corin's amber eyes snapped to Mezzo, his jaw tightening. "If you so much as lay a finger on me, I'll rip your arm off."

"Not if you fall under his spell first," Vex quipped, then let out a loud guffaw. "Get it? He won't be able to move...when he keels over...sleeping."

The courtyard door swiveled open. Ash stepped out first, flanked by Zephyr and his men, their weapons directed at his back. Behind them, Rae carried a small box and a tablet, scowl forming as she spotted Vex still laughing, his shoulders shaking from residual laughter.

"Why do I have a feeling I need to chide you?" Rae asked, arching a brow at Vex, though her lips twitched in amusement.

The fissure continued to drone the same haunting tune. We gathered at the edge, our breaths misting in the cool evening air.

Ash cradled the sleek, metallic jammer in his hands. The compact device, no larger than an apple had grooves carved into it. They pulsed ominously. "Ready?" he asked.

Kole, Vex, and Zephyr plus his men stood rigid, gazing down the chasm. Rae's fingers darted across her tablet as she prepped to monitor the fissure's changes. Even Corin watched with acute intensity, his wings flexing slightly.

Ash nodded to himself and took flight, his wings beating steadily as he hovered over the center. The unnatural light radiating from the rift cast eerie hues across his features. He extended his arm and released the jammer. Then rejoined us, his boots scattering loose rocks upon landing. "Now we wait."

The seconds dragged. Rae crouched near the fissure, her eyes glued to her tablet.

"Frequency levels are...fluctuating," she said, her voice tight with concentration. "Dropping...but they're unstable."

The fissure's resonance began to change, its pitch lowering to a faint, vibrating whisper that made the ground tremble beneath our feet. Small rocks tumbled into the chasm. Every nerve in my body screamed in warning.

Then, silence.

A heartbeat later, a high-pitched note tore through the air, like a saw driving straight into my skull. I clapped my hands over my ears, wincing. Around me, Kole snarled under his breath, Rae dropped her tablet with a grimace, and Vex cursed loudly, his teeth bared against the assault.

The sound cut off. The fissure fell silent, and an eerie still-ness descended.

"Is it over?" I asked, my voice hoarse.

Rae picked up her tablet and scanned it. Her brow furrowed. "I... I'm not getting any readings."

The sound of wings slicing through the air drew our attention skyward. Mattias and his team descended, their crimson wings catching the dying light.

"What the hell was that?" Mattias asked when he landed.

I barely registered his question. I darted toward him, my chest heaving. "Where's Xavier?"

He grimaced. "He's meeting with Donovan," he said.

I eyed him, not believing. The Invicta Earthbounders and the Soaz were capable of anything, and Xavier walking into their den felt like a dangerous gamble.

"Arien..." Rae's gasp drew my attention to her.

She waved the tablet toward me, her face pale. "There's nothing. No frequencies. Nothing."

Everything seemed to slow. Then the sound of swords being drawn shattered the stillness.

I spun around to find Kole and Vex standing between me and Corin and Ash, their weapons raised and stances wide.

"It's time for you to return to your precious realm," Kole growled. "You're no longer welcome here."

Corin didn't flinch, his gaze calm as it slipped past Kole to me. "We will wait nearby," he said. Without another word, he and Ash spread their wings and took flight, disappearing into the darkening horizon.

"Arien!" Kole rounded on me, his voice like a whip. "What the fuck did he mean? What did you say to them?"

"N-nothing," I stammered, pedaling backward until my shoulders collided with Mattias's chest. The warrior steadied me with a hand on my arm, but the reassurance was fleeting. He leaned down. "I don't meddle in disputes between mates," he murmured, stepping back and leaving me exposed.

My tongue tangled up, the words caught in my throat as Kole's glower bored into me.

"Hey," Rae said, bouncing in between us. She pressed a hand to Kole's chest. "Back off. She's not going to tell you anything if you keep snarling at her like that."

Kole's gaze burned into Rae next, but she didn't waver. After a tense beat, he exhaled sharply, some of the heat leaving his eyes.

He addressed me again, his tone softer but no less serious. "Can I fly you back to P6? We need to talk."

My heart thundered as I nodded.

I stepped into his space, wrapping my arms around his neck. The gesture seemed to calm him, his arms sliding around my back as he held me close.

Kole launched us into the air, his wings beating steadily as we soared above the treetops. The wind whipped past us, but I'd have endured more for the warmth of his body against mine.

Our gazes met, and for a brief moment, the chaos of the world below fell away.

THIRTY-FIVE

I didn't know how to navigate my relationship with Kole from here. My time no longer felt like my own. My life had become the consequence of my mother's choices and Lirael's plot to save the Earthbounders. The implication crippled my mind, my abilities. Was I even my own person?

But right now, none of that mattered.

I closed my eyes and let the thoughts drift away as I brushed my lips over his, savoring the firm warmth.

The wind rushed past us, ruffling my hair and tugging at the edges of my clothing. Kole's wings beat in steady, powerful strokes, creating a rhythmic whirr that blended with the rushing air. His body provided heat against the high-altitude chill, his muscles flexing with each flap, keeping us aloft.

I pressed closer, my palms against his chest, feeling the solid strength beneath my fingertips. His arms cradled me securely, his grip unwavering even as the world blurred into a vast expanse of greens and browns below. The horizon stretched out in hues of deep orange, the sun casting long shadows over the landscape.

Lately, the only times I felt alive or truly myself were

moments like this—Kole's touch ignited every part of me. Or when Xavier kissed me. The thought of Xavier sent an ache through my chest, so I shoved it aside. I didn't want to worry in this moment. I wanted *Kole*. I wanted him to occupy my every thought and command all my senses.

Kole deepened the kiss, his control sending a thrill through me. I wrapped my legs around his waist and hoisted myself higher against him. The wind whipped past my ears but soon faded into the background as I lost track of time and space, my world reduced to his touch and the warmth of his body pressed against mine.

The sensation of something padding my back jolted me from my haze. I blinked, looking around. Kole had laid me down on soft and warm blanket.

The rush of the wind stilled, replaced by the rhythmic crash of waves. The sea shimmered with deep shades of pink and indigo, reflecting the horizon. I squinted into the tropical sun, recognizing the secluded spot on P6's lands—the same place I had learned my savior's name when I'd first joined P6-ers after my banishment from Invicta. The same place where I had once threatened him with a marshmallow stick.

Kole hovered above me, his wings folding against his back, his stormy eyes regarding me with an intensity that stole the air from my lungs. The fated-mate connection of *Ashanti Rosa* that we'd lost all those weeks ago had given way to something stronger, something unshakable—something that didn't rely on destiny but on choice. It was as if the sky, the sea, and the earth itself had conspired to lead us here, to this moment of perfect, fleeting stillness. What we did with it rested with us.

"Don't move," Kole whispered before flashing into the nearby palmettos.

I blinked. *Now?* Seriously?

The entire plant shook, rustling violently. My brows

furrowed. Then Kole emerged, a rolled-up blanket tucked under his arm.

I laughed. *Of all the things...*

Kole arched a questioning brow as he spread the blanket beside me.

"Vex mentioned leaving one here to make date planning easier," he said.

I smirked. "Should I be worried that you keep supplies here for *your* dates?" I teased.

Kole's eyes darkened. He didn't have to answer—I knew this wasn't his style. Kole never courted women. He never had to. I could imagine them flocking to his dangerous aura, no invitation needed

Instead of replying, he rolled me over, pinning me on my back again—but this time on the blanket. I bit my lip.

"What did you wanna talk about?" I asked in a small voice.

Kole's forehead wrinkled. "I can't predict the future..."

I shook my head. "No one can."

"Maybe this is selfish, but I want you to promise me something." His grip on me tightened slightly. "Don't engage in combat unless it's self-defense. You've had only basic training. Any Pure will have you bleeding in seconds. A demon—" His body tensed, vibrating with restrained emotion.

"Shhh." I pressed a finger to his lips. "I promise to be more careful."

His chest rumbled with a quiet growl. "Then why do I still have this nagging feeling...?"

I cupped his face. "I came from nowhere and had no one until you," I said softly. "Death doesn't scare me anymore. But being away from you does. I will do whatever I can to keep *us* safe. And I know you'll do the same."

Kole exhaled, his tension easing. "My greatest honor is protecting you, my love," he whispered.

His head dipped, his lips finding mine. I drew his tongue into my mouth, greedy for his touch. I put on a brave face for him but on the inside, I was falling apart.

Then—he stilled.

Kole broke the kiss, rising onto his elbows, his gaze searching mine.

"Don't do this," he whispered.

I frowned.

"Don't kiss me like it's our last time together."

I slid my fingers into his thick walnut-brown hair, biting my lip.

"What if I kiss you like I *love* you?" I asked.

His pupils blew wide. "I am all yours. Take what you need," he rasped, his voice husky and strained.

I gaped at this beautiful warrior surrendering completely to *me*. I'd never taken full control before. Finally, I whispered, "Make love to me."

The warmth of Kole's fingers brushed my cheek, sending a pleasant shiver down my body. I stretched, the hem of a shirt sliding up my thighs. Then I stilled as awareness crept back in.

We were on the beach.

We had been kissing, touching...and then—

Heat flooded my cheeks as I glanced at Kole. He rested beside me, shirtless, his trousers the only thing covering his lean, muscled form.

I peered down. Oh. I'd forgotten he'd draped his shirt over me to keep me warm—even though his body heat, combined with the tropical weather, had left me breaking out in a sweat.

"I fell asleep?" I asked, propping myself on one arm. "Why didn't you wake me?"

Kole smirked. "I selfishly watched you sleeping in my arms." With his deft fingers he tucked loose locks behind my ear, caressing my jaw as he retracted his hand.

A blaring beep ruined the moment.

His expression darkened.

"What is it?" I asked, sensing his hesitation as the beeping continued.

His brows furrowed as Zaira's voice erupted through the comm smartwatch.

"Kole! Get your ass to the mission center, stat!"

His jaw tightened. Then he tapped his smartwatch. "I hear you." His tone was clipped, his warrior instinct kicking in.

Adrenaline spiked through me. I scrambled to my feet. "What's going on?"

Kole stayed silent, but the grim set of his mouth was answer enough.

"Here." I began pulling his shirt over my head to return to him.

His hands shot out, gripping my wrists.

"Angels," he growled, his eyes glazed over with need. "Don't do that again unless you *want* me to lose all control."

My breath hitched.

He exhaled sharply, pushing the shirt back down over my thighs. "Keep it on. P6 is on red alert."

Red. Probably not a good sign.

I swallowed hard. "What does that mean?"

Kole turned toward the horizon, his wings flexing.

"The enemy is coming."

THIRTY-SIX

Within minutes, we landed in the courtyard, the cool air snapping around us. Kole's grip tightened on my hand as we sprinted to the elevator. The mission center loomed in unsettling silence. Rae stood at the center, her face pale, fingers clenching her tablet. Zaira's gaze flicked to us as we entered, her lips pressed into a thin line.

"The Soaz issued a bounty for Arien's capture," Rae said, her voice taut.

"What?" I gasped.

Kole slammed his hand on the table, disbelief flashing into fury. "Did the council approve this?"

Rae shook her head. "No. He acted alone. Our insider says the warriors no longer abide by the council. After everything that's happened, they see them as weak."

Damian's plan was working. He wasn't just a threat anymore—he was becoming the leader of all Earthbounders.

Zaira's grimace deepened. "Kole, he named P6 as a possible location. The warriors are already on their way. It's only a matter of time."

Anhelm scrutinized me in a silent assessment that twisted my stomach.

Vex, seated at a nearby terminal, swiveled a monitor toward us and cleared his throat. "Guests just arrived."

On the screen, four dark vehicles rolled up to the front gate. A warrior exited, scanning the area with a sensor-like device, sweeping it in slow arcs as he measured the allura's activity. He smirked, then motioned for the others. A second later, the gates groaned open, and fourteen warriors strode onto P6 grounds, their movements efficient and predatory.

The air thinned. My chest clenched, panic clawing at my throat. My foot instinctively retreated. They had come for me. This happened because of me.

Kole stepped into my line of vision, gripping my forearms.

"No," he said firmly, his voice cutting through the storm in my mind. "I know what you're thinking. I won't let you sacrifice yourself."

"They're here because of me," I argued, my voice shaking. "If I leave, they'll—"

"No." His tone shut down any argument. "This is our fight now. They come for one of us, they come for all of us. Anyone who disagrees can leave."

His words hung in the air, a challenge as much as a declaration.

I twisted away, reading the room. Rae and Vex stood side by side, their stances unwavering. Zaira crossed her arms, her fierce stare daring anyone to question her loyalty. Anhelm and Mezzo exchanged a neutral look but didn't move, shoulders squared with resolve. Even Zephyr and his men stayed, their solemn expressions giving way to calculated resolve.

No one moved.

Disbelief hit like a shock wave but quickly hardened into something steadier—acceptance. I bobbed my head. "But you can't stop me from fighting, Kole. I mean it."

He tensed, frustration flashing in his thundering eyes, but he didn't argue. Instead, he inched closer, fingers grazing mine.

"Don't do anything reckless," he said, his tone softer now, edged with quiet warmth.

Rae crossed her arms. "Arien and I will fire the depressant I've been working on. We will surprise the enemy by launching from inside the cabin." As a madeborn, my feisty friend had the raw strength of a secondborn but none of the Pures' wings or heightened abilities. What she lacked in supernatural gifts, she made up for with her scientific mind.

"If we get overpowered...retreat underground." Kole fixed everyone with an authoritarian stare, lingering on me. My former protector wrestled with his instinct to shield me from all danger. I understood his worry—I felt the same for him, even knowing his skill in battle—but trying to keep him from the fight would be like asking him to be someone he wasn't. The same was true for me. I held my ground, locking eyes with him. Wherever he went, I would follow.

Vex smacked his hands together, snapping out of his shock. "Let's go kick some pretty Invicta boys' asses."

The fourteen warriors poured onto the grounds, their sleek, black uniforms swallowing the last light of dusk. Their weapons—swords, staffs, and discs strapped to their bandoliers—gleamed with lethal intent.

Vex and Mezzo took position at the front of the house, blades drawn, bodies coiled for battle. Zaira and Talen stationed themselves on the roof. Zephyr and his men hid out of sight.

Rae crouched behind the open window, pulling me down beside her. She shoved a handful of canisters into my hands.

"Only throw them when you're sure of your aim," she warned. The powder inside could cripple a Pure, grounding them if they inhaled it.

"They've got numbers," Vex said.

"They don't have us," Kole said, assuming a stance at the very front. His wings unfurled with a thunderous snap, charcoal feathers stretching wide and shadows rippled across the ground.

The invaders spotted him and surged forward, their leader barking orders. Kole launched skyward, cutting through the air with blistering speed. He collided midair with the first attacker, their swords clashing in an explosion of sparks. The force sent shock waves rippling outward, the clash of weapons ringing through the space.

Vex darted forward, dodging and parrying before spinning into a brutal slash that tore through his opponent's midsection. The warrior crumpled, but two more charged to take his place. Mezzo absorbed a staff strike with his wing, his hulking frame unmoving. With a grunt, he shoved his attacker back, then swung a massive fist. The blow sent the warrior sprawling. Zaira loosed an arrow burying the shaft in one warrior's shoulder, forcing him to drop his weapon with a snarl and lower to the ground.

Above, Kole and the group's leader clashed in a vicious aerial battle. Their wings cut through the air, creating gusts that whipped through the front yard. The leader's blades flickered like lightning, but Kole met every strike, his onyx sword an extension of his deadly arm. They rose higher, silhouetted against the deepening twilight. Kole's dark wings seemed to swallow the sky, his movements a deadly blend of power and control.

The enemy feinted left, then twisted into a downward slash that sliced across Kole's shoulder.

Blood sprayed.

My legs wobbled.

My warrior roared and countered with a vicious upward strike, knocking his opponent's sword from his grip. The leader's eyes widened—just before Kole's boot slammed into his chest, sending him hurtling toward the ground. I let out a long breath.

A Pure slipped past the first defense line, his gaze snapping to us. Rae pulled back her arm, ready to hurl a canister. A silver disc struck her square in the chest. She crumpled with a choked gasp, stunned.

"Rae!"

I bolted toward her, but the warrior lunged through the window. My fingers tightened around the short sword Rae had thrust into my hands earlier. My pulse pounded as I lifted the blade, drawing his attention away from her.

He charged, an onyx staff whistling through the air. I ducked, the weapon slicing past my head so close I felt the air shift. Heart hammering, I slashed upward. The blade caught his side, cutting shallowly but enough to make him stumble. I spun away, my breath ragged. A snarl twisted his angelic features and my stomach clenched.

Then, out of nowhere, Zephyr dropped behind him. His sword plunged deep into the warrior's chest. The enemy crumpled. Zephyr's golden curls fell into his eyes as he blinked at me, then vanished through the window before I could speak.

I whirled back to Rae. She sat on the floor, gripping her launcher. Her hair stood on end with static but I didn't spot any injuries. She fired, the concussive blast hurling two warriors to the ground. "Stay close!" she ordered me, her voice cutting through the chaos around us and in my head.

The sky churned with wings and steel. Warriors clashed midair, blades sparking as they struck and parried, sending embers raining to the ground. The air reeked of blood and metal.

Vex and Mezzo fought back-to-back, their coordinated strikes keeping the advancing warriors at bay. Above them, Zaira loosed arrows when an opportunity arose, the projectiles always finding their mark.

"They keep coming!" Vex growled, slicing through an attacker in one swift motion.

A distant car door slammed. Reinforcements.

"We hold," Kole called from above, his voice steady as bedrock. Our eyes met—a fleeting connection, piercing, assessing—before he turned back to the Pure he'd been locked in battle with since this brawl began.

Then the ground convulsed. A thunderous explosion tore through the earth, hurling debris into the air. I stumbled, throwing an arm up to shield my face from the dust.

When the smoke cleared, Rae crouched beside her launcher, a small crater in the floor next to her. "That one was defective," she said, scowling.

I darted to the window. The warriors paused, searching for the cause of the deafening sound. They squared their shoulders, ready to resume fighting, when a menacing whistle sounded.

Every warrior froze, heads snapping toward the road. The remaining enemy warriors parted, stepping aside as a figure emerged from the shadows.

Damian.

His black-as-night eyes locked onto mine, and a wicked smirk tugged at the jagged scar slicing across his lip.

"Hello, nightshade," he said, sneering.

A tremor shot through me. Kole dropped between me and my nightmare, his sword raised.

"You'll have to go through me," he said, his voice a low, dangerous growl.

Damian cocked his head, his smile stretching. "Kolerean. Always so protective." His eyes gleamed with cruel amusement. "How did that work out for your last protégé?" He meant his and Xavier's mother, Kole's former charge. She had been wrongly imprisoned and executed while her protector, Kole, watched helplessly.

Kole's shoulders tensed as if pulled by an invisible string.

He met Damian halfway, their blades colliding in a deafening clang. Damian moved with terrifying speed, his strikes savage. His blade was a blur, every blow meant to kill, not wound. But Kole was as fast, as relentless, countering each attack with brutal power.

They fought like forces of nature—Damian, a serpent striking with no mercy, and Kole, a tempest crashing against him. Damian feinted left, then slashed low. Kole blocked, twisting into a counterstrike. Sparks flew. Their footwork stirred dust. Kole's wings dragged against the ground, upturning dirt and pummeling Damian's face with it to obstruct his vision. The mutated Pure didn't unleash his wings, keeping his true identity secret. But the snarl twisting his lips said he'd have enough of this skirmish.

Damian's pupils dilated for a flitting second, and his claws shot out. Kole deflected the next punch, but the moment his claws scraped his forearm, blood welled in angry streaks.

Damian leapt back, disengaging. But why?

His lips twitched. The ghost of a smirk. Kole lunged but barely managed two steps before his body jerked to a halt. He wavered, his head shaking as if trying to clear unseen fog. A sick realization slammed into me. *Poison.*

"No!" I shouted, scrambling over the half-wall.

Rae's fingers clamped around my arm, her boots digging into the floor. "Don't."

Kole's breathing had gone ragged, his grip tightening on his sword as he fought to stay upright.

Amusement flickered in Damian's cruel eyes. He propelled himself forward. His boot slammed into Kole's chest, launching him backward. Kole crashed into the front door with a sickening thud, the impact rattling the cabin and sending splinters spiderwebbing across the windowpanes.

Rae's grip loosened. I tore free, sprinting to Kole's side and dropping to my knees. His eyes rolled back, his body convulsing in violent spasms—its reaction to the scratch. My gaze snapped to Damian, fury rising like bile.

A strangled cry from the roof yanked my attention upward. Zaira dangled in an enemy's grasp, a wickedly sharp throwing knife pressed against her throat. More Invicta Pures emerged from the shadows, surrounding us.

I shot to my feet, pointing straight at Damian. "He's not an Earthbounder. He's mutated—part demon."

Silence. The Pures didn't even flinch.

I scanned their faces, heart pounding. "Didn't you see what he just did? We fight demons, not obey them," I growled through clenched teeth.

Damian clapped, a slow, mocking rhythm. He sauntered toward me, smirking. "Good performance." Spreading his arms, he gestured to the warriors. "They all know about my gift. I revealed my special abilities to the council this morning. They were very...receptive." His lips twisted into a manic grin.

"Gift? He's lying to you—"

Say another word and I'll take the feisty redhead to my personal cells. His voice slithered into my mind, cutting off my breath. My mouth snapped shut.

Only a few feet separated us now. Damian extended a hand, his smile triumphant and delirious. "Shall we?"

I glanced at Kole still motionless on the doorstep. My *chosen* mate. Rage detonated inside me, hotter than fire. A red filter slid before my eyes and searing heat flared along my arm. Through my sleeve, the lines of my tattoo ignited, glowing with an unnatural light.

Damian's eyes widened just as lightning bolts erupted through the air, slicing through our enemies. The Pures disintegrated into ash before they could even scream.

I slumped over, drained by the outburst. Ashes floated down from the roof where the warrior had held Zaira. *Did I do that?* I peeked at my marks—they throbbed with an orange glow. My breath caught in my throat.

Damian roared, wings thrashing as he staggered back. The lightning shards had scorched his leathery wings in different spots, but they failed to pierce through. He bared his teeth, his expression twisting into something near madness.

"Once they see what you're becoming," he sneered, "they will turn on you." He licked his lips, dark amusement flickering in his eyes. "I look forward to watching you crawl back to me."

With a powerful beat of his wings, he shot into the sky, vanishing into the dusk.

I fell to my knees beside Kole again, my hands trembling as I pressed them against his chest. "Kole," I whispered, my voice breaking. He didn't move. His lips were tinted blue. Was he cold? I touched his forehead, then yanked my hand back. He was burning up.

Vex and Talen bounded over. They lifted Kole's limp body while I circled them, worried about Kole's other injuries and his comfort.

"Medical unit," Rae said.

I could only watch, tears spilling down my cheeks while they carried him away.

Zephyr descended from the sky, scanning the battlefield. "No one else is coming. This was all of them." His brows knit together as he turned to me. "How did you do that?"

"I... I..." I pressed a hand to my forehead, expecting the same feverish heat Kole had, but my skin was cool and clammy. Shock. Yeah. That had to be it.

Zephyr squeezed my wrist. A half-smile ghosted across his face. "Go."

My eyes locked on Kole's handsome face. But my legs wouldn't move. The scent of disintegrated flesh wafted toward me. I swiveled in a circle. Piles of ash lay on the ground. *I did this.* Bile kept rising in my throat. I dashed around the corner and dry-heaved. *I don't want to feel this pain.* My plea awakened a dormant part of me, one I'd been trying to squash. The trembling subsided and my eyes dried. I blinked, seeing red.

THIRTY-SEVEN

The warriors carried Kole into the elevator, his wings dragging, feathers slick with blood. I pressed myself into the corner, barely breathing. My mate —once unshakable, fierce—hung limp in their arms, his strength reduced to nothing.

My left eyelid twitched with the storm inside me—pressure built in my chest, a ticking bomb of rage and helplessness.

"Stay with us, you ugly bastard," Vex growled through clenched teeth.

Kole groaned. His wings shuddered, then slowly retracted with a wet, sickening squelch. More blood dripped onto the floor.

The doors slid open with a mechanical hiss. I followed closely, my pulse hammering so hard it rattled my ribs. My fingers flexed, my body wired for action. *Not now.* Revenge would come—but Kole needed me first.

The thought hammered into me with every step. My eyes dried and prickled along my eyelids.

Rae had a table prepped when we arrived, her usual jolly self replaced with grim determination.

"Put him down," she said.

Vex and Talen obeyed, easing Kole onto the surface. He hissed, his jaw locking against the pain. Sweat slicked his forehead, trickling down his temples. Shadows hollowed his eyes, his dark hair plastered to his face.

Rae turned to me. "Scanner."

I grabbed the handheld device from the tray, placing it in her outstretched palm. Our fingers brushed. She gave my hand a brief squeeze before focusing back on Kole.

The scanner hummed as she ran it over his chest. A swirling mass of dark tendrils pulsed on the screen.

"What is that?" I asked, my voice brittle.

Rae didn't answer right away. Her lips pressed into a thin line.

"Rae," Vex pushed.

She swallowed. "It's an infection. And it's spreading."

Kole's fingers curled into fists, his knuckles white. "I'll heal," he rasped, but the strain in his voice betrayed him. He wasn't improving. I placed my hand over his fist.

Rae shook her head. "Whatever Damian's claws were laced with, it's stopping your body from regenerating." Her expression darkened. "It's—" She hesitated, glancing at me.

"Say it," I whispered.

"It's killing him," she said.

The room tilted. This was my fault—I'd let Damian in, let him manipulate me, let him mark me with his twisted connection. And now Kole was paying the price. I blinked the tears away.

"Can you give him something? What about the serum?" I asked, desperation creeping into my voice.

"We can try…" Rae didn't sound convinced. Her hesitation made the reality sink deeper, twisting the knife. She motioned for Vex, who grabbed serum pouches from the fridge and set them on the tray.

I returned my gaze to Kole. His eyes fluttered open, dark and glassy.

"Hey," he whispered. "Not...your fault."

A lump wedged itself in my throat. A tear slipped free, burning its way down my cheek.

"I'm sorry," I murmured, brushing damp strands of hair from his face. "I should've—" The words stuck.

Kole's hand found mine. His grip was weak, too light for someone as strong as him.

"You don't need me," he whispered.

I stiffened. *What!?*

"That's a lie, and you know it," I shot back. "You can't die. Period." My vision blurred.

I squeezed his hand tighter, my mind racing. I had power —something inside me, raw and untapped. The fae spear injury gave me abilities I barely understood. Sky Ice had shielded me once, but I had no control over it.

But what if...

What if it can heal Kole?

The only way to find out meant returning to Ariada—to Sylvan—to a planet where every step could be my last. I bit my lip, my gaze snapping to Rae as she finished hooking up the IV. She met my eyes, silent questions flickering across her face. Kole's hand slackened. His body stilled, features smoothing out.

"He'll drift in and out," Rae said, adjusting the drip. "The serum will slow the spread. Buy us some time."

We stepped into the main medical room, the four of us standing in tense silence.

"How much time?" I asked.

Rae exhaled. "Since his body is accepting the serum...I'd say a week."

A week. Would that be enough?

I lifted my chin. "We need to explore all our options. We know someone powerful. Someone who can grant my heart's desire..." I said, twisting my lips. There were no guarantees he would help me, but I had to try. Between him and Sylvan, right now, the fae king was a safer option.

Rae's eyes rounded. "You mean—"

"King Cygnus."

Vex let out a low whistle. "You're seriously going to ask the fae king for help?"

"You can't," Rae said. "He wouldn't want you to."

"Kole would've died for me. That's what mates do." My voice came out clipped.

Vex waggled his eyebrows. "Making it official, huh?" Rae socked him in the bicep.

I folded my arms. "Unless you've got a better idea, I'm tracking Cygnus down."

Talen frowned. "And if he says no?"

"Plan B is to steal Sky Ice from Sylvan," I said, biting my nail. I sounded insane.

The warriors gaped at me.

"Oh...uh..." Rae forced a laugh, but it quickly turned to a strangled choke. "Angels, you mean it."

Talen rubbed his chin. "I don't know... This could work." His eyes darkened. "If she survives."

Rae flung her hands up. "Do you hear yourself? *If* she survives?"

Vex grabbed her forearm, pulling her close. "You can't stop her, my love. There's no length I wouldn't go to for you if something happened. She can jump allura and navigate the void—it's like she was made for this."

I inhaled deeply, then extended my arm. The lightning storm I had unleashed inspired an idea and this was as good time as ever to test it. The tattoo lines along my skin glowed

—soft at first, then brighter, the air crackling with energy. The light surged down my arm, pooling in my clenched fist. *Easy*. A heartbeat later, a spear materialized—a weapon forged of pure lightning.

Vex took a step back. "What...the...hell?"

"I wasn't expecting it either," I admitted, rolling my wrist, and testing its weight. It felt...natural. An extension of me. "It's fae—Cygnus's weapon." I turned the spear, its energy whirring beneath its surface. "Maybe if I return it, he'll grant my wish." Most likely I would also pay with my essence, but I didn't want to worry Rae any more. The truth was, the king could demand my life for Kole's, and I would give it to him with pleasure.

Rae sidled up beside me, eyes locked on the weapon. "This is... I don't even know *what* this is."

"It's power. Power I can't control," I said.

Talen studied me. "Maybe you can learn?"

I shook my head. "I'd need him to teach me. And that's not happening." Exhaling, I pulled on the energy, drawing it back into my arm. The spear dissolved, light threading back into the intricate tattoo. "Look, I know this is reckless. I know the risks. But do you see another way?"

No one answered.

I lowered my head. "I can't sit here while Kole is dying. I have to try. If Cygnus refuses, fine. If I die trying, at least I'll know I didn't give up on him."

Vex raked a hand through his hair. "You're impossible, you know that?"

Talen smirked faintly, though his eyes were solemn. "I think it's called *convincing*."

Rae inched closer, resting a hand on my shoulder. "If you're set on this, we'll back you. But you better come back." She didn't wait for my response before turning and disappearing into Kole's room.

Vex slung an arm around my shoulders. "She'll be fine. Come on."

The three of us took the elevator down to the alluron level. The chamber pulsed with an eerie quiet, the portal's burnt-orange light flickering like a heartbeat as if it sensed us.

I approached the barrier.

"You sure about this?" Talen asked.

I met his gaze. "No." I turned back to the swirling vortex. "But I'm doing it anyway."

Vex chuckled, but there was no humor in it. "Sounds about right."

I skimmed my fingers over the electric surface. The hue coalesced, stretching into a dark, gaping hole. I pictured the blue ribbon on the other side—the only marker leading me to Cygnus. My pulse pounded.

Then I lunged forward, the portal's pull wrapping around me like a shroud.

THIRTY-EIGHT

The void churned around me, endless black streaked with flashes of crimson—gollums closing in. The wind howled, tearing at my clothes, clawing through my hair like it wanted to rip me apart. I forced my mind to focus, scanning the emptiness for the faint blue ribbon that would lead me out.

A blue shimmer appeared in the distance—a soft, other-worldly light undulating like a wave. My pulse quickened. *There.*

Snarls rattled through the void. Gollums' red eyes blazed, closing the gap. I propelled, hurling myself into the ribbon's glow just as claws slashed the air behind me.

I crashed down hard. The impact jarred my knees, sending a sharp clang echoing through the chamber. Gold and silver platters skidded across a vast banquet table, goblets toppling, jeweled dishes tumbling to the floor.

"Damn it," I muttered, collecting myself and rising to my feet. The rich aroma of roasted meats, spiced fruits, and honeyed wine flooded my senses, stirring an unnatural craving.

The fae warriors froze mid-conversation. They stood around the table, dressed in their finest—sleek black and deep emerald uniforms trimmed in silver, with runes stitched along their sleeves in glimmering thread. Their beauty was unnerving, too sharp, too perfect. Like I'd fallen into a painting.

After the initial shock wore off, their expressions darkened. Growling and hissing, warriors leapt onto the table, their movements fluid. The wooden surface groaned beneath their weight.

"Wait!" I lifted my hands, but they kept closing in.

With a burst of panic-fueled energy, I called on the spear. Heat flared along my arm, and the double-edged weapon appeared in my hand.

The fae halted. Eyes narrowed. One muttered under his breath. Others simply stared, the menace in their posture shifting to something closer to curiosity.

"Well, well." The voice sent a shiver down my spine. Smooth, commanding, and laced with conceited danger.

The fae parted to let King Cygnus through. Gold runes embellishing his simple black attire pulsed under the light like they were alive. An antler-shaped circlet rested on his jet-black hair, an intricate design crowned with a citrine gem. It was understated, a quiet declaration that his power needed no symbolic ornaments. A deep green mantle swept the floor behind him, fastened at his chest with a starburst clasp.

His saffron eyes flicked over the wreckage—toppled bowls, scattered fruit, spilled wine pooling like blood. One brow arched.

"I know, I know," I said quickly. "You were going to eat that. Maybe consider moving the portal next time you sit down for a meal."

His mouth twitched. Amusement? Annoyance? I couldn't

tell. He lifted a jeweled goblet from the edge of the table, took a slow sip, and studied me over the rim.

"To what do I owe the pleasure of seeing you again?"

I straightened, extending the spear. "I've come to return this—and to ask a favor."

His upper lip curled, as if suppressing the urge to bare his teeth. "Making demands, are we?" He flicked a hand toward his warriors. "I could have you beheaded before you took your next breath."

Not interested in the spear then. I had prepared for this.

"And what if I could help you reclaim your place on Earth?" I asked. "No more hiding."

Cygnus's jaw tightened. "I'm not sure I even *want* that anymore." His voice cooled, his danger-filled eyes sweeping across the hall. "We've made progress—avenging our history, reclaiming what was taken. In fact..." He gestured to the feast. "Tonight, we celebrate our latest conquest."

Sweat prickled at my brow. *This isn't going well.*

"Earth is under attack," I pressed, my voice raw with urgency. "Hordes of demons mass behind a crumbling veil, and the Earthbounders are too scattered to hold them back. If the dam breaks, your realm will be next. It's tethered to Earth, isn't it? Your warriors are strong, but can they withstand *thousands* of demons?"

Cygnus's eyes flashed neon yellow. His fingers tapped the hilt of his sword. Slowly, he unsheathed it. The blade caught the light, and for a moment, my own reflection stared back at me in its warped gleam.

"Interesting," he murmured. Then, with a sharp click, he slid the sword back into place. He motioned to one of his warriors, who barked an order. A group of fae loped toward the table. I jumped down, giving them space. The air hummed as the portal expanded. One by one, the fae stepped through and vanished.

My questioning gaze swiveled to the fae king. His power had grown exponentially since our last encounter when his warriors couldn't yet travel through portals without an allura-wielder such as me initiating the jump.

"Sit," Cygnus said, his words a command.

"I'm not hungry—"

His glare cut through my protest. I clenched my jaw and lowered myself into the empty chair beside him, the spear resting across my lap.

His gaze flicked to the weapon. He reached out, tapped the shaft with a single finger, and it dissolved. Light surged up my arm, seeping back into the intricate tattoo along my skin.

Cygnus's eyes gleamed as he watched the glow fade.

The warriors resumed their meal, piling roasted meats and glistening fruits onto their plates. The scent curled through the air, rich and intoxicating. My stomach twisted. Fae food was addictive. Dangerous.

I clenched my fists beneath the table, forcing my hunger aside. No distractions. I had come for one thing—Kole's life depended on it.

Warriors stepped from the portal one by one, their boots whispering against the table's surface as they disembarked with unnerving grace. I scowled. *How do they do that?*

One of them bent low, murmuring in Cygnus's ear. His expression hardened to stone.

"The threat is real," the fae said aloud. "Something powerful waits to be unleashed."

The king rose in a single, fluid motion. "Follow me."

Two warriors flanked me as we entered the armory. Weapons lined the walls—blades, spears, axes, bows—some encased in glowing tubes of light, humming with restrained power.

The warriors fired two cylinders into the columns of light,

testing their weapons. Cygnus turned to me. "Summon yours."

I extended my hand, the spear forming instantly in my grip, its weight solid, familiar. Hope flared. *Take it, Cygnus. Accept my deal.* He didn't move. Instead, one of his guards drew closer and grasped the spear. The moment he tried to pull it away, my arm jerked with it. My brows furrowed. I switched hands, shifting the spear effortlessly between them, but when I twisted my wrist, the weapon refused to drop, as if gravity had lost its hold.

My fingers trembled.

"The spear has taken on organic properties," the guard said, awe creeping into his voice. "It's alive—and bonded to her."

Cygnus cast a thoughtful glance. "It chose you."

No. No, no, no.

"I don't want it," I said.

Cygnus tsked, his head tilting. "A rare honor. When a weapon chooses its warrior, it cannot be undone. Accept it." His tone left no room for argument.

I closed my eyes, shoulders sagging.

"Why the despair?" the king drawled.

"My mate is dying." I exhaled sharply, meeting his eyes. "I hoped...to bargain with you. Take my essence, all of it if you must, but please...heal him."

Cygnus straightened. "Wish-making is dangerous. I can't control the consequences." His expression flickered with something unreadable. "And I have no use for your essence. I've recovered my full power since our last encounter."

Rage coiled tight in my chest, then snapped free. Red. I saw red. Heat burned through my limbs, my breathing ragged. Cygnus lifted an eyebrow, intrigued. With a cry, I lunged, driving the spear toward his chest. He moved like liquid shadow, sidestepping with ease. A flick of his wrist twisted my arm, redirecting my own attack. The spear's edge skimmed my shoulder.

Boom.

A force slammed into me, hurling me backward. I hit the floor, dazed, blinking stars from my vision. Oh gods. What had I done? I turned on the ruthless king. Scrambling to my feet, I braced for the killing blow.

Cygnus strolled over, hands clasped behind his back, a scowl shadowing his face. "I stand corrected. The spear didn't just choose you—it's protecting you. From yourself." His gaze sharpened. "Tell me, how long have you had the demon lurking inside you?"

I wobbled upright, shaking my head. "I made a deal..."

His lips pressed into a thin line. "Of course you did."

What the hell does that mean?

He studied me like a puzzle waiting to be solved. "The fae spear pulverizes demons. It should have incinerated you the moment it made contact."

I examined my now empty hands. "Then why didn't it?"

He exhaled, pensive. "My best guess? The spear bonded to you before the demon took root. It still reacted to the demonic presence—but it didn't kill you." His eyes darkened. "That won't be the case with any of our other weapons. Don't think you can wield fae weapon again. You got lucky."

A cold weight settled in my gut. "What now?" I asked.

Cygnus shrugged off his cloak. "Since you're already here, and I'm in a celebratory mood, I'll teach you a few commands to amplify the spear's power before you return to your war."

I blinked. "Wait, seriously?"

His eyes flashed. "Don't waste my time, angel."

I shut my mouth and activated the spear, waiting for his instruction.

Cygnus placed his palm over my fist and whispered,

"*Solvren.*" The twin spearheads flared, blazing white. "Solvren drains an Archon of its power."

He shifted my grip, his voice steady. "*Veythar.*" Lightning crackled across the spear's length, releasing dozens of lightning bolts similar to what I'd done when Damian attacked the P6 compound.

He pried my fingers open. "Draythos." The spear lifted, floating effortlessly. Cygnus spun me, my hand guiding the weapon in an arc that cut the air in a lethal sweep.

My pulse thundered. "This is...incredible. Than—"

Cygnus spun away. "Time to send you back."

Just like that.

He strode from the chamber, and his guards nudged me forward. I practiced the commands in my head, my pace quickening. Kole's face burned in my mind. Minutes here would cost me hours on Earth.

We entered the grand hall. The guard steered me toward the portal immediately, but I twisted free and faced the king.

"When this threat reaches Earth, we'll need everyone— including the Andromeda fae."

A single wrinkle appeared on his forehead. Then, with a flick of his fingers, the world lurched, and the portal swallowed me whole.

THIRTY-NINE

I hurtled through the tunnel, faster than ever before, thinking of locating Corin. Darkness obstructed the exit, giving me no warning before I crashed into a solid body, knocking us both to the ground.

Corin's amber eyes widened beneath me.

Strong arms hauled me upright. Ash and Corin loomed in the abandoned tunnels of the former Underground base, their minacious postures signaling trouble.

"What are you doing here?" I asked, pretending to not notice their murderous glares.

"We could ask the same," Ash gritted out.

I dusted myself off. "Clearly, I was looking for you. Your turn."

Corin ran a hand through his hair. "We were planning to find you. This is the closest allura we can access right now."

"Oh." I spread my arms wide. "Well, I'm here. Let's go back to that desperate leader of yours."

Corin barked a single snicker. "Didn't think you'd actually follow through."

"Or survive long enough," Ash said. His shrewd eyes

roamed over me, narrowing. "Something's different about you."

I lifted a brow. "What?"

He shrugged, wings flexing. "You don't act like someone walking to their death."

I rolled my eyes and gestured toward the portal. "Are we going, or do you want to keep analyzing me?"

Ash strode toward the allura, extending his hand. The barrier rippled violently, shuddering like water about to boil. "It's ready."

"After you," Corin murmured, his iron grip locking around my arm.

He didn't have to tell me twice—I leapt forward.

Corin's hold steadied me and I landed without face-planting. Then, without hesitation, he scooped me into his arms and flew us across the chasm to the exit.

Ash waited by the pool in the next chamber, his eyes filled with tension. The underground halls were eerily silent. Too silent. I stilled. No hum. No pulse of magic. The entire place felt...lifeless.

Ash let out a low growl. "Something's wrong. Let's find Sylvan."

We took off down the corridor, ascending the staircase to the main floor. No movement. No voices. Not even the shift of fabric or wings. Corin and Ash slowed, scanning every open space, bodies coiled with unease.

We reached the war room. Beyond the open wall, the vast valley stretched toward the horizon. Mountains loomed in the distance against the sepia sky. Above, Ariadans clashed in midair—wings flashing, swords striking.

Were they sparring?

Corin reached the windowless wall first, knocking over a chair in his rush.

"Stay here," Ash snarled low in my ear. "If we find you

anywhere else when we return, you'll regret that Sylvan didn't kill you when he had the chance." He shoved me against the painted wall before bounding out the opening with Corin at his side.

What the hell had them so on edge?

I wasted no time. The moment they disappeared, I sprinted for the double doors—then stopped. A fragment of the map caught my eye. Burned at the edges, but still legible: "NE" with a navigational symbol. Northeast? My fingers traced the faded letters, then darted upward. Another marking—"SE." I whirled, heart hammering, and scanned the opposite end of the wide wall. "NW" and "SW." A pattern.

I stepped back until my hip hit the grand table, then bent sideways, twisting my head upside down to see the entire map from a different angle. The lands...looked familiar. I gasped.

Ariada wasn't just another realm. This planet—Sylvan's domain—was Earth. Earth's future.

Sky Ice's—or maybe Lirael's—whispered words suddenly made sense.

"Future proves past."

The force trying to conquer Earth wasn't just after my world. It was after every version of it. Ariada. Earth. Every variation in between. The battle on Earth was only the beginning of something larger and temporal.

I slipped through the empty chambers, senses on high alert. The silence and emptiness gnawed at me.

The ornate cabinet came into view and I darted for it. Sky Ice lay on the pedestal, daring me to take it. I inspected the cabinet for latches or a hidden mechanism. Nothing. The entire structure was seamless, a single unbroken piece.

Instinctively, I placed my palm flat on the glass. The stone trembled, then floated to the surface. It calmed me. *Hold on. I'm getting you out.*

I stepped back, preparing to summon the spear, when a sword whistled past my legs and buried itself deep in the cabinet's base.

Crack.

Glass exploded and everything, including the crystal, plummeted to the ground.

I leapt back, heart hammering. My spidey senses had malfunctioned—I hadn't felt Sylvan's presence.

He launched downward from the balcony above, armored head to toe—golden breastplate, shoulder guards, a skirt of layered plates. Leather straps bound his sandals, gleaming gold shin guards catching the dim light. A deep red tunic peeked from beneath the metal, marking his station, and a gold-leafed circlet rested against his brow.

His voice thundered through the chamber. "The sacred stone belongs here."

"Then why does it react to me? It's part of me as much as it's part of her. And you know it."

His jaw clenched. "No. You're only an extension of who she was. You don't exist without her."

I closed my eyes. I used to believe that. Not anymore.

When I met his gaze again, my voice was steady. "Lirael had a hand in my creation. So did my mother. So did whatever force governs life itself. I am my own person—separate and independent. Can't you see that?" I hesitated, then added quietly, "She's not waking up."

Sylvan roared. "Liar!" His second blade flashed as he unsheathed it, eyes burning with fury and desperation.

I threw my hands in front of me. "You don't want to do this!"

His voice dropped to a chilling whisper. "Yes. I. Do. Once

you're dead, she will be whole again. She will return to me."
He spun, casting his sword in an arc as if he aimed to chop
my head off. I summoned the spear and swung it to counter
him. The impact sent me skidding backward, feet barely
keeping purchase. I darted behind a column just as Sylvan
struck—stone shattered under his blade, dust choking the air.
He was too strong. Too fast.

His sword lodged deep in the marble floor. He yanked at
the hilt, struggling to free it. Panting, I dove across. If I could
grab the crystal and reach the allura... I got the stone. The
contact zapped but didn't hurt me.

A vicious growl split the air.

No!

I rolled onto my back, Sky Ice clutched tight against my
chest. I raised is above me. Maybe—just maybe—he'd stop to
save it.

PING.

A shrill note pierced my skull. Time slowed down—
Sylvan's sword had connected with the stone, then hurtled
away, flung high into the air as if the stone had repelled it
with brute force. Sylvan's fury morphed into awe.

Sky Ice pulsed, its brilliant azure glow expanding outward.

The sword clattered against a distant wall. Sylvan
collapsed to his knees, breath ragged.

His whisper barely reached me. "It chose you..." His chest
heaved, eyes squeezing shut as if in agony.

Then the ground trembled. Chunks of stone rained down
from the ceiling. Cracks split the walls.

"What's happening?" I asked.

Sylvan shot to his feet. "No..."

He grabbed his fallen sword—for a moment, I thought
he'd attack again. I staggered back, keeping the stone
between us. He eyed the crystal, his lips pressing into a thin
line.

"The stone chose you." His voice was hoarse, resigned. "I grant you safe passage back to your world. With the stone." Then he spun and jogged down the hall.

My mouth fell open. That...was not how I'd expected this to go.

He peered over his shoulder. "Are you coming?"

I snapped out of it and rushed after him. I took in his armor again and frowned. "Why are you dressed like that?"

"Coup d'etat," he hissed.

"What? Who?" I had a feeling I knew the answer.

"Half my warriors. Callista leads them. They lured us outside—her tactical move to seize the sacred chambers."

Another tremor rattled the ground, sending cracks skittering across the stone. Sylvan broke into a sprint. I chased after him, down a spiral staircase. But his speed was unmatched—I lost him.

The steps ended at a single exit. I slipped into a small, empty chamber, heart hammering. Where had he gone? Another quake split the floor. *Holy shit, this place is falling apart.* I jumped the widening crack, bolting into the next room.

Sylvan knelt over two lifeless bodies, hands glowing as he pressed them to their chests. Water pooled beneath them, red with blood. The priestesses. I slapped a hand over my mouth, shuffling closer.

Sylvan's shoulders shook. "It's no use. They're gone."

His light flickered out. He rose stiffly, grief etched on his face.

"Callista took her forces through the allura." His gaze slid to me. "I think I know where they're going."

My throat bobbed and I tightened my grip on Sky Ice.

"Let's stop her. You and your army—"

Another quake fractured the wall, sending rubble down on us. Sylvan spread his wings, shielding me as debris slammed into his back.

He peered into my eyes. "There's no time. Take the small passage in the corner; it loops around to the allura. It's reinforced but be quick."

More stone rained down. Sylvan pressed a ruby at the base of the pool. The bloodstained water began to drain.

"What are you doing? You can save yourself!" I shouted over the roaring collapse. The floor split between us, and I staggered back.

His unshakable devotion carved a loving expression on his face. "I'm not leaving her." Then with a powerful beat of his wings, he plunged into the Celestial Volt. A slab of ceiling the size of a car crashed over the basin, shattering it.

I dashed for the passage. The stone's glow lit my path as the corridor shook violently. The exit flared ahead—I sprinted, leaping onto the platform.

The allura flickered wildly—unstable. The frame pulsed angrily, ragged lightning snapping inside, converging into a massive surge.

Walls crumbled and a chunk of platform chipped away.

Clutching Sky Ice to my chest, I swayed back and then hurled myself into the allura.

FORTY

I slammed onto the solid floor, my breath ripped from my lungs.

"She's back!" someone shouted.

Strong arms scooped me up, pressing me against a firm chest. "You're bleeding. How bad is it?"

"Just scratches. Crawled through glass," I muttered, already shifting to standing. My fingers tightened around Sky Ice, scanning its surface for damage. Its glow had dimmed, but the crystal remained smooth, unscathed.

I swallowed hard. "Kole?"

Unlike Sylvan, I couldn't control time—only my destination. But I had thought of Kole when I jumped. He had to be alive.

"You made it just in time," Talen said. "He's worse, but still with us."

I rushed to the medical wing. Eerie quiet met me there, save for the steady beeping of monitors. Antiseptic stung my nose as I burst through the doors on rubbery legs.

Kole lay in the same bed I'd last seen him in—pale and motionless. His chest rose and fell in shallow, strained rhythms. Sweat slicked his forehead, dark hair matted to his skin. He looked—wrong. Too still and too fragile. The sight of my invincible warrior was like a punch to the gut. My knees wobbled, and I clutched the side of the bed to steady myself.

"Kole," I whispered, my voice breaking.

Rae adjusted the IV drip, her face grim although relief had crossed her features when I entered. Vex leaned against the wall, his arms crossed. His eyes were clouded with worry, though he tried to mask it with a stoic expression.

"How long has he been like this?" I asked.

"Too long," Rae muttered. "The infection... It's spreading faster than I can stop it. His body can't heal like this."

My gaze dropped to his neck. Veins—black and sickly—crept like poison through fragile glass. Nausea twisted my stomach. I clenched Sky Ice tighter. Its cool surface pulsed gently, like a heartbeat against my palm. *Please*.

I leaned over Kole, pressing the crystal to his chest. My fingers shook as I let go.

"Don't let them take him," I whispered, tears stinging my eyes.

Light exploded from the stone, flaring so brightly I flinched. The energy shot into his skin, sinking deep. Instead of fading, it spread, a soft blue glow rippling outward like waves across water. The black veins recoiled, retreating as the light chased them away. His breathing deepened, chest lifting in stronger, steadier rises.

Rae's sharp inhale broke the silence. She leaned over the monitor, eyes wide. "He's...improving."

"Really?" A chuckle escaped me and sobs followed.

She nodded, tapping the vitals screen. "His heart rate—his oxygen levels—they're stabilizing. Whatever this crystal is doing, it's working."

Relief slammed into me so hard my legs almost gave out. Kole's color returned, his skin warming beneath my touch.

Vex's quiet chortle drew my attention to him. He pushed off the wall, halting beside me. "I think you just brought him back from the dead. What other talents are you hiding?"

I let out a shaky laugh, blinking away the last of my tears. Vex sported bruises along his jaw and deep scrapes on his arms. "What happened to you?"

He shrugged. "Tried talking sense into Donovan. Let's just say he wasn't in the mood for a heart-to-heart. Talen stole more serum while I played distraction though."

I winced. "You got yourself beat up for him?"

"Yeah," he said, lips twitching into a smirk. "But don't worry—Rae kissed every single bruise better when I got back."

I stifled a laugh, stealing a glance at Rae. Her cheeks flushed scarlet. Then my attention snapped back to Kole. His hand, once deathly cold, felt warm. His breathing had evened out. He was unconscious, but I knew—he was fighting to come back to me. I bent down and brushed a soft kiss against his full lips.

Vex's eyes softened. "He's stronger than you think," he said. "But you already know that."

I nodded, swallowing the lump in my throat. Then Sky Ice dimmed. My brows furrowed. I'd never seen it do that. Gently, I lifted it. My eyes bugged out as the stone began crumbling into the tiniest of particles that dissolved into wisps of blue smoke before vanishing into nothing.

"Why did it do that?" Rae asked.

"She's dead," I whispered. Tears streamed down my cheeks for Lirael and Sylvan, and for their tragic end. Kole's healing was the last gift Lirael had given me. I wondered if she'd always known the Celestial Volt would become her and her mate's tomb. My thoughts swirled to Callista.

I wiped my cheeks, forcing my focus back to Rae and Vex. "Is the fissure still holding?"

Rae exhaled. "The Ariadan block failed. Yesterday, the fissure split—wider and longer. Earthbounders and our allies are preparing for an invasion."

"She's amassing her troops." I spoke my thoughts out loud.

"Who?"

"Callista, a warrior from Ariada who betrayed Sylvan and half of her people. She's tired of the status quo and peace. She chose this time in Earth's history because Bezekah's invasion destabilized the ley lines. She's been secretly traveling to different timelines to find one she could explore. Lirael, the priestess, tried to halt Callista's plans."

Rae stiffened. "What do you mean, timelines?"

"Ariada isn't just another realm," I said. "It's Earth. Millions of years in the future."

Vex's entire body locked up. "Are you saying...we're about to fight our own race but from the future?"

I nodded grimly. "And the demons she's bringing with her." A puzzle piece clicked into place, dread pooling in my stomach. "Damian's in control of them. They're working together."

Vex cursed under his breath. "The Soaz hasn't been seen or heard from since he showed up here." His jaw tightened. "Who's running command?"

"Zaira. With Anhelm," Rae said.

Vex shook his head. "Anhelm and Mezzo are planning a mission. I'll ask Zaira to send a wide alert."

He marched toward the door.

I followed fast. "What mission?"

We stepped into the elevator together. Vex punched in the code, his lips twisting. "I shouldn't have said anything..." he muttered.

"Vex."

He sighed, then tipped his head my way.

"They're going to get Xavier."

FORTY-ONE

"Wait!" I threw myself on the hood of the Jeep just as Anhelm turned on the ignition. The warriors exchanged *what-the-fuck* glances.

Mezzo cracked open his door, one boot hitting the ground, the other still inside. "Are you reenacting a bug's last breath on the hood?"

I slid off, rubbing my hip. "I'm coming with you."

"No." He shut the door. A man of few words.

I scowled, planting myself in front of the grill. *They wouldn't run me over. Right?*

Anhelm threw his hands in the air, rolling down his window. "Get in."

"How do I know you won't floor it the second I step aside?" I asked.

"Because Zaira is now coming too." The moment he spoke, Zaira strode into the garage, helmet in hand, fiery hair pulled into a tight ponytail.

I grinned at her. She swung onto her bike, gaze lingering on Anhelm in the driver's seat. The warrior straightened under her scrutiny.

I hopped into the Jeep's back seat. Zaira revved her engine. Dressed in a sleek black suit and heavy boots, she looked like a force of nature. She tore into the tunnel.

"Oh, it's on," Anhelm muttered.

The Jeep lurched forward, slamming me against the seat. I fumbled for the belt as Anhelm and Zaira engaged in a reckless cat-and-mouse chase all the way to our destination —a winding back road through dense woods. Then we went completely off-road, barreling over fallen logs, the impact rattling through my ribs. By the time we stopped, my chest ached from the seat belt, and the back of my skull throbbed from smacking the headrest. I climbed out on unsteady legs.

Zaira projected a holographic map of Invicta, peeling away layers until the underground tunnels came into view. I only recognized a fraction of them.

"Where did you get this?" I asked.

"Me." Nelia's voice drifted from a small cave entrance swallowed by thick vines. She stepped into the muted light, wrapped in a stylish oversized sweater, skinny jeans, and winter boots. I yanked her into a tight embrace. Memories of our imprisonment resurfaced—Nelia, beaten in front of me, blood on the floor.

"How?" was all I managed through my clenched throat. We pulled apart.

"Donovan negotiated my release."

"He did?" I whispered. The stubborn warrior had acted like he didn't care. All this time I had blamed myself for leaving Nelia behind.

Anhelm and Mezzo brushed past us, weapons ready.

"Rae contacted Roan, who connected us with Xavier's sister," Zaira said, pausing by us.

A loud yelp rang out from the tunnel. Nelia dashed past me.

"He's with me," she yelled. I followed her. Zed began brushing off his shirt after Anhelm released him.

"I told you I'd be fine," Nelia said to the secondborn medic whom I'd met when I first arrived at Invicta.

"I'm not letting you out of my sight again," he said in a steely tone. He caught my gaze and dipped his head. "Arien."

I smiled. "Good to see you, Zed."

He nodded. "Dez is manning the monitors and security. We have ten minutes."

"This way." Nelia took the lead. Weathered stone walls and an arched ceiling formed a narrow tunnel. At the far end, an iron door stood with a keypad lock. Nelia scanned her watch. The locks released with a hiss.

"Stay close," she warned. "The allura is deactivated but lately they doubled patrols."

A singular corridor stretched ahead similar to the last. Another set of security doors blocked the path. Nelia scanned in again. The next tunnel forked into five directions. She veered down the second passage on the right. The rough stone walls transitioned to reinforced concrete and iron beams. We rounded a spiral staircase, descending fast. At the bottom, a vast cell system greeted us.

"They keep him—" Nelia began.

"Stop," a deep voice boomed.

Two Invicta guards appeared, stunned to see us. Mezzo and Anhelm drew their swords.

"Go," Anhelm barked. "Get him. We'll hold them off."

Nelia sprinted ahead, and Zed, Zaira and I followed, turning a sharp corner.

"Check these cells," she said. "Xavier?"

We scattered, rattling doors.

Banging.

Then we froze.

Our eyes snapped to a cell in the far corner where we

heard someone scraping against the door. Nelia reached it first, swiping her card.

A red light blinked in error. She tried again. And again.

"They cut me off," she growled.

"Stand back," I said. The spear materialized in my grip. I raised it high and slammed it into the lock. Metal screeched with sparks flaring in the air. The door tilted open.

Bloodied masculine fingers gripped the edge and heaved it ajar.

A towering figure stepped forward, dirt and blood smeared across his skin and clothes. But his aquamarine eyes burned brighter than ever.

"Little one," Xavier rasped.

Then his legs buckled. I caught him but started slipping to the floor under his weight. Anhelm hefted him over his shoulder and broke into a sprint.

Mezzo stood guard over unconscious bodies. Zaira stayed close at my side. We raced into the narrow tunnels, but Nelia and Zed had disappeared along the way. I halted.

"Go!" Zaira snapped. "We need you to take down the last barrier."

I threw a lightning bolt at the first lock, then sprinted ahead, frying the security system on the final door. They flooded through.

"I'm going back for them!" I shouted.

Mezzo whirled, fury darkening his face. "Arien!"

I spun my spear, casting a lightning web across the entrance and sealing it shut.

His face flushed red on the other side.

I didn't know how long the barrier would hold, so I whipped around and ran, arms pumping.

My old habit of mapping places in my head came in handy. I pictured the web of tunnels from Zaira's hologram—most familiar, but one stood out. A dead end. That didn't sit right.

Boots thundered above. More echoed in the distance.

I slipped through the last narrow passage and veered left at the first fork. The tunnel narrowed; the stonework looked rougher, older than the others. It was supposed to dead-end, but if I was correct, a cellar stood on the other side of the wall. The one Damian once took me to after he threatened my best friend's life.

The spear's glow cut through the dark. My steps slowed as the wall loomed ahead. I hurled the spear into it. Rock blasted in all directions and I dropped to the ground, arms shielding my head. Dust stung my eyes. The spear hovered above me, humming with energy. I snatched it from the air and studied the round opening carved into the rubble—just big enough to squeeze through.

My boots pressed into compacted dirt. I traipsed toward a crooked door and peeked through the crack. During my stay at Invicta I'd rarely seen anyone come here. I knew the way to the infirmary from here, but what were the chances my friends would still be there? More likely, Donovan had already locked them away. I wouldn't have put it passed Nelia to try to distract Invicta warriors from us, even if it meant their own capture.

I groaned, bumping the back of my head against the wall. *Here goes nothing.* I squared my shoulders, lit up the darn spear with the *Solvren* fae command, and climbed the steps to the higher levels, intent on speaking to the new Magister and waltzing in like I owned this cursed place.

FORTY-TWO

Power and courage ruled the Earthbounders. To earn their respect—or at least get them to listen—I had to show both.

The demonic presence inside me coiled, uneasy. Walking into a den of angels set it on edge. I had ignored it for a while, the trip to Ariada and touching the crystal stripping away much of its power. I had hoped all of it. But...

Red flashed before my eyes. I blinked hard, grinding my teeth. Not now. Not here. Damian had convinced the Seraphs to accept his mutations somehow, but I doubted their tolerance would extend to me.

A rustle of boots and wings echoed from above. I straightened, shoulders squaring, chin high, and climbed the final steps. Invicta's warriors scrutinized me. Their eyes weighed my worth, lingering on the lightning spear in my grip. That's right; this weapon was like a lightsaber—I'd advise caution.

The guards stood at even intervals, directing me toward a wide, open chamber. I rounded the corner.

Donovan leaned against a column, casual, smug. Nelia, Zed, and Dez sat on a nearby couch near the tall fireplace,

unharmed but tense. Nelia pressed her lips into a tight line—
she'd let me have it later for coming back.

Seraphs had encircled the space. Among them, Mattias.
His red mohawk made him impossible to miss.

"You're so predictable," Donovan sneered.

I cocked my head. "That's rich coming from you." My
bounce back earned me a few snickers.

Donovan's eyes narrowed dangerously. He pushed off the
column and loped toward me. "Think you're funny?"

I flicked a wrist, gesturing to the angels around us. "I
don't, but I can't help it if they do." More unrestrained
snickers followed.

"Silence!" Donovan snapped, glaring them into submis-
sion. Then he turned back to me, voice dropping to a low,
dangerous drawl. "Damian's missed you. He'll be happy to
know you've returned."

Cold flooded my veins. Donovan smirked. He saw the fear
flash across my face.

I clenched my jaw. "He's not on your side. Damian's
orchestrating all of this. He wants to wipe out the entire
Earthbounder race."

"And?" Donovan shrugged. "He can't defeat Invicta. And a
little cleanup now and then is necessary." His jaw tightened.
Arrogant. Blind. He had no idea what Damian was capable of.

"You should care," I said. "Your father's death doesn't
have to be for nothing."

His eyes flashed, and for a moment, I thought he might
lash out. "Why would I listen to someone like you?"

Oh, he did not just go there. My chest heaved. "Someone like
me?" I stepped closer, my voice rising.

"You have power," I said. "Invicta follows your orders
now. They *believe* in you. But you're wasting it by refusing to
take a side. If you don't act now, there won't be anything left
to lead. You've seen the reports from the fissure—you know

what's coming. They will slaughter us all unless we stand together."

Donovan's gaze flickered—hesitation, doubt. He looked away.

"Leave," he said, voice tight. "And take these traitors with you."

Nelia's eyes widened. She nudged the twins, and they all hurried to my side.

Donovan peered at me again with numb eyes. His gaze drifted to the spear in my grip for the first time. Then, without another word, he turned and strode out.

Mattias appeared at my side. "It'd be my honor to escort you out."

I lifted an eyebrow. "Maybe you can explain what the hell just happened on the way?"

A smirk tugged at his lips, and he gestured for us to follow. We entered a wide corridor.

"I finally figured it out," he said. "It's both."

"Both what?"

"Naïve and brave. Lethal combination."

A small smile ghosted my lips.

A grand staircase opened up, leading to the foyer with the fountain and the council chamber. My gaze locked onto the double doors with their intricate carvings.

"Mattias?"

He faced me, curiosity in his gaze.

"What if I needed to...borrow something from the council chamber?"

His brow furrowed. "What exactly?"

"The divine armor. It kills demons, right?"

His expression closed off. "Sacred objects can't be removed—"

Yeah, I figured he'd say that.

"*Veythar*," I whispered. A single bolt of lightning struck

him, sending him to the floor, stunned. He blinked up at me, paralyzed from the neck down, but the effect wouldn't last long. "Nothing personal. I hope you understand," I said.

Nelia beat the twins to the bottom of the steps, already yanking one side of the door open, on board with my plan. I sprinted past her toward the dais. Atop a white pillar, pure gold armor stood on a display stand—an ancient Power's last relic.

I paused with my fingers an inch away. A searing pain shot up my arm, and I yanked my hand back with a hiss.

"I can't touch it. Damian's blood tipped the scale..." I said.

Nelia stepped beside me. "When? Never mind. Let me carry it." Although appearing fragile and delicate, Nelia had the drive and skill of a Samurai. She could lead armies into battle. She made a perfect choice to bear such a powerful artifact.

"Hide it under your sweater," I said. She stripped it quickly and pulled the breastplate over her head. The metal shifted, reforming to fit her frame.

"Whoa," the twins breathed.

"Did you know it could do that?" Nelia asked.

I shook my head and handed the sweater back to her.

"There's no record of anyone wearing it," Zed muttered. "We only knew it repelled demons."

Dez nudged him. "What if the first Power was a girl?"

I rolled my eyes. Then footsteps sounded outside the chamber. We stilled, listening in.

Nelia studied the holographic map, then led us into an adjacent room—a space resembling a dressing area. We peeked through the window. A line of black SUVs rolled in, their tinted windows reflecting sunlight. Warriors from various institutes emerged, clad in full combat gear.

"Damian called in reinforcements," Nelia whispered.

"So he can wipe them all out in one day..." I muttered.

Zed crouched, ripping off a vent cover. "This leads to the alluron chamber, right?"

Nelia checked the map, then nodded, her gaze flicking to me.

I hesitated. "Uh, no..."

The twins eyed me.

Dez scratched his head. "The way I see it, we either jump with you or get trapped here with a horde of Pures." He shrugged. "Odds look better with you."

FORTY-THREE

We scattered like bowling pins, sprawling on the floor of the P6 alluron in a star shape.

Laughter bubbled up, and I clutched my sides, breathless.

"Oof, that was rough," Dez said.

"Is she alright?" Zed asked.

"I think that's her way of burning off the anxiety," Nelia said.

The door burst open and unfamiliar warriors stormed in, with pulse weapons drawn. Their comms crackled with an urgent voice barking an order and they relaxed their stances.

One angel arched a brow. "I guess you're expected?"

Fighting off the last of my laughter, I rolled to my knees, crawling toward the shimmering barrier. My friends placed their hands on my back as we stepped through, the alluron granting us passage. Inside me, the demon recoiled, retreating to the deepest recesses. Like it was...working with me. Yeah, right. More likely, it just had strong survival instincts.

"Is Xavier here?" Nelia asked the guards.

"In the infirmary. I can take you," one warrior said.

Zed followed them. His twin hesitated, glancing at me.

"Go," I said. "I know my way around." And I sobered up. He jogged after them.

A lingering warrior studied me, eyes calculating. "You're the one."

Goosebumps skittered up my arms. What did he mean? I forced a small smile and brushed past him.

I rounded a corner for the elevator and slammed into a wall of hard muscle. His scent of pine, sandalwood, and thunder filled my nostrils.

"Kole," I breathed.

Steel arms wrapped around me, lifting me off the floor. I latched onto him, legs winding around his waist as he backpedaled into the elevator and punched the door-close button. His lips pressed to my neck, hot and needy, his tongue trailing up my jaw.

"Kole," I moaned, threading my fingers into his thick hair. A low groan rumbled from his throat, vibrating against my skin as he rolled his hips into mine.

The elevator lurched to a stop. I tensed, starting to pull away, but Kole held firm, striding forward. He marched out with me still wrapped around him and climbed the steps to the library. There his magnificent wings snapped open, and he crossed into the seating area buzzing with dozens of warriors. A hush fell over the crowd. I stared into Kole's chocolate eyes and his gaze never left mine. I had half a mind to ask how the hell he wasn't tripping over things, but his spatial awareness had always been ridiculous. Good thing he was carrying me. I'd have already tripped over. I bit my lip and smirked at him.

The double doors leading to the patio stood wide open. The second we cleared the threshold, Kole kicked off the ground, wings driving us skyward. The wind whipped around us. The sun had begun to sink lower, streaking the sky in shades of burnt orange and dusky pink.

Kole landed atop the cabin's roof, lowering us onto the angled peak. I straddled his lap, breath still unsteady.

He tilted his head forward, brushing his nose along mine, lips parting, but I leaned back, studying him instead. Healthy. Whole. Even a little flushed. I couldn't believe he had fully recovered, that he was here with me now.

Kole growled, impatient. His arms tightened, locking me against him with no escape. I smirked, then brushed my tongue against his lower lip before tugging it between my teeth. He flinched, crushing his mouth to mine, stealing the breath from my lungs. Our bodies found their rhythm.

Boots hit the roof with a thud at the other end. I pulled back, heart hammering. Kole went rigid.

Xavier stood at the far end, his red wings catching the last light of the setting sun, painting him in scarlet. Relief rushed through me.

"You're healed," I breathed.

Scrambling off Kole's lap, I rushed forward, squealing like an idiot. Xavier's scowl wavered. He loped across the space between us. The crease between his brows smoothed. I threw my arms around him, pressing my head against his chest, feeling the steady, strong beat of his heart.

An awkward silence settled. I put some space between us, glancing at Kole.

My mate reached into his wing, plucked a single charcoal feather, and held it out to me.

"In case we get separated again." The reality hit me like ice water—Callista and Damian could launch their attack at any moment, with an army of future Earthbounders and sophisticated demons.

I sank onto the roof next to him, taking his feather and

turning it over between my fingers. A rustling sound followed and Xavier stuck his red feather in front of me.

"Take mine, too." His voice carried a pleading note. He'd already given me his feather once—did he forget? I swallowed past a lump and accepted his gift. Without thinking, I tucked Kole's feather behind my right ear, Xavier's behind my left. I didn't know what possessed me to do it. The warriors ogled, making my cheeks burn. Oh, well, the feathers would disappear soon until the time I called on them.

Xavier settled beside me.

"Once this is over, if—" I cut myself off. There were no *ifs* in this scenario; we would survive and defeat the enemy. "Once this is over, what happens to us?"

"You'll have to choose."

"You don't have to choose."

Kole and Xavier spoke at the same time. They glanced at each other, frowning. Did they think they were on the same page?

"I'll take a wild guess—you've never discussed *this*," I said with a dry laugh. I shook my head. "Never mind." I stared ahead, avoiding their questioning gazes. What did it matter when tomorrow wasn't promised?

Xavier covered my hand with his. I glanced down. His knuckles were still healing, deeper cuts forming pale scars. I lifted our joined hands and pressed a soft kiss to his fingers. Then I lowered our hands to the space between us and leaned my head against Kole's shoulder.

The three of us admired the fiery sky. This could be the last sunset we saw together.

Or the last one, ever.

FORTY-FOUR

A caravan of vehicles—trucks, SUVs, sedans, some beaten and rusted with age—crested the hill leading to the cabin. My muscles locked and my instincts sharpened.

Kole's hand landed on my thigh, firm and grounding. "Stay calm. It's Exiousai Seth. I convinced him to return. We need his strategic mind—and his rebels' brutal force. He's been preparing for this battle for centuries. And I no longer want to kill him for letting you leave the Underground alone." He said that last part with a sidelong glance in my direction.

What did he mean...centuries?

"The prophecy..." The whisper left my lips. My gaze snapped to Xavier. "Your mother gave him a feather. He had visions of me, but didn't know it was me until I got my wings."

Xavier's forehead tensed, his brows pulling together. "I don't like where this is going..." His voice dropped an octave.

"Why?" Kole asked.

Xavier exhaled sharply. "Because it means our girl is

important to this war. And that puts her in even more danger than she normally finds herself in."

I scoffed. "Hey. I can't help it if danger finds me."

"More reason to keep her under lock and key," Kole said like I wasn't even there, his gaze on Xavier.

Xavier cocked his head. "Did I mention I own an island in the Caribbean? No neighbors."

"Y-you're kidding." Words sputtered out before I could form a proper response. Both warriors smirked. Xavier squeezed my hand, then pulled me to my feet. They were kidding, right? Neither answered the question.

We leapt from the roof. Xavier's hands steadied my waist until my feet met the earth.

"Roan," I called. The warrior had just stepped out of his sleek car, grinning wide. Kole got in line with Seth. The former P6 leader acknowledged me with a nod when they passed us.

"Not dead yet?" Roan asked, and a growl rumbled from behind me. Roan's smile widened. The Underground rebels proceeded inside the cabin, among them many Powers—Pures and secondborns—and shifters. The real kind. Not the mutations from the Fringe. They carried a different sort of aura around them, more primal.

I elbowed Roan and fell back in step beside Xavier. Walking by his side felt...natural. Too natural. He kept stealing glances at me, and I kept catching him. The closer we got to the mission center, the tighter my stomach twisted.

A holographic map flickered to life over the massive war table at the center of the room. Leaders clustered around it, others hanging back, waiting. Rae stood among them, petite yet unwavering, holding her own with sharp intellect. She'd become an expert guru on frequencies among the Earthbounders. No one shunned her because she was a madeborn anymore. It meant she wasn't born an Earthbounder but somehow had been made into one. I suspected it involved a sacrifice from Vex, but I'd never asked them about it. I never understood why her status was such a big deal to begin with.

Xavier brushed his lips against the side of my neck—so brief, so subtle, I might have imagined it—before striding toward the table. Kole's intense gaze swept over me once before shifting back to the map.

Zephyr, son of Elyon and Magister of the Northeast, pointed at a location. "My father sent our best warriors to join the fight, against Invicta's orders. They're in flight now and will arrive in an hour. They can handle the first line of defense here."

I craned my neck, trying to see over the cluster of shoulders. I already knew the terrain well enough, but the monitors along the wall displayed real-time footage. Scouts lingered at the fissure's edge. If the barrier failed, they would alert P6 immediately.

"Arien."

I stiffened. My name had been spoken, the voice clear and direct. My head snapped toward the center of the room.

Seth was staring at me.

Oh, shit. The crowd shifted, parting for me. I forced my pulse to stay steady and stepped forward.

"Can you track the Soaz?" Seth asked.

I hesitated. My tongue darted over my lower lip. "I—I don't know. I blocked him last time, so I...don't know?" *Great. That was completely useless.* My mouth clamped shut before I could embarrass myself further.

"You will try to contact him at my signal. I want to separate him from his allies." His gaze didn't waver. "Describe the Ariadan leader."

I nodded and described Callista along with the Ariadan men who stood seven feet tall and were built like war gods. "Their wings will give them away—silvery-white with golden accents." *"Like mine"* hung at the tip of my tongue. I swallowed at the painful memory of losing them.

Seth studied the map, then zoomed in on a small hill at the tree line, away from the fissure. "I want you stationed here. Our men will hide in the trees, armed with divine armor. When the Soaz gets close enough, they'll strike."

Someone cleared their throat.

"What?" Seth barked.

Zed and Nelia approached. She still wore the armor.

Seth's irritation flared. "Why haven't you taken that off?"

Nelia's eyes flickered to Xavier. "It won't come off."

Xavier was at her side in an instant, hands skimming over the breastplate, knocking, tugging at the seams. His jaw clenched.

Seth's brows furrowed. He exhaled through his nose, nodding once. "She goes with Arien and the unit." Then he asked Zed: "Can you camouflage it?"

The secondborn nodded. "No tech needed. Show him."

Nelia inhaled, then murmured, "Hide."

The gold darkened, black spreading from the center outward like ink spilling over the metal. Within seconds, the armor matched the shade of her tactical shirt, its shine vanishing, though the material remained solid.

Seth rapped his knuckles against it. "Interesting." Then his attention shifted to me again. "One more thing—you can't fire the fae spear while you're waiting for my signal. Its energetic print can draw him to it. We can't risk it."

Xavier gripped Zed by the front of his shirt, yanking him forward until their faces were inches apart. "You stay close. Bring modulators, zappers—anything that slows demons down. If anything happens to my sister..." He snarled into the secondborn's face.

Zed met his stare without flinching. *Whoa.*

Nelia peeled Xavier's hand away, unfazed. "I'm trained. I can take care of myself."

Xavier held Zed's glare a moment longer before releasing him and returning to the center. Seth continued assigning teams on the holographic map, but my attention drifted to the monitors again.

Scouts sprinted from the fissure as black ooze burst from its depths. A voice thundered through the speakers, "The line's been breached."

FORTY-FIVE

I had exactly two reactions when the invasion began. First, I patted my hip to make sure my short sword was still there. Second, I looked to them—Kole and Xavier. The two forces that grounded me.

Their eyes swirled with emotions they rarely showed. Orders rang out, warriors flooding from the room in a coordinated rush.

Kole strode toward me, brushing a loose strand of hair behind my ear. "We're all flying from here. I'll take you to your position." I nodded, but my mind felt distant, disconnected.

Outside, tires screeched as secondborn warriors and shifters tore down the dirt road in armored vehicles. Two massive trucks, loaded with weapons and tech, trailed behind as part of Seth's convoy. They'd get there after the Pures landed, but Seth didn't seem concerned about the delay.

Roan crossed the courtyard, whistling as he passed. "The scouting team deployed the last of those little gadgets your giant friends left. Sealed the fissure back up—for now. Won't hold long, but it bought us some time."

He unfurled his wings, preparing to launch. I caught his arm.

"Be careful. You can't enjoy your newfound fame if you're dead," I said, offering a small smile.

He chuckled. "True. Same goes for you." He winked before rocketing into the sky. I watched until he was a speck.

"Ready?" Kole's deep velvety voice came from behind me setting an avalanche of uncontrollable shivers. No, I wasn't. I spun on my heel, letting my eyes say what my lips wouldn't. His gaze softened just enough before he scooped me into his arms.

I buried my face in the crook of his neck, inhaling his scent, wishing we could stay like this forever. I hated when his feet touched down. But I was a big girl. I forced myself to step away and inspect the surroundings. Vast open space stretched between my position and the fissure, separated by sparse bushes. Enough to camouflage us for a while. Nelia, Zed, and a team of Underground warriors emerged from the trees.

Kole's wings bristled with agitation. "I'll come back when Seth's ready to use you as bait. There's no way, across all of Heaven and Hell, that I'm letting you face this monster alone," he growled. Relief crashed through me—followed by fear. Kole had already barely survived Damian once. And Damian was cunning. Ruthless.

"Xavier will keep an eye on you and Nelia too," Kole said. "As long as you stay here, you'll be out of harm's way. If I had any doubts, I wouldn't leave your side." His voice darkened with the last words, his expression thunderous.

"Oh, I'm not afraid," I said, scowling.

Kole sighed. "That's what keeps me on edge." His smoldering eyes captured mine. "Fear makes people hide. It makes them listen. It makes them think about their own safety. But that's not you."

My scowl deepened, but he didn't let me argue. Instead, his lips grazed mine—a soft touch, barely there—before he crushed my mouth with his in a kiss that left me breathless. And then he was gone, vanishing into the sky in one powerful stroke of his wings. I stood there, lips tingling and utterly dumbfounded.

"Ahem."

I blinked. Nelia's brows lifted to her hairline.

"So...how does my brother fit into all this?" She waved her hands before I could answer. "You know what? I don't want to know."

"Good, because I don't know...yet." I let out a dry laugh, wiping my clammy hands on my pants.

"Our great-grandfather had a harem of sorts," she mused. "Women only."

I shuddered. "I don't want a harem." The words slipped out, but my throat tightened around the rest. *I'll be happy having one of them.* But, to be honest, my heart and soul craved both and I'd be devastated if one of them didn't choose me back. Was I selfish thinking that way?

Nelia smirked like she'd read my mind. "I get it. And for what it's worth, I wouldn't trust anyone else with my brother's heart."

I exhaled, trying to shake the unease curling in my stomach. A prickle crawled over the skin of my arm closest to her. I jumped two steps back, clutching it.

Nelia held up her hands. "Sorry." She backed off. At least we knew the divine armor was still working.

A deep, guttural tremor rolled through the earth. Cracks skittered across the open field like veins of glass. The ground swelled beneath us, groaning. The last barrier inside the fissure ruptured with a deafening crack.

A furious wind howled, thick with the stench of sulfur and decay. Sickly yellowish light speared skyward, ripping the dusk open. Shadows twisted and stretched in impossible directions, twisting over the battlefield like writhing specters.

Nelia scaled the small hill beside us. I followed, flattening myself to the ground.

A chorus of blades rasped against leather followed as our warriors drew their weapons.

Then a shriek erupted from the depths, followed by another. And another. The air vibrated with an unholy cacophony of things that should never have been born. Clawed hands and grotesque limbs scrabbled against the edges of the fissure, dragging themselves free. Their eyes burned like coals, mouths yawning wide with hunger.

The Earthbounders barely had time to brace themselves before the horde surged forward, the ground trembling beneath their charge. My pulse slammed against my ribs. Hulking, grotesque forms poured from the fissure, their beady eyes glinting with malice, jagged teeth snapping at the air. Their guttural snarls rattled the ground. Among them, feral hamangi—monstrous creatures with thick, webbed wings—launched into the air, gliding short distances before landing with bone-shaking force. Their wide, gaping jaws snapped viciously, black, hairless heads swaying as they scanned for prey. Their meaty legs coiled before they sprang, soaring multiple stories into the air before slamming down into the chaos below.

I didn't spot a nefora—the enormous, serpent-like demons whose sheer size made them nearly impossible to kill in their corporeal form. A rare stroke of luck. But that luck was short-lived. Rhinoquiem, borelli, and dozens of creatures I couldn't name spilled from the abyss. Secondborns and Pures worked in tandem, hurling energy discs that detonated at the demons' feet, erasing them before they reached our front line.

The P6 warriors fought like demons themselves, their

wings slicing through the smoke-filled air. Kole was a storm, his dark wings carving through the haze as he brought down demon after demon with deadly precision. I had seen him fight before, but this was something else entirely.

The sight of cheruse demons that resembled vermilion arachnids with eight appendages made my hair stand on end. I thought King Cygnus had dispatched them all, but some had survived, long enough to answer Damian's call.

The devil himself rose from the pit in his full demonic form—leathery wings and claws on full display. I had no doubt his eyes fully bled black too. He spun in a circle assessing the battle and revealing a white-winged angel in golden Ariadan armor by his side—Callista.

Tall and sinewy, she held her head high. She clutched a clear crystal sword in her hand and looked more like a savior than the harbinger of the chaos now spilling into the world.

The Ariadans—her personal army—emerged next, rising through the fissure like sentinels sent to Earth by the Heavens. Except these Earthbounder swore their allegiance to the darkness. Callista's gaze swept over them, one by one, before she gave the silent command.

They vanished into the trees.

My pulse thundered.

"This isn't good. They're surrounding us," Nelia whispered. She activated her smartwatch and recorded a short message. "Send to the Exiousai and team leads," she murmured.

My attention snapped back to the battle. P6 warriors held their ground, standing shoulder to shoulder with Xavier and his men. Kole moved like a storm wrapped in human flesh, a blur of dark wings and deadly focus. A hamangi sprang over the front line, aiming for an attack from above, but Kole met it midair, his blade a silver arc slicing through the beast in a whirlwind of motion.

Howls erupted from the forest. I spun toward the sound, scanning the tree line.

"It sounds like the Exiousai sent werewolves to track the Ariadans," Nelia muttered.

"Arien." Kole's voice snapped me out of my daze as he landed beside me, his blade dripping with demon ichor. "Move down. It's almost time."

Nelia gasped.

I followed her gaze—a cheruse demon lunged, its sharpened limb impaling Zaira. Another demon tore down Mezzo. Anhelm rushed to Zaira's side, abandoning Xavier—who was too preoccupied fending off two spider-like demons to notice the hamangi above him, wings folded and preparing to drop.

My fingers tightened around Kole's forearm. There was no time...

The demon plummeted toward Xavier...

A red-winged blur slammed into it, knocking it away just feet from Xavier's head. The two figures crashed to the ground.

Donovan.

He drove his knee into the hamangi's chest, pinning it, then stabbed his massive onyx blade through its throat. The creature convulsed, then liquefied into black sludge.

Seraphs descended from the skies. Dozens of them, warriors from Invicta and allied institutes, touched down in formation, bolstering the front lines. More streaked through the air, pushing Damian into the fray. With Donovan's troops, we finally outnumbered his army.

I inhaled sharply, pulse hammering. Kole watched in quiet amazement.

I met his gaze. "Go," I said, breathless. "It's time to send them all back to hell."

His eyes lit with danger, and he launched back into the fight.

Nelia and I dropped to the ground, waiting for our moment. I clenched and unclenched my fists, ready to draw Damian out and sever the connection between us, permanently.

"Nightshade..." His voice wrapped around my thoughts like vines, tightening. The blood bond between us shuddered awake.

I winced, my breath hitching. "He's trying to locate me."

"Too soon," Nelia hissed. "Are you blocking him?"

"For now," I gritted out. "But...he feels stronger..." Pain exploded in my chest. I crashed to the ground, gasping as a pulse of energy ripped through our connection. It dragged me under, drowning me in his presence. Nelia's voice blurred, urgent as she spoke into her smartwatch.

White-hot light erupted beside us. The air shimmered, then split apart. I shielded my eyes until the glow dissipated —and when I lowered my arm, King Cygnus stood in its place.

His circlet caught the pale light, his dark armor, etched with golden runes, pulsing with raw power.

I sucked in a breath. "Cygnus?" The moment he arrived, the weight of Damian's presence vanished. I could breathe again.

Cygnus glanced my way, lifting an eyebrow, and then without a word he strolled directly into the fray. As if the battle raging around him didn't exist.

"Angels..." Nelia whispered, wide-eyed. "What is he doing here?"

I scrambled to my feet, still unsteady. "Not a clue." I exhaled, rubbing my temples. "But he severed Damian's hold on me."

Nelia shot me a wary look.

Then a body dropped from the trees with a thud.

FORTY-SIX

An Underground warrior lay on his back, eyes vacant, blood seeping from a deep puncture wound in his chest. Silence followed.

"Do you think—" I swallowed, my voice barely above a whisper.

We both edged backward, pressing against the mound behind us.

"Those spiders have us surrounded," Nelia murmured, drawing her sword in one fluid motion. "They hunt in small packs." Her grip tightened. "Get behind me."

"No." My short sword was already in my hand.

"I have the divine armor, remember?" she hissed.

"It's useless if they take out your legs or slit your throat."

We waited. No sound of fighting or struggling broke the stillness.

"They must have taken out the others," Nelia muttered.

Long, jointed appendages with wicked-looking stingers emerged from the brush, the creatures advancing in a coordinated, deliberate effort. One made a chittering noise.

"They're communicating," I whispered.

"They're hesitating... I think they were ordered to keep you alive. You need to run," she said.

My fists tightened. If I ran, she'd become a spider food. There was no way in hell.

A cheruse demon swiped at Nelia's legs. She leapt away, landing by me. My side heated up being this close to the armor Nelia was wearing.

The demons hissed, slamming their stingers against the ground—an intimidation display, or maybe something worse.

Nelia's breath turned ragged. My own heartbeat drowned out all other sounds. I counted six cheruse demons, but who knew how many more lurked beyond the trees? A wet glob landed on my cheek. Slowly, I tilted my head upward. A hamangi perched at the top of the mound, its jaws gaping, thick saliva dripping from its fangs.

Another sharp click rang out, the leader giving an order. Then one of the demons broke rank, lunging. In that instant, the fae spear blazed to life in my palm. I barely had time to register the shock before I flicked it forward, the spear impaling the charging demon through the chest. It let out a horrid wail, its flesh charring and curling in on itself before its body collapsed, still smoking.

The remaining demons reared up, mandibles snapping. Then they leapt all at once.

"Veythar, draythos!"

Lightning burst from the spear, the bolts arcing between the creatures, freezing them in midair. I swung my arm across, and the spear cleaved through them all, severing bodies in one sweep.

Nelia's eyes rounded, her expression caught between shock and something unreadable. The hamangi demon plummeted into the space between us, its body still twitching from the electric shock. With a roar, Nelia drove her sword into its chest.

We exchanged uneasy glances. Then a whip snaked around my wrist. The fae spear clicked off, melting back into my tattoo. I wrenched against the bind. Nelia jumped in to help, but before we could free me, a brutal force yanked me upward. My shoulder wrenched painfully, and suddenly, I was airborne. A strong, unyielding body wrapped around me, pinning my arms in place. The leathery wings gave him away, but I still snapped my head up, glaring at his stone-set face.

"Arien!" Nelia's voice rang out from below.

Damian weaved through the aerial battles, then angled his wings and dove. Straight into the fissure.

Wind screamed in my ears, carrying the snarls and shrieks of the demons festering below. They reached for me, clawed hands stretching, molten eyes gleaming with unsatiated hunger. Damian angled his descent, his grip like iron, his wings beating against the currents as we tore through the cavernous depths. Ledges flashed past, each one crawling with watching, waiting creatures.

Then he hurled me into a crevice. I hit the stone hard, knees buckling. I tried to summon my spear.

Nothing.

Panic stabbed through me. My tattoo refused to respond.

Damian landed before me, his silhouette massive against the pulsing glow of the abyss. He sidled closer, towering over me, his eyes fully black. A wave of nausea hit me.

"*Stop fighting it, nightshade.*" His voice coiled around my mind, soft as silk, yet strong as iron. His fingers ghosted over my cheek, trailing lower, skimming my collarbone. Fire bloomed beneath his touch.

"I don't—" I started, but the words died in my throat as his claws pressed into my skin.

His fangs pierced my neck next, and I gasped, my body arching as a rush of heat poured through me. His mouth was cold, but the sensation burned, sending shock waves through my veins. Stealing something from me.

I tried to resist.

Tried to pull away.

Tried to remember who I was.

But my mind fractured. Damian's presence seeped into the cracks, filling every space.

The pain faded. The fear dissolved.

And when I met his gaze again—I wanted *him*.

Every rational thought drowned beneath the bond thrumming between us. The red halo around my irises flickered and then spilled over.

I pressed against him, hands splaying over his chest. His scent of smoke and blood was all-consuming, his power an intoxicating force that demanded surrender.

I barely registered the flurry of white-gold wings descending from above. Callista landed with grace even among this chaos, her golden armor reflecting the sickly yellow.

"Control the demons," she said, tone clipped. "They are attacking my warriors."

Damian grunted, reluctant to do her bidding.

A simper curved my lips. "Leave her," I whispered. "She'll never let you rule."

"Damian!" Callista roared before flinching away from a hamangi and launching herself upward.

Damian's regarded me, admiring my blown red eyes. He licked my lips that I offered freely before plunging his tongue inside my mouth like he owned it. His lips were cold and possessive, his hold tightening as I sank into him, losing myself to the bond tethering me to him. He pried my hands off his chest and tugged low, breaking our kiss. I whimpered at the loss of contact.

"First, you're going to beg for my forgiveness. On your knees," he said in a gravelly voice.

A thud echoed behind us. Nelia rose from a crouch, her breath ragged, sweat beading her forehead. Her body swayed, exhaustion pulling at her frame from the climb down here, but her eyes never wavered. Her gaze flicked to mine, her resolve hardening. Then she charged him.

Damian's face twisted with rage. He struck her before she could reach him. The crack of his slap split the air. Nelia's body whipped sideways, crashing against the rock. A pained gasp burst from her lips and something snapped inside me.

The haze lifted.

For the first time since Damian's bite, I felt something other than wanting him. I felt a spark that was me. But I didn't let it show. Instead, I slowly circled him, keeping my expression serene.

"Forgive me," I murmured, sinking to my knees before him. The red halo around my eyes dimmed but I held onto just enough of the demonic presence to keep it visible.

Damian smirked, tilting my chin up with his fingers. My right hand drifted toward his leg, gliding higher. His gaze followed, dark and expectant.

Then I dropped the red curtain from my eyes and twisted, slamming my left hand over Nelia's chest.

Agony gripped me, the demon shrilling inside me. Fire ripped up my arm, consuming every nerve. Damian's body jerked violently. He tried to kick me off, but I tightened my grip, my fingers locking around his belt. My other hand fused to the divine armor, the connection so strong he'd have to tear my arms off to break it. And with every passing second, he weakened.

His snarl twisted into a scream. His skin cracked and burned, and welts erupted along his arms as divine energy ate through him. He slammed his fist into the back of my head.

Pain burst through my skull, but I didn't let go. Wouldn't. The armor's glow intensified, fiery white, pulsing in rhythm with my heartbeat. Damian's flesh blackened, oozing blood. He collapsed to his knees before me.

And then his eyes changed. Not the empty black void of a demon, nor the dark human pupils I knew. Deep ocean blue.

Like his father's.

For the briefest moment, I saw past the monster. I saw the man.

His body convulsed, smoke pouring from his wounds. Then lightning tore from my chest. The force hurled me backward, the armor finally releasing me.

Damian crashed onto the stone, body charred and smoking.

My arms trembled. I stared at the armor, its surface still scorching hot from the energy that had consumed our demons. My fingers blistered and raw. I waited for my skin to char like Damian's had. But nothing happened. Maybe most of the armor's power traveled through me to Damian and not into me, my body acting like a conduit. Yet I couldn't feel any demonic presence in me and something about my body felt off.

Above, the Earthbounders waged their final battles against Callista's forces, but the noise was muffled, as though my senses were pulling inward.

The edges of my vision blurred, and a wave of dizziness swept over me. Blood trickled down my temple, and I could feel the pull of unconsciousness creeping closer. My chest heaved as I tried to draw in a steady breath, but it was no use.

I thought of Kole—his strong arms holding me like I was his anchor to the world.

I thought of Xavier—his fierce loyalty, his unwavering belief in me, even when I doubted myself. They had always been my constants. My protectors. And now...

I reached into my pockets, my fingers closing around two precious feathers. One—dark as midnight. Kole's. Its softness comforting even now. The other—crimson. Xavier's. It caught the faintest glimmer of light, even in the gloom.

They had given them to me as symbols of their feelings for me, their promise to always be there when I needed them. And now, I needed them more than ever.

My vision darkened further, the world tilting. Too weak to call out, too spent to lift my head. But they would find me. Tears blurred my vision as I clutched the feathers tightly.

"I'm sorry," I whispered, my voice breaking. With the last of my strength, I crushed them. They disintegrated, bursting into charcoal and crimson barbs, their energy flaring outward like a beacon. The plumage swirled around me, warm and pulsing—two heartbeats in sync with my own.

My head tipped back, and I swore I felt them, Kole and Xavier, like a breeze on a sunny day brushing against my soul.

"I'm scared," I whispered, a stray tear slipping down my cheek.

I inhaled in chopped gulps, grasping for something familiar, something solid to hold on to. The words came before I could stop them—words I never understood until now.

"Do not go gentle into that good night..." My heart stuttered. *Do not go gentle...*

The light faded, and the darkness closed in, claiming me. My body slumped. The wind whispered against my cheek, carrying the sound of wildly beating wings. My soul cried out for them. And with one final, shuddering breath, I surrendered to oblivion.

FORTY-SEVEN

KOLE

The cheruse demon faltered, steam huffing from its nostrils like a broken forge. I drove my onyx blade into its gut and ripped upward. Flesh split. Gore spilled. It collapsed with a shuddering groan. Screeches tore through the battlefield. I surveyed the chaos. My demon wasn't the only one falling. Warriors struck fast, exploiting their hesitation. In one coordinated push, we cut down half of them. The rest wavered, some retreating.

Oh, hell no.

I raised my sword and roared. The other commanders echoed my call, their signals ringing across the field. We surged forward like a storm. Our secondborns—trained with our tech—struck ahead of us, stunning or paralyzing the enemy before we crashed into them.

Only a few yards away, King Cygnus broke through Callista's defenses, cutting down Earthbounder giants and leaving them to bleed out. The last one standing charged Cygnus—only to fall under his spell. In a trance, the giant drove his blade into his wounded brother's gut, twisted it deep, then turned and threw himself into the fissure below, wings folding as he free-fell.

Callista bared her teeth, fury darkening her face. Her crystal sword gleamed, her stance widening. Cygnus extended a glowing hand, trying to breach her mind, but she had fortified herself against fae magic somehow. Had she known he'd be here?

With a single beat of her wings, she surged off the ground and shot toward him.

Cygnus parried with an effortless flick of his arm, runes on his sleeve repelling the crystal blade. The force threw Callista off balance. He seized a fistful of her feathers and wrenched her down, slamming her against the ground. Her pretty sword clattered away.

"No!" she cried, struggling.

Cygnus pressed his boot against her chest, pinning her. "Beg for mercy."

I cut the legs out from under a fleeing demon, letting Talen finish the kill while I closed in on Callista and the king. If I'd read him correctly, he had no intention of letting her live, but if she survived this, I'd be on standby.

She thrashed under his weight, fury burning in her eyes.

"You have no mercy in you," she spat. "We're the same. Look around you. You're fighting for the weak, for fools who delude themselves into thinking humanity is worth saving. We could rule together. Take what's rightfully ours."

I ended the last of the Ariadan traitors still breathing. Cygnus didn't acknowledge me, but he knew I was there. I waited.

His foot eased off her chest. A smirk curled Callista's lips. She sprang to her feet.

I gripped my sword tighter.

Cygnus studied her, his dark eyes narrowing. Then he removed the circlet from his head.

"Every ruler needs a crown," he said, placing it atop Callista's.

She accepted it with a victorious sneer. Rage boiling inside, I spread my wings, ready to challenge her. But I halted when her expression twisted. A choking sound tore from her throat. Her hands flew to the circlet. The metal seared against her scalp, burning through her hair, her skin. Blood poured from her eyes, her nose, her mouth. She collapsed, convulsing. A final, wet gurgle—and then she stilled.

Cygnus nudged her body over with his boot and retrieved the circlet. The metal had cooled again, its brass sheen innocent.

For the first time, his gaze swung my way.

"Only the righteous can bear the weight of fae crown."

I acknowledged his actions with a nod.

A sudden gust ripped from the fissure, howling and slamming into my chest. It carried a familiar scent of wildflowers on a summery day.

I stopped breathing.

"Arien!"

FORTY-EIGHT
KOLE

I blasted into the sky, heart pounding, soaring high above the battlefield. In all my long years, I had never known fear. But what I felt now—this twisting in my gut, this tearing in my soul—was what it must have felt like.

Xavier dove into the fissure beside me, his expression murderous.

Her scent guided me.

A ledge jutted from the fissure's wall below, opening into a carved-out shelf. I zeroed in on blond waves splayed across the stone. Nelia lay beside her near the charred remains of a slain creature I suspected was the Soaz.

I gritted my teeth and pushed harder, landing at a sprint before falling to my knees beside my love. Xavier rushed to his sister. I pressed two fingers against Arien's throat, then her wrist. No beat. No warmth.

Xavier got Nelia sitting upright and regaining consciousness. Then he was listening to Arien breathing. Or the lack of it.

"She touched the armor," Nelia rasped. "To kill him." Tears spilled down her soot-streaked face.

Xavier and I locked eyes. Whatever differences we'd had, there was one thing we'd always agree on—keeping her alive. I pressed my hands over her breastplate. Xavier tilted her head back and breathed into her mouth.

"How long?" he growled.

"I don't know," Nelia whispered, wiping her cheeks and forcing composure. "He knocked me out before I could get the armor near him." She peeled the divine armor from her chest and set it aside, then wrapped Arien's scorched fingers in her hands, massaging life back into them.

My throat tightened. The demons we'd fought on the ground retreated because she killed him. But she had remained alive—for minutes. Alone. In agony.

I slammed my fist into the dirt beside her head and roared.

"Come back to me!"

Nelia took over the compressions, sensing my control slipping. Xavier's shoulders shook. He was barely holding on himself.

"Why isn't she recovering?" he asked, his voice raw.

"Don't stop," Nelia murmured. "Keep going."

I stared at my mate's face—delicate but unbreakable, even now. Even like this. Too striking to be real. Too strong to be gone. My eyes roamed over her body, memorizing every detail, too afraid to forget a single freckle. The lightning tattoo had disappeared completely. Was it due to her state or something else?

"The divine armor burned him, but not her." My voice felt hollow, distant. "She's still there." Was I lying to myself? Prolonging the inevitable?

Nelia bit her lip, holding back words I refused to hear. Xavier trailed his fingers over Arien's forearm, over the place where her marks had once been.

"She said the fae spear annihilated demons," he

murmured. "The armor must have drawn her demon out. If that's true, they could have...canceled each other out." He continued to trace his fingers over her skin.

I didn't feel my legs moving when I strode over. I simply lifted her small fragile body, spun around, and flew to the surface.

Warriors drove the last demons into the fissure, their bodies toppling into the abyss. My gaze scoured the battlefield in search of one creature.

The druids.

Their leader stood at the tree line, waiting.

"We feel when a sister calls for us," he said as I landed, Xavier and Nelia close behind. His words sent a fresh pulse through my heart.

"She's not dead?" I said, hope underlying my tone.

"Define death," the great druid said, then turned toward the trees. "Meet us at the Everlake." His voice dropped to a murmur. "Water magic is potent..." Then he was gone, his druids vanishing with him.

Drums pounded in my ears. *They can bring her back...*

I looked down at her—her lips pale, her body slack in my arms. My chest tightened.

"Stay with me, love," I whispered.

Nelia took off toward our army, calling for reinforcements. Xavier met my gaze, his eyes sparking with something fierce. He gripped my shoulder then we launched into the air together, flying hard and fast.

The great druid waited at the Everlake's edge. He gestured for us to enter. We waded in up to our chests, holding Arien's body floating between us.

The druids surrounded us from along the shore, on the rock ledges, in the caves. Their leader raised his hands. Wind churned through the trees. The lake, always still, rippled outward like something ancient had woken beneath its surface.

I never looked away from her. Neither did Xavier.

We both wanted her. We both loved her.

She had burrowed into our souls with her defiance, her righteousness, the way she lifted her chin before a fight, the way her head tilted when lost in thought. She had no idea I noticed all of it.

But I'd tell her now.

If only she came back.

I narrowed my eyes at the Seraph. *Was he right for her?* I wanted her for myself, selfishly, entirely. But if she chose him, I would step aside. As long as she lived.

I threw my head back, closed my eyes, and prayed.

A subtle pull tightened in my chest—faint at first, then insistent, like an invisible thread winding through my rib cage, tethering me to something just beyond reach. To her.

Xavier sucked in a sharp breath, his lips parting. Whatever this was, he felt it too.

Then her scent hit me.

Not a memory. Not a ghost of what once was. *Real.*

It curled through my lungs, warm and familiar—like rain-soaked earth after a storm, like something untamed but alive.

My pulse thundered.

I surrendered to it, to the pull of her, letting go of the last sliver of myself I'd held back.

The lake stilled.

FORTY-NINE
ARIEN

I pried my eyelids open. Light poured in and my eyes watered. The outlines of two exquisite faces I knew all too well hovered above me. Powerful arms lowered my body and my bare feet touched a mushy floor. I stood submerged up to my neck.

Flurries danced around us, carried by unseen hands, drifting like silver dust in the air.

I exhaled slowly, my lips curving. My gaze flicked right—to Kole's godlike features, sharp and commanding. Then left —to Xavier's deceptive boyish beauty, masking something dark and dangerous.

"Is this a dream?" I breathed.

Kole's lips tilted into that slow smirk, carving a single dimple that always made my stomach tighten. "The best dream there is, love." His voice, deep and growling, sent a shiver straight to my core.

Something in me responded. A hum low in my belly, awakening something I had no name for. I gasped at the odd but achingly familiar sensation.

Both men went still, inspecting the sides of my neck.

I lifted a hand, fingers grazing the spot. "What?" My voice wavered. Had someone slashed my throat? Had I... *Ohmagod, I died.* The memory slammed into me. The unbearable heat, the divine armor searing through my veins, frying me from the inside out. My breath hitched.

Kole's featherlight touches grounded me in an instant. I melted into the sensation, my eyes fluttering closed. If I was dead, then this was my personal brand of heaven. Then Xavier joined him, tracing the same spot on the other side of my throat. A shudder raked through me.

It was subtle at first—just a whisper of sensation—but then it surged, like a thread connecting us, weaving through my chest and into my very bones. My eyes flew open. My lips parted.

"Do you...feel it?" I whispered.

Xavier swallowed, his Adam's apple bobbing. "I saw this mark on you in my vision," he murmured. "But I never understood..." His hands skimmed lower, fingertips gliding to my collarbone, his touch both reverent and possessive.

My breathing quickened in response.

Kole growled. A dark, low sound that sent another shiver rippling through me. His gaze glazed over with lust. My eyelids lowered halfway. The pheromones the three of us were emitting, the closeness of their bodies to mine, were like a drug.

I lifted a trembling hand to Kole's cheek. He leaned into my palm. Xavier nosed the back of my neck, inhaling my scent.

"If this isn't a dream..." I moaned softly, my knees weakening. "What's happening?"

"The Everlake brought you back," Kole said, his voice thick. "And awakened our *Ashanti Rosa* bond."

"And ours," Xavier added from behind me.

I stilled, trying to fight through the hormone haze clouding my mind. "How?"

Kole swept wet strands of hair from my neck. "You bear my wing under your right ear," he said, then nodded to Xavier. "And his under your left."

My heart stalled.

Xavier's lips left my skin as he pulled back, peering at Kole over my shoulder. "I've never seen marks like these before."

"Me neither," Kole said.

I turned, cheeks flushed, and the world came into focus. People lined the shore—Earthbounders, shifters, warriors from every base and rank. Nelia clutched Zed's arm. Dez stood beside the P6-ers, Zephyr and Donovan just behind them. The druids stood solemnly to the side, their robes rippling in the wind. A massive black crow perched on a gnarled branch, its beady eyes gleaming. Cygnus. Even in his shifted form, I could feel his cold, oppressing presence.

I gulped. So many eyes.

"What now?" I asked.

Xavier's lips quirked. "You belong with us." His voice dropped lower. Tempting. Dangerous. "Both of us." His fingers skimmed my arm. "The possibilities...are endless."

Heat coiled in my belly. I bit my lip. I wanted to kiss them. Needed to.

As if he read my mind, Kole yanked me back against his chest. Xavier's cerulean eyes pulsed as he dipped his head lower. My tongue flicked out, wetting my lips involuntarily. Then reality crashed in.

I cleared my throat. "We have an audience."

"Perfect, I like making a statement. And I hate repeating myself," Xavier purred against my lips. Kole grunted in agreement, his fingers digging into my midsection and setting my core on fire.

My former nemesis gathered my face into his large hands. The first brush of his lips sent a jolt of pleasure skittering through me. I gripped his soaked shirt, clinging like my life depended on it. He groaned and deepened the kiss, his mouth owning mine.

The kiss was fire. Fury. Devotion. Claiming...

When he finally pulled away, my breath came in sharp gasps. Then Kole gripped my jaw, twisting my neck gently. His chocolate eyes were like a thunderstorm, intense and foreboding. His gaze alone made my stomach flip. He crashed his full lips into mine.

This kiss was different.

Xavier kissed like a promise. Kole kissed like a war.

I melted, my body molding against his. My knees wobbled, and my core pulsed with the undeniable bond sealing between the three of us, with me at the center.

The sensation surged, racing up my spine and settling below my shoulder blades.

I gasped, breaking away.

Kole's brow furrowed. "What's wrong?"

I clapped a hand over my mouth, unable to speak.

Xavier's voice dropped, dark with a warning. "Little one..."

I stepped back.

A mass exploded from my back. Water rained down in a glittering spray, drenching Kole's and Xavier's stunned faces. I blinked, breathless. Wings.

They unfurled, silvery white with golden undertones. I tested a flap and sprayed more water at Kole.

A slow, wicked grin spread across his face. Xavier wiped a hand down his face, eyes blazing with something almost...

feral. Their wings expanded possessively to their fullest in response to mine.

Kole fixed me with a dark stare. "You get a minute head start," he said.

I swallowed, my body thrumming with anticipation.

Then I took off.

DEAR READER

If you enjoyed this last installment in Arien's journey, please consider leaving a review. Reviews help authors reach more wonderful readers like you.

While Arien's story ends in Marble Sun (for now), the Earthbounders saga will continue with spinoffs.

The first spinoff standalone will tell Brie and Donovan's story in MADEBORN.
You can expect the following tropes:

- He falls first and harder
- Single young mother
- Enemies to lovers
- Groveling
- Alphahole in need of taming
- Shadow daddy
- Strong FMC

Sign up for my newsletter and follow me on social media for the release date: https://www.egsparks.com

May you soar high always!

ABOUT THE AUTHOR

E. G. Sparks is an award-winning dark fantasy romance author. Her debut novel, "Sky Ice," won the Silver/2nd Place award in the 2024 Feathered Quill Book Awards for the Fantasy category and was a Finalist in the 2024 Wishing Shelf Book Awards.

She delights in sharing fantasy worlds and making her heroines' lives difficult. When not in her writing cave, E. G. can be found hanging out with family and friends, traveling, gardening, doing yoga, and (you guessed it!) reading.

E. G. resides in sunny Florida with her husband, three beautiful daughters, two dogs, and a cat.

She invites readers to get first looks, bonuses, and more by subscribing to her newsletter at: www.egsparks.com